LOVE IN THE RUINS

LOVE IN
THE RUINS

TALES OF ROMANCE IN THE DEINDUSTRIAL FUTURE

EDITED BY

JOHN MICHAEL GREER

FOUNDERS HOUSE PUBLISHING LLC | 2020

CONTENTS

LOVE IN THE RUINS

Introduction

John Michael Greer

The future's a foreign country, and they do things differently there. That's one of the recurring lessons of history, a lesson that science fiction sometimes learns and sometimes manages to forget. At the same time, even in a country as foreign as the future, some things remain the same, and this anthology is about one of those.

Back in 2014, when I was blogging at *The Archdruid Report*, I challenged my readers to try their hand at short stories set in the kind of future we're actually going to get. Much of my nonfiction writing and blogging in those days focused on sustained critiques of the rigidly binary vision of the future that pervades contemporary pop culture and the media: the one that insists that the only possible paths for humankind are endless progress leading to a Star Trek future metastasizing across the galaxy, on the one hand, or sudden apocalyptic collapse on the other. Neither of those futures are especially likely, and a good case can be made that neither of them has any reasonable chance of happening—the way that believers in both insist on some kind of *deus ex machina* gimmick to bring them about is as good a demonstration of this as any.*

It struck me, though, that it would help people think their way past the utopia-or-oblivion dichotomy if there were more stories talking about the kind of future we can reasonably expect, the kind in which our species has to deal with the consequences of its mismanagement of its resource base and its natural environment over the long term; in which our civilization follows the same trajectory of peak, decline, fall, and revival as all its predecessors; and in which human beings go on to lead interesting, complex, and occasionally successful lives, just like their ancestors did in preindustrial times. I put out a call for stories, and the result was an anthology, *After Oil* (Founders House 2012), which included the best of the stories submitted to the contest. Three other anthologies followed in turn—and eventually, so did this one.

The decision to put together an anthology of romance stories and poetry set in the deindustrial future was partly one of those things that happens on the crowded, lively comments page of a blog where ideas get batted back and forth like volleyballs. Like the themes of the earlier anthologies, though, it also reflects an important point. Only in bad propaganda and worse science fiction, after all, do ordinary people spend all their time gazing boldly off into whatever canned future they've been told to want. Most people are far more interested in meeting those needs they share with other human beings in every time and place. For most of us, the need for love is one of the most important of those.

All the short stories and poems you're about to read, accordingly, are tales of love and romance set in futures that you won't find in today's corporate mass media—futures in which people are busy dealing with some stage of the decline

---

* My nonfiction books *The Long Descent*, *The Ecotechnic Future*, and *After Progress* make a more detailed case for this assertion.

and fall of industrial civilization and the emergence of new, deindustrial human societies. Some of those futures are grim, some are gritty, some are relatively pleasant, and the characters who inhabit them are just as diverse—but some of them fall in love.

—John Michael Greer

Working Together

Daniel Cowan

Alex took a moment's break from packing the remains of the harvest, along with some tools and other belongings into a large trailer, and took a drink from his canteen in the cooling autumn air. He looked out across the field at his journeyman, hoe in hand, making some finishing touches in the garden before they left for the season. A wiry, middle-aged man with a thick dark beard, he was wearing a wide straw sun-hat, and dressed in a billowy white work-shirt, a long kilt that he'd sewn for himself from cotton broad-cloth, as well as a pair of homemade tire sandals. He did not exactly accord with the image of fashion that Alex was used to at least aspiring to approximate.

Alex had made the trip back to the city twice since the late summer, to transport into town the vegetables and grains that he had helped produce, for the most part to be preserved for the winter by those few who remained in the city for the summer months. He was glad his boss let him make the trip instead of taking it for himself and leaving Alex with a set of chores on the farm. His journeyman, Phillip Ducharme, seemed to him a bit odd, unconcerned with the months of isolation, and welcoming the three days of solitude that these delivery trips would afford him. Alex would have preferred some more time in the city as, aside from these trips, there were only two local dances out in the country to break up the hot summer months. After delivering the produce and arranging for their preservation, and spending a night at his mother's house, he was obliged to make his way back out to the Central Maintenance Union farms.

Harvest would be over soon enough though, and he would have time on his own to enjoy some of the return parties in the city, to play some music and meet up with his friends before winter set in and a new season of work began.

ONE OF THOSE WHO remained in the city for the summer was the chef at a lunch counter next to the law courts. Between orders, Rose was getting two young teenagers set up at a long wooden cutting block next to some baskets of vegetables. Her own cutting block was adjacent to the two hammered-steel woks she cooked at, set back a little from the counter where her customers ate, or at which they could pick up their orders to eat at the tables. From her station she could keep an eye on everything in the restaurant, as well as deliveries being brought down to the cellar.

A regular pushed through the screened door and made his way to a stool at the counter, a bundle of papers under arm, wearing thick round glasses, a loose linen dress shirt, khaki pants and some leather sandals.

"Chicken soup?" Rose asked him. He pulled his lips to one side and gestured with his face "Why not?", while setting out his papers in front of him. "And a light beer."

Rose slid a lever beneath the woks over with her knee, opening the gas valve, and the burners fired with a whoosh while she flicked a spoon of lard into the wok. Once it melted and shimmered, she tossed in a handful of sliced onions, bell peppers, and celery root, and then a few chicken pieces. She tilted the pan, and pushed them up along the cooler back slope of the wok to make space for another little pool of fat, into which she added some ginger, garlic, and dried lime peel. Chicken bones and necks were slowly simmering in the other wok, with a few aromatics and chilies swimming around at the surface. She took a few ladles of broth to add to the vegetables. It came to a quick boil as she added a scoop of cooked rice and a pinch of green herbs. She ladled the mix into a deep clay bowl and brought it to the counter, then pulled a cork stopper from a jug of cool-ish beer to pour him a glass.

"Thank you Rose," he said, only just barely pulling his eyes from his long sheets of handwritten notes. She smiled at him, and moved back to scrub the wok and get ready for the next order.

Rose was deft and quick in every movement she made. Years of kitchen work, the constant activity, slinging around the cast iron cookware, the sacks of grains and the crates of vegetables had made her healthy, fit and strong for her slight frame. Working in a food business helped as well, as there were always nutritious meals to be had from what wasn't sold in the day, which she cooked up to eat with her sister and her helpers.

Their restaurant had been set up by her mother when Rose was young. After Rose's father passed, her mother took over his restaurant supply business, which imported goods that weren't grown locally, various grains, legumes, coffee, spices, an so on, mainly for the few restaurants in the city, as well as for some inns and institutional kitchens. It was successful enough, but grew harder to manage as time went on: demand in the city was always diminishing, and there were continual disruptions in supply. Certain orders would just stop arriving, and their suppliers never heard from again, though Rose's mother, Natalia, would write letters, left to wonder what had happened to her connections.

Natalia kept her ears open for an opportunity to open an establishment of her own, to augment and to diversify away from her import business. She was offered a chance to go in on a roast house that was opening on Wellington Avenue, a wealthier neighbourhood in the city, but instead she took a commission to run a cafeteria in the city centre, right beside the law courts and near city hall and the hospital. It was a good decision. The high-level staff that worked there were a captive clientele of professionals requiring a meeting place that offered interesting meals, which added a steadier income stream to Natalia's family.

Compared to the outdoor ovens at the roast house, her fuel costs were minimal. She had decided on installing the wok stations, as good quality Chinese pans and tools were available from her northern supplier, and the wide pans could be heated quickly for a stir fry as the order came in, and then turned off as quickly again. This helped keep the kitchen from heating up excessively. (In cooler weather, they would sometimes set up an iron grate over charcoal for a change of pace.) The commission came with the ability to buy city bio-gas at a decent rate, as a supply line had already been piped over from the central physical plant across the street.

It was an economical way of cooking. They could use shavings of whatever meat was available (pork, poultry, rabbit, goat, beef, bison) to serve over whatever dried grains or legumes that they had in dry stock (rice, millet, wheat, sorghum, lentils, beans.) To these proteins and carbohydrates they could add whatever vegetables might make sense, incorporating fresh produce from city garden beds, or the onions, cabbages, beets, Brussels sprouts, carrots, garlic and ginger that were stored in the root cellar. Next to some canvas cots along the cool walls of their basement, sauerkraut, kimchi and mushroom mixes fermented in large ceramic crocks. Thin strips of meat could be quickly fried in the woks, or they could steam tougher cuts in bamboo baskets, couching them in garlic, ginger and lemongrass, to be sliced on top of a bed of grains and doused in a flavourful sauce.

With the seasonings and sauces made possible by the imports that Natalia was able to arrange, it amounted to a versatile culinary style. Over the years, Rose had developed a sense of how to combine the varying inputs into one or two coherent dishes to offer per day. Her cooking style was based on traditions her mother had passed on to her, as well as her intuitions on how various regions might have composed flavours and arranged meals. She had a small shelf of old cookbooks near her bed that her sister had slowly collected for her, with faded glossy pictures of restaurants and dishes from early in the century. Over time, groups of immigrants had introduced plants better adapted to the new patterns of temperature and rainfall than some of the traditional crops. The elements of what people ate and of how they cooked it were also settling into new patterns, formed under increasing limitations on available ingredients and cooking fuel, edited by shortages of all kinds.

After her regular had finished his lunch and bundled up his papers on his way out, Rose collected the bowl and the pint glass that was sitting on top of some bills and coins. On her way back to the dish pit, out of the sight of customers, she dropped the money into a slot in a cast iron chute that dropped down into a safe in the cellar. City centre was a relatively well-policed area, and some of their clients who were in a position to do so made sure that the security of the restaurant was given special attention. Still, Natalia had taken whatever precautions she could think of to make her businesses as unattractive as possible to anyone contemplating a break-in or a robbery. She had learned from the economic crises and periods of chaos that had she had seen come and go, and planned her operations accordingly.

IN THE EARLY MORNING Alex rolled up their bed clothes and bug nets, and loaded them into the trailer along with their generator and their pump. He checked the air pressure on the tires, harnessed their two mules to the trailer's makeshift hitch, and with that they were ready to go. Philip climbed into the open cab, dressed today not in his gardening wear but instead in his city work uniform, a dark collared shirt, dark denim pants, cuffs rolled up, and some leather shoes. His hair had grown out about a quarter-inch from when he had recently shaved it. No socks though, for whatever reason, Alex noted. The younger apprentice had put on some nicer clothes for the journey himself, wearing a newer red plaid shirt and some blue jeans. He had shaved his deeply tanned face, though he barely needed to. His blonde hair was nearly down to his jawline at this point, and he planned to get a haircut once he got back into the city.

Not tending the reins on this trip, and his journeyman morose and silent as usual, Alex had plenty of time to reflect on his first summer out on the union farms, which could have been the first of many. He did not relish the thought. It wasn't that he minded the work, and it was pleasant to be out in the country over the hot summer months, when the heat was especially oppressive in the city. It felt dead in town over the summer anyways, as so many people closed up business for the season and headed out to work on the land and grow food, in various arrangements. Alex doubted though that many in either the city or the country had to endure the spans of deadly quiet that he did that summer, assisting his journeyman, who had no wife or family to bring out with him to help their camp feel more like a home.

They rolled slowly down the highway. Alex watched the ruined houses, clustered together every so often not too far from the road. In a few places though along the path leading into Winnipeg, there were a few homes that were maintained year round. Some family had obviously stayed in place over the decades of disruptions, to patch, paint, caulk or tarp as needed to keep the elements out.

"How long since most of these houses were put up?"

"Hmm. I'd say about eighty years for most. Sixty maybe for the last ones."

And silence again for a while between them. They approached another camp, about eight people working in the field. Alex didn't know these people's affiliation, but he did feel a touch of longing at the idea of working in a group like that. He noticed too that, like the camp Philip and Alex had just closed down for the season, they were making use of some of the poured concrete basements that had been left intact beneath these collapsing chipboard structures. If a basement could be found that wasn't too big, and where the house had been built on higher ground where drainage wouldn't be a constant problem, these could be covered and used as in-ground shelter. Retreating frequently into the cool ground was pretty much the only option to pass through the summer's devastating heat.

At the site they had stayed at in the Maintenance Union's grounds, some debarked logs had been pulled across the top of such a concrete dugout. Moss had been pounded into the crevices where the logs came together, and on top of that were some loosely-filled sandbags that had been arranged into an A-shaped roof, aiming to move standing water away from their shelter. Some fence boards and brushwood had been woven together over the sandbags. They had a piece of corrugated tin, weighed down with cinder blocks on three corners, to cover over the hatch at the front where they climbed down

11

into their quarters. And though the original houses that had been built on these concrete foundations were gone, the original well casings were often in good shape, pipes of about six inches in diameter that had been drilled many feet deep into the earth to access water in the ground. The Maintenance Union used jet pumps and portable generators to draw water from these wells, filling large clay vessels they had commissioned from the city's Clayworkers Union.

Watching this group in the field, a few men and a few women, Alex wondered how they arranged their sleeping spaces, and how they spent their downtime. Alex and Philip had gotten up early nearly every day of the summer, working from the cooler hours of the morning until about noon, when the heat would become unbearable. They would take a break on their cots for a few hours. If he didn't sleep, Alex would practice quietly on his mandolin, writing down lyrics and chords in his notebook when a new song was coming together. He didn't ask if Philip minded, and Philip never mentioned it, so he worked on his songs throughout the summer, but kept it muted nonetheless. A row of clay cisterns separated their sleeping areas somewhat, and kept the air around them a bit cooler over a radius of a few feet.

The summer was behind him now. Next year, maybe he could have more time working in some of the other, larger camps of the Maintenance Union's? For seeding, harvest, and for a little bit of building, Alex had helped out some others for a few days over the summer. As he got to know Philip more, and so long as he put in his work on Philip's plots, maybe he could spend more time living in another camp? Alex didn't think his journeyman would mind the time alone.

Overall he liked working for Philip, and was actually quite grateful to have been taken on at all. A lot of his fellow apprentices had harsher work conditions than his. He managed to get along with Philip for the most part, but it was a hard transition into the working world from how he had been living. His parents had allowed him, a little unusually, to follow his own interests late into his adolescence. His father, Bill Roche, was well off, having worked as an official in the upper ranks of the city's bureaucracy. He was a competent man, and had carved out a place for himself organizing various essential services and dealing with the unions that were supposed to provide them, along the wealthy families whose interests were also always involved. He was a good negotiator. He managed his connections and his influence with skill, and balanced his own security with the demands of the city and of the unions, well aware that these were all connected. The long hours that he put in, the constant dealing and the precarious obligations that he struggled to fulfill, inclined him to let his son move along a different path. So Alex had finished the tenth grade and focused on music, making some money with a band of friends, playing the coffee houses and pubs around Osborne street and any other occasion for which they managed to get hired to perform.

Those coffee houses all sold several local newspapers along with a few books, and often had a rack of pamphlets and zines on offer for a few cents each, covering everything from art and poetry to politics and religion. These venues had developed an atmosphere of discussion and debate, and so as well as playing shows, Alex had taken an interest in politics. He met frequently with a group that was heavy into political discussion, as well as occasional actions and agitations. They picked apart and debated proposals and essays written by thinkers of various persuasions, focusing especially on distributist, communtarian, and syndicalist tracts.

Alex hadn't at all mastered the details of the common positions held in this group, but he enjoyed immersing himself in this scene, and all philosophy and history that was being introduced to him. To some extent the ideas being discussed aligned with his father's politics. Various schemes were entertained, but in general the idea was to somehow limit the role of money in the economy, with the most essential, locally produced goods and services to be portioned out to the unions and workplaces of the city, according to the number of their members and what they provided to the economy. Maybe a council with representatives from the city's many workplace unions could meet to arrange how these essential goods would be apportioned.

Recurring depressions and a lack of coordination between local and regional governments had given rise to periods of economic chaos, where the money supply and credit could never seem to cover local requirements. People were left scrambling to find ways to earn enough to get by, and were looking for security in meeting their basic needs. Wealthy families often had the savings and the food stores to weather these periods with ease, but a lot of ordinary people were wondering if there wasn't a way for an essential economy of things like food, housing and medicine to continue locally and uninterrupted even when the national economy was out of order. At the same time, the wealthy families of the city were not keen to see the idea of distribution based on labour rather than ownership take root.

When Alex's father had fallen ill and eventually had to leave his position, it seemed to mark the end of Alex's youth. His parents didn't press the issue of him finding a more stable means of income, but when some protests had descended into rioting, and Alex had gotten in some trouble with the police, it was clear even to Alex that his family's circumstances were requiring him make changes and take on more responsibility. His father didn't live to see Alex begin as an apprentice in the Maintenance Union, but Alex felt he would've been proud to see him work his way into the ranks of one of the organizations his father had worked with for so much of his own career.

Even without regretting his new line of work, he did miss all the late smokey evenings in the village creating music, with all the culture and the characters he'd gotten to know. It seemed distant to Alex at the moment, but he was looking forward to a taste of it again, and to some respite during this short gap between summer and fall, when the city as a whole paused and celebrated for a moment before changing gears for the colder seasons.

He turned to Philip, "Do you think we'll ever build out here again?"

Philip took a moment, and looked up and off in the distance, turning the question over.

"Yeah, I think so. Once all the troubles die down, I could see people building out here again. If the wars died down, and we could get supplies easier, I could see it."

A noisy pickup truck with some sort of hand-painted company logo on the passenger-side door overtook their trailer on the highway, and then moved slowly on ahead.

A PAIR OF SURGEONS were finishing up a large meal at a corner table, eating their way through some bowls of meat and vegetables, with some small dishes of sauce, a sambal and a mayonnaise dip, and a platter of thin flatbread. They're celebrating something, Rose thought, or maybe indulging after a difficult ordeal at the hospital. She had sent the food out on a new set of dishes she had bought from the nearby potter's gallery, all with a mottled deep-blue glaze.

"Hey Rose!" one of them called out across the restaurant, a little overly loud. Rose looked up from her cutting block. "I love these bowls! What do you say we take them with us?"

She raised her cleaver up into their sight-line and bobbed it in the air. "What do you say I take a few knuckles?" She paused and then gave them a slight smile. They grinned, as did an administrator who was eating at the counter, a woman wearing an elegant long dress, with a thin, light grey fabric that she wrapped around her shoulders.

"Alright, they stay here!" Rose returned to her work.

Rose was a definite favourite among those who had business in the city centre, as her mother had been. She was a beautiful woman with a commanding presence, not hesitant to speak her mind. She ran the business with intelligence, and was attentive to the needs of people she dealt with, the restaurant's customers and all the others that she purchased from or supplied. She had long dark hair, that she usually had her sister braid and tie up, to sit behind a black baker's cap. Her daily uniform was a black t-shirt, loose checkered kitchen pants, a long black apron tied with some cloths at the waist, and a pair of rubberized clogs on her bare feet. In her appearance and personality, as well as in her capabilities, she was a radiant figure to those who knew her.

Her mother had passed earlier in the summer. Though Rose didn't show it, talking with doctors made her uneasy, she had mixed feelings and held some resentment towards them. As helpful as they had been with her mother, they had scheduled her surgery for the winter, after the hospital resumed full operations and they starting working through their back-list of non-urgent procedures. She had no way of knowing, but of course she had to wonder if her mother would have survived with more timely attention.

Her mother had been in poor health for awhile, so Rose was used to running the restaurant and the import supply on her own, along with overseeing her sister's small side-business. When their mother had passed, the burden on Rose was lessened somewhat, not having to care for her on top of the long days at work. But she couldn't help feeling the weight of responsibility increase on her, particularly for her sister, and for the network of relatives and cousins that often looked to her mother for help for help. The city was always falling into periods of desperation in recent years, especially as industry and the government began to focus more to the north. A lot of things were being neglected, and Rose felt the strain of keeping things together in lean times.

Katerina was at her usual table off to the side of the restaurant, as her morning duties in the kitchen and the store room were finished, and the small animals in the building's courtyard had been fed. She bussed tables as needed in the afternoon, while she caught up on paperwork, among other things. Rose never exactly knew what Katerina was working on. Her sister was a much quieter person than herself, and a bit secretive, you had to pry if you wanted details from her. Looking over at her table, three or four books beside a notebook and some papers clipped together, it was clear she was busy with something.

Katerina had kept the books for their businesses for years now. She had been pulled from school to work a little less early than Rose had been, but her mother knew Katerina was not going to take to physical work as readily as her sister had. She was reading whenever she had a chance, she was shy and lived in her head a lot more than she focused on the details of daily life. As a younger teenager, Katerina had mentioned some vague ideas of wanting to work in the city's office complex, as a secretary perhaps, so her mother got her a subscription to *Modern Professional*, a small quarterly publication that catered to these sorts of aspirations, aimed mainly at young women, with articles about making it into, and succeeding in, the professional classes. It was mostly a vehicle for selling correspondence courses, of which her mother purchased a few to further Katerina's education: bookkeeping, penmanship and various scripts, applied math, short-hand, basic legal studies.

Katerina devoured these courses, receiving the lesson materials by mail, and usually sending back the tests and assignments far before they were due. Natalia was pleased with the system she'd set up for her younger daughter: she could put in some work with basic chores and attend to her courses later in the day. She gave over to Katerina more of the administrative work, writing letters to suppliers, paying taxes, and so forth, and Katerina talked less about wanting to get a job in the government or industry. This pleased Natalia too, as while she wanted her daughter to be happy, she was averse to the idea of working for wages, and liked to keep her family working together.

Over time, an idea came to Natalia of a business for Katerina. Constantly interacting with the various professions and government officials at the restaurant, from time to time they asked Natalia if she could maybe source a certain book from her contacts in Chicago or Minneapolis, with some sort of technical information they were needing, regarding things like medicine, geography, or engineering. Sometimes she was successful, bringing the books in along with some other supplies, and she wondered if maybe she could start up a small bookstore beside the restaurant that Kat could manage. The space she had in mind was more an alcove than a full shop, it had been once been the front desk and lobby for some offices there. But it could fit a few bookshelves, and they could build some stock slowly. There was a need for information that was getting harder to access these days, maybe she could carve a niche for her daughter in supplying that gap.

Mind was another magazine that Katerina had a subscription to, a lot more fun than the professional journal, which was filled with logic puzzles, crosswords, and a diverse array of articles on topics like code breaking, mnemonic systems, Latin etymology, and speed reading. It was an amusement, but it helped immensely in dealing with the requests that the professionals grew accustomed to placing with her. A lot of the specifics they mentioned were alien to her, but she could make an image with her mnemonic system to keep a track of it quickly, even if she was busy. She couldn't always arrange for a book to be ordered, but she developed some work-arounds: sometimes materials could be loaned, and she could write up a neat manuscript for her client, or an article could be mailed, or she could even arrange a long-distance phone call, and take notes dictated by a specialist. Her short-hand and her practice with mnemonics made that possible.

Katerina would sometimes practice her short-hand and her concentration from her table in the restaurant, eavesdropping on conversations, singling them out through the noise of a lunchtime service. No one noticed, and even if they did, no one would be able to read her personalized notation of what they had said. She was good at working from the sidelines, and didn't mind letting her sister take centre-stage.

"Hey Kat!" Rose called from behind the woks. Kat looked up from her book. Rose gestured to the dishes on two tables in the corner that had been vacant for awhile.

"Oh yes, thanks," Kat replied, marking her place and getting up. She had known they were there, but had tried to finish up her chapter first.

MOVING TOWARDS WINNIPEG FROM the east, Philip and Alex took a short detour off the highway when they saw off to their right the tops of the lime kilns above the prairie horizon, smoke rising from several spots in the vicinity. As they moved towards them, their road passed through an open quarry, and Alex looked out over the men down in the rocky pit, working with hammers and shovels, filling carts with the blasted stone. Though they were heading into autumn, the direct sun coming down on field of white rock beneath the cliffs was intense. As much as he had struggled over the past year, he saw clearly how much harder some lines of work were compared to his own.

A sign on the path read 'Manitoba Limeworks and Colliers Union', leading into the complex of kilns, the central plant and the workers' barracks. And as hard as the work in the quarry must be, Alex couldn't imagine adding to the summer heat with the continual fires that were burning here, roasting the limestone and producing charcoal from the massive piles of chopped wood stacked in the field beyond. There were men in gloves and long-sleeved shirts, with goggles and scarves over their faces, raking the the quicklime from the bases of the kilns, and others, blackened with soot, collecting the charred wood into large sacks tied onto wooden pallets. Maybe they worked mainly night shifts during the heat spells? There were lamp posts set up throughout the grounds. Alex couldn't imagine any other way.

Their trailer was more than half-way full at this point, but there was room to load in some of these building supplies that their Union used in such large quantities. Philip would be reimbursed for the materials when he dropped them off and credited for the delivery. Every little payment helped to make ends meet. They pulled up alongside a loading dock, and arranged for a worker to cart out four kegs of quicklime and three larger sacks of crushed charcoal, which he helped Alex load into the trailer while Philip went into the office to pay.

There were two other vehicles at the dock doing the same as them, making building supplies a part of their cargo on their way into the city. Leaning up against the trailer, Alex couldn't help but eavesdrop while they conversed with another worker about city news. His heart sank at what he heard. The two councillors who had been working in networks related to the political circles he'd been a part of last year had been arrested. The charges were unclear, but Alex was sure that it would be something entirely unrelated to the fact that the ideas which these politicians were promoting were gaining popularity in the city. He had no idea if these two might in fact be involved in corruption or something like that, but whatever the case, it wasn't good news for the movement that he realized now he still had some hopes for. After the months out in the country, overhearing this conversation about the murky intersection between politics, the legal system and the industrialists left Alex feeling somewhat glad that he had left his involvement in all that behind when he started his apprenticeship.

"I think we'll stop here for the day," Philip said, interrupting Alex's thoughts as he passed around the mules, heading toward the trailer's cab. "They said it's alright to camp in the grounds over there. We'll eat, and have a good sleep, and make it back into the city later tomorrow."

They drove the trailer to a site beyond the workers' barracks, with a few fire pits spaced out around a well with an iron hand pump. Alex wanted to take a look at the kilns, so he said he'd take a walk and pick some firewood from the lot they'd seen on their way in. He reached over behind the lime kegs to grab some cloth to use as a sling to carry the wood. Philip started putting up their two canvas pup tents, and set out some hay and water for the mules.

It must have been dinner time for the kiln workers, as the lot was empty and quiet, except for the crackling of fires in various kilns. The lime kilns were towers made themselves out of limestone, while the charcoal units were made of thick steel, painted black, in which logs were stacked behind heavy metal doors. The charcoal units were paired with the kilns, with pipes directing the gases let off by the charring wood into the fires of the lime kilns.

Alex had heard that the Limeworks had been built in the twenties and thirties, during the drawdown efforts undertaken back then. He had no idea if those old projects, with all those countries working together, might still be in operation, but whatever the case it was good they had invested in all this, through his work this last year he had seen how useful it had proven to be. Philip was nominally a member of the plumbing division of the Maintenance Union, though more often than not they were removing people's plumbing systems instead of installing them, capping off connections between buildings and the sewer system. The treatment plants had become unreliable, and especially in the heavy rains, basements were continually underwater.

Alex's main task was usually taking a sledge hammer to the concrete floor above a building's main drain, so that he could dig down to cut the main sewer line, and plug the pipe with a mix of sand, gravel and lime mortar. Cement was unusual these days, and to replace the hole they'd broken in the floor, they made a mix of quicklime, clay and char to cover it back over. The lime and char also worked well for repairing leaks in the old foundation walls made from river stone, they could chisel out the old mortar and replace it.

The old concrete though was harder to replace. Cracks could be tarred over for a while, but eventually, when the steel rebar swelled and turned to powered rust in the centre of the concrete walls, structural strength was lost, and the buildings had to be abandoned and taken down. They would salvage all the rusted rebar they could, collecting into sacks all the pieces or reddish flakes they could gather together, to sell to the Metal Workers, who would melt it down to solid iron products once again. The pieces of concrete would be carted away and crushed down to be used as filler in other projects like road repairs.

The city would cover some of the cost of the plumbing maintenance work if the building's bathrooms were set up for the collection of wastes by the night-soil men. This was a common project for Philip and Alex, building compartments to house the receptacles that would replace toilets and hold cover materials like sawdust and charcoal pellets. In wealthier households they sometimes installed systems where small amounts of water moved the bathroom wastes down the maintenance room for collection, by workers from the city's main powerhouse.

Another legacy of the sustainability measures of the twenties and thirties were some giant anaerobic digesters that were constructed in the city's core, as well as a number of facilities that recovered heat from the composting process. Food scraps, garden wastes, night soil, shredded brushwood, and livestock bedding were all collected and used to provide energy for the city: the digesters produced bio-gas for space heaters, cooking facilities, and electrical production, while the compost systems provided base heat to certain dormitories and industrial buildings, the heated water circulating into iron radiators, reducing the need for fuel in the colder months. Both systems created fertilizer for the city's gardens and the surrounding farms, and both incorporated crushed charcoal from the Collier's Union. Adding char to the soils over time helped with both the drainage of the heavy spring rains, and also to retain moisture in the ground over the drier months of late summer.

Touring through the kilns had Alex loosely contemplating the connections between the parts of the city and the country that he'd been to exposed to over the last year, the farms, the households he'd worked in, the larger industrial plants. When he got to the piles of logs and straw and branches, restless from the day of driving, he ambled around in the stacks, thinking, balancing on some high points, taking some precarious leaps from one point to another. By the time he'd collected up their firewood and headed back to the trailer, the kiln workers were coming back onto the site. Alex steered wide around them. Even from a distance some of them looked rough and unfriendly. The sight of this haggard crew and their isolation out at this camp once again made Alex feel grateful for position he'd secured.

As the evening light faded, Alex started the fire. They pierced some pieces of sweet potato on metal prongs to roast, to eat along with a bit of beef jerky and pickled eggs and beets.

ROSE SLOWLY CLIMBED THE stairs in the courtyard up to the landing outside their family's second floor apartment, and took a moment to look out at the sky. The evening sun was casting dark pink hues up on the heavy clouds resting on the city's skyline. Kat heard her unlock the deadbolt, and looked up from the kitchen table at Rose coming through the door. Rose paused when she saw her, and something in Rose's eyes made Kat nervous right away.

Rose slipped off her black clogs onto the mat and came over to the table. She seemed like she was going to say something, and then paused again. "We need to talk for a minute."

"Sure."

Rose took a seat on the chair, angled a little away from facing Katerina directly. "That position they were talking about, up north, they awarded it to me." She looked up. "They want me to move up there, this week."

Kat was silent. A friend of Rose's hearing the news would've at least tried to put on show of being glad for her getting this commission, and to cover over their sadness to see her go. But the sisters, close as they were, especially after losing their mother recently, were both overwhelmed with trying to process the implications.

Rose started again, "We're going to have to leave the restaurant to you, at least for a bit."

Kat wiped a tear from her face, Rose's eyes started to well up. "Why do they want you so soon?"

"Ah," Rose began to reply, trying to steady her shaking voice, "I guess it's the same up there as it is down here, their city's starting up again in full for the fall. There are big dinners planned, politicians from Asia are coming in to stay in the consulate. I have to get up there to organize everything, the supplies, the menus, and train people in the kitchen there. You know how it is with staffing, people get sick or go missing last minute, things turn on a dime." She leaned on to the table and rested her chin on her hand. "It's a really good opportunity for us though."

Kat's eyes had dried a little, she was trying to think everything through. "It's going to be busy next week here, with everyone coming back into the city, the parties and all. You know I don't do the work that you do Rose."

"I know, Kat. But you have seen it all so many times, and you don't have to do it just like I do, you can make the things that you want to. If people don't like it, too bad." She paused for a moment. They both knew that Kat wouldn't take well the complaints she was bound to receive. "You've got the helpers, and you can hire more if you need. You don't have to open every day right away either, I'm going to be bringing in plenty of money up north, we can afford it. And with the return parties and everything next week, people are going to be out of their routines anyway."

Kat stared down at the table. There were so many details left out of these directions that they both knew there wouldn't be time to work out before Rose left. Kat would just have to figure things out as she went. She looked at Rose again, "Are you going to come back?"

"Not for a bit, Kat. I don't know how this is going to go. I'd really hate to lose this restaurant and our other accounts unless I knew for sure that things will be good up there, but

if things turn out, we could give this place up, or have someone else in the family take this over, and you could come up
with me. Maybe I could come back to train someone, and get
things in order."

"But what about the bookstore?"

"I don't know. Maybe you could do something like that
up there."

Kat's took a deep breath, her head was spinning. She got
up and put her arms around Rose, and leaned her head into
Rose's shoulder. "I'm going to miss you."

PHILIP HAD CIRCLED THE trailer around the edge of the city
to the nearby town of Charleswood to drop Alex off at his
mothers' house. Philip paid his respects, and they made some
vague plans to meet in about ten days to start up their winter
maintenance work, before he left to head into Winnipeg.

He had considered having Alex help him unload the trailer in the city before dropping taking him home, but he sensed
his apprentice's patience wearing thin over the last stretch of
the summer, and felt his restlessness growing the closer they
got to the city. Best that he let loose for a bit, then calm down
again. Overall, Alex had done well over the summer, he was
glad to give him the time before they set to work again.

On his way out of Charleswood, Philip stopped at a store
to buy a little tobacco, and dug out a pipe from a bag of his in
the trailer. He hadn't smoked anything all summer. His habit
was to use the move out to the farm in the spring to shed
whatever vices he'd fallen into over the winter. There was a
period of withdrawal anyways switching from city life to the
quiet of the country, it worked to mask the withdrawals from
any other indulgences that had crept into his life. Indulging
with his pipe today though he allowed himself, marking the
changing of the seasons.

Philip himself really wasn't that excited to get back into the city, though a change of pace from working on the farm plot was welcome. It wasn't his aim to isolate himself over the summers, but he'd found the gatherings on the union farms a little too close and open and intimate for his liking. Ironically, there was a bit more space between people in the city, and that touch of formality suited him. Watching Alex happy to join up with other crews for a few days at a time, Philip felt a little ashamed. Maybe he should try to be more outgoing? He was resigned to the idea that this wasn't likely. Once your habits and your reputation have reinforced the faults in your nature, it's hard to make a change.

Looking ahead at another winter in the city, headaches seemed to line up one after the next. It was getting harder to function in his trade. Not that there weren't a lot of repairs and a little construction for them to do, but finding a way to pay for these was getting harder. People were doing without, or abandoning their buildings altogether to move elsewhere. Proper parts could be hard to come by, and patches and impromptu fixes were not the way he liked to work. He didn't always have a lot of choice. Keeping an apprentice was another expense, even just one was a struggle for many in the union to afford . He saw promise in Alex, he wanted to keep him on: when Philip took on an apprentice, he did his best to see them through learning the trade, when they'd be recognized and could take on jobs and apprentices of their own. It was not only his work, but the general violence and the theft in the city that had been weighing on him for the last few years. Desperation had introduced a sense of lawlessness into daily life, and not just among the poor, it was at all levels. At what point would he decide to give it up and try for a better opportunity?

Philip exhaled deeply, pulled back his shoulders tightly for a moment, and tried to release all this worry. He'd be alright. As long as he worked hard, and stayed vigilant, and made himself useful, there would be a way to make a living. It was a matter of managing problems as they arose, and that was done moment by moment, when the time came.

When he got into Winnipeg proper, he pulled the trailer over, hitched the mules, and bought a bottle of soda. He sat in the cab for a moment and watched the people in the street. Two women were leaving a hair salon together. That is one business that will never fail, Philip thought, when it comes to people's looks they'll always find a way to come up with the money. In a studio to the right, some grunting and slamming could be heard from the open windows out on the street below. One large young man was working out combinations on a canvas heavy bag, a few others were on the mats practising some catch-wrestling. Henderson's Fight Club. From further down the street Philip could hear a church choir in an afternoon rehearsal. Always a lot of noise and activity to acclimate to in the city.

As Philip made his way to city centre, a little further north than the old rail-yards, just after passing the law-courts he came across a woman leaning up against the post of a fence, her face buried in the sleeve of her long white dress. There was bit of blood splattered across her apron. He noticed her light-brown hair tied up loosely, resting on the stiff white collar of her dress. A cleaver dangled from her hand, on his side of the fence. He pulled back on the reins, and brought the cart to a stop.

"Ma'am, is everything alright?"

Katerina sniffled, and pinched the bridge of her nose with her fingers, and then drew her fingers across her closed eyes to clear away the tears. She looked up at the stranger, not knowing how to answer. "I... can't.... I don't like doing this," she said as started to cry again. Philip looked at her again, and then through the fence to further in the yard, and saw a chicken's body dangling from a thin rope, it's head cut off. There was also a goat chained to the fence.

He took a moment, and sat there while she collected herself . "Well, if you don't like to do it, do you have to? You couldn't bring them to the butcher's maybe?" he said, thinking aloud.

She turned her head slightly and looked askance into the yard. She hadn't thought of that, Rose had always done it herself, but maybe that was an idea?

She didn't quite meet his gaze. "It's only that... The restaurant there, nothing's set up, I can't get the burners to work right..." She looked up at him, "Just not a good day."

He wasn't sure how to respond. She wasn't quite asking for help, but she wasn't indicating that he should move along either. "What kind of burners?" he asked.

"Oh, um, they're under the wok pans we cook with."

"Well, I could take a look at them if you like. I work in the maintenance union, with that sort of thing."

She looked up at him again, scanning his face to see if she felt she could trust him to let him into the closed restaurant alone. Rose's two helpers were kept late today working at the back table, but they were still fairly young, they probably wouldn't be a lot of help if he was to rob them.

"Um, sure," she said, thinking it over, "you can pull your trailer in here." She walked over and unlocked the long gate they opened for delivery carts.

She stepped up on the back dock, and hung up the bloodied apron and the cleaver as well, fitting the hole in the corner of the steel blade over a thick nail in the wall. She washed up over the outdoor sink, and took a cloth from her pocket and wiped it by her reddened eyes, trying to get a hold of her emotions and deal with this day. "Just a moment," she said as he paused by the back steps. "Ok, right in here."

"I didn't get your name yet, ma'am."

"Oh, Katerina. Chovnyk." She held out her hand to shake.

"Philip Ducharme. Nice to meet you," he said, giving a slight nod with his head.

Two young faces looked up at him blankly as they came through the back end of the kitchen, halting the conversation they were having while slicing some onions and cabbage. The air was pretty smoky, the wok on the right had a fair amount of suet rendering and spitting out bits of oil or water. Philip didn't know much about cooking, but this looked way too hot, and dangerous. Katerina walked up to the pan, tilting it carefully away to try to avoid being hit with splatter. "This pedal here, it seemed pretty stuck this morning," leaning down to the gas lever at knee height, "I forced it to come on but it doesn't seem to work anymore."

He bent over to move the lever back and forth, it was very loose. It looked like the shaft had snapped off inside the valve, you couldn't regulate the bio-gas with it anymore. Philip stood up to take a look at which direction the steel pipe was running from. Just as worrisome were the hood vents above the woks, they didn't seem to be taking up the exhaust very quickly. Not such a danger today, with the breeze from the open windows and the iron grate doors, but with colder weather that would be a problem.

"Do you need these on for the rest of the day?" he said, gesturing to the woks.

"We'll be here for a while, but we're not opening 'til tomorrow morning. I guess they just need to be on to finish this."

"Ok, good, well if you want... I'm just getting back into the city today, I'm not really set up for this at the moment. But if you want, I could come back in the morning and probably get this lever working. For today..." He trailed off, moving over to look behind some shelves at the gas piping. "Ah, yes" he said, as he bent down near the far wall, throttling the gas supply with a shut-off valve on a pipe coming up through the floor. The flames beneath the pan with the suet dropped down towards the burner nozzles, heating the woks far more gently. "I'll leave this bar here mostly down like that, and when you're done, move the bar right down towards the floor, and make sure those flames go out."

Katerina took a look in behind the shelf to see the valve. She hadn't ever paid much attention to the details of the restaurant, that was always Rose's domain. She was realizing today how much she ignored the daily operations of their businesses, focusing only on her limited tasks so that she could attend to her own interests. Maybe she should have taken more notice of how things were done over the years: with her mother gone and Rose moved away, it was so much to take on this abruptly. There was no way that Rose could've prepared her in so short a time.

"I'm hoping too that there's access to the roof around here," Philip continued, "I'm thinking there is something not right with these hood vents. You should probably have those looked at before the weather gets colder outside."

Katerina looked at him, feeling overwhelmed with him piling on these issues. "Can you do that?"

"Oh yes, sure. No problem. I'll try to make up something for that lever tonight, and like I said, I can be back in the morning." The pedal was a specialty device that had come with the unit that those woks were sitting on, probably a long time ago, but Philip was thinking of ways he might attach it to a regular gas valve with something he could find in the union shop.

"Ok, then, do we pay you, or the Maintenance Union, tomorrow then, or do you need something today? We're ok for the money," Katerina said to reassure him. "I don't normally deal with these things."

Philip looked at her, and thought a moment. "You know what? I'm just coming in from the country today, I've got a lot of vegetables in that trailer, and more I had brought in a few weeks ago. I'm thinking maybe I could do the repair, and the cleaning, no need for pay, and your restaurant could buy some of the food I've got stored from the summer?"

He really should not have offered that. The food was really more the union's than his own. Those who spent the summers in the country were credited for what they produced, but what was produced on the farm was more for the security of all the union's workers, not just those that grew it. He might be able to buy some of this back, in order to sell it, pointless as that would be. Philip's mind was racing through some ideas as to how he might make good on this strange deal he had proposed. Nonetheless, on this day, coming back into the city after months of isolation, and not expecting to be taking on his role as maintenance worker yet, his impulse was not to make this repair a transaction for pay, but rather to strike up some relationship with this woman and her restaurant. He'd worry about providing the vegetables later.

"Well, we might be able to do that. We do run a food supply business here too, it's not hard for us to make use of extra food," she said, with a slight smile, pleased to be able to offer something other than wages in return herself.

"Great. Ok then, I'll be back tomorrow, first thing." He smiled and nodded, and started for the back door. "Oh," he said, and looked back, "that chicken—I'll to be passing a butcher's on my way, would you like me to drop it off and bring the meat back tomorrow?"

Katerina's heart dropped a little, being reminded of the stress of dealing with the animals, at the same time as she was touched by his attention to detail and his helpfulness.

"Please. Thank you."

PHILIP HAD PARKED THE trailer in the Union compound for the night, and slept the night in a dorm room there, to get up early to deal with the contents of the trailer, and to gather a few parts and tools to complete the repairs at the restaurant. It was no hardship, he was used to getting up very early over the summer, trying to get some work done before the heat became overwhelming. Katerina had been on his mind, lightly, over the night. Something about her and the atmosphere of the restaurant had caught his interest. He didn't feel like hanging around the union hall today. He felt a call to get involved with something new, and wondered if there was any way for that to happen.

The trailer and the mules were left in the compound. After a light breakfast of rough-cut oats, Philip borrowed a worksman tricycle with a deep cargo bin, and packed it with a basic tool kit, some varied lengths of threaded steel pipe and rod, some pipe wrenches, and some brushes for cleaning out the vents. An energizing cool autumn breeze met him as he set out below the garage door and headed towards the butcher's shop.

When he arrived at the restaurant, he tapped on the metal window screening to be let in. One of the helpers he'd seen yesterday, the younger sister of the pair, came to let him in. On the dock, some charcoal was heating up an iron grate.

"All cut up," Philip said to Katerina, placing the packages of chicken, neatly wrapped in brown butcher's paper, on the back counter.

"Thank you so much. Did you find what you needed to get the wok going?"

"Yep, I think so. I'll get to that first, I'm sure you'll be needing it soon."

"Yes! Thank you."

Philip carried the tool kit to the woks and started to work. He watched Katerina move about in the kitchen, somewhat frantic and lost, bringing things up and down from the cellar, working with the helpers on the large cutting blocks. The older boy, maybe fourteen years old or so, was offering his advice, and helped her out with a large pot of water to the charcoal stove.

By the time he'd installed the new valve and turned the bio-gas back on to the woks, a few customers had already been let in and had taken seats at the counter, reading newspapers, conversing and drinking some tea. Katerina was trying to set herself up at the woks as Philip was gathering his tools. He went up on the roof to check on the vents while she started making a few of the dishes she'd planned for the day.

By the time Philip had carried his tools back down off the roof, the restaurant had gotten pretty busy. He tried to make himself scarce as he tested the hood vents, twisting up a sheet of newsprint, and reaching in beside Katerina to light it from the flames beneath the wok. He blew it out, so it would issue a little stream of smoke near the hood vents, to see if it would be quickly drawn up and out through the vents.

Despite trying to be unobtrusive, he could sense that Katerina was stressed by the cooking, and was a little irritated by the interruption, though she tried not to let on. Once he was sure the vents were working, he stepped off to the side, taking a look at the customers at the tables, and back at the two helpers working at the cutting block and minding the stove out back.

"Katerina," he started, and hesitated.

"Yes?"

"Is it possible I could help out in the kitchen?"

She looked at him with questioning eyes. Was he wanting a job? Was this part of what he'd mentioned yesterday, about buying the vegetables? She was getting confused about what she was owing him at this point. "Alright, um—were you wanting to be paid separate from the repairs, or..?"

He took a moment. "You know, I'm not too worried about pay right at the moment." He was thinking how he could phrase this, and raised his eyes to meet hers. "I've just got back into town yesterday, and I've got some time off for the end of the season. I'm just interested in the restaurant, I've never really seen in a place like this, how it works. And the kind of food you make."

She looked back at him, and her face softened. "Yeah, alright. That's fine." She looked at his hands and clothes, marked with soot and dust and grease. "You should probably wash up, the sink's out back." She smiled. "There's an apron on the hook back there." She didn't know what to make of the offer, but she supposed it couldn't hurt and she didn't have a lot of time to consider it, being currently swarmed with orders during her first lunch service.

After he got cleaned up, they set Philip up with a chef's knife where the young man had been working, while he went up to the woks to help Katerina and to deal with the customers. He moved back and forth to get Philip organized when he had a moment. The younger helper, the young man's sister, gave some pointers on how to hold his knife, on how thick to slice the various vegetables, or how fine to dice them, passing on some of the instructions she'd been taught by Rose.

Over the afternoon, all of them had a little fun taking on unfamiliar tasks. The lunch service was right on the edge of falling apart, but they were being creative, and made to relate to each other differently than their normal roles dictated. For the first time since Rose had left earlier in the week the gloom had lifted in the kitchen. Philip didn't say a lot, and focused on the various jobs he was given, but he was glad to have a place in the restaurant for the day. Katerina appreciated his help and his presence, especially that he was able to quietly blend in with them unobtrusively, strange as the circumstances were having him working in the kitchen out of the blue.

Over the next few days, while getting settled back in his apartment and dealing with belongings and equipment he'd brought back from the farm, stowing them away for the winter at the union compound, Philip kept coming by the restaurant for a few hours at time, helping out with the various crises as they arose, in the restaurant, or with their stores and the supply business. He was interested in how the restaurant operated. He'd been involved in growing food for quite a few years now, but his own knowledge of cooking was very basic. He enjoyed seeing how they processed all the meats and vegetables and other foodstuffs. The little adjoining bookshop, and the professionals who were regulars at the counter gave the restaurant an atmosphere that Philip found interesting, it was a world outside his usual routine.

Questions of pay fell into the background. Possibly they were working under the pretense he was coming by the kitchen to secure the sale of the vegetables he'd grown. With the preparations underway for the return parties coming up, and in the wake of the shock of Rose leaving so abruptly, Katerina and her helpers were in a holiday mood, the addition of Philip's presence in their operations sort of blended in with all the other changes of the week.

That Friday in the late afternoon, when the helpers were washing up outside, Philip approached Katerina before leaving for the day.

"Hey Kat, I was wondering if you'd want to go the return party on Osborne street tomorrow, together. I didn't know if you were going or not."

She was taken aback. She hadn't really thought of the weekend yet, or expected to go to the festivities at all, it wasn't something she normally would do. This was the first weekend since Rose had left, it occurred to her, and now that he had brought it up, it would be good not to spend it entirely alone.

"Sure, that would be really nice. Thanks for asking," she said, smiling.

KATERINA TOOK AN EXTRA hour of sleep the next morning, and then planned to take care of all the tasks she hadn't managed to get to over the week. Deliveries were stacked up out of order, they had fallen behind on their own shipments, and a pile of paperwork was building on the apartment's kitchen table. She hadn't even opened the lock on the bookstore since Rose had left. Exhausted, aching, and a little depressed, she was unsure how she could continue with this. She was keeping the restaurant closed today on account of the return parties, and they nearly always took Sunday off, so she was glad to have the weekend to catch her balance. Before she got to work, she took a seat downstairs in the restaurant with a cup of black tea that she'd added some dried citrus peel into, enjoying the quiet morning and the sun spilling in through the shuttered windows.

Later in the afternoon she laid out some clothes on her bed that she was considering for the evening. She was quite nervous. Just for this moment she was glad that Rose was away and she had the apartment to herself to think, she would've been quite embarrassed by all the comments that Rose would've no doubt sent her way. She hadn't been out with anyone for a very long time, not since she was a teenager anyways. Rose had the occasional suitor, but it had been hard for her to match with someone who wouldn't be a disturbance in their lives.

Katerina was reserved by nature, and she'd always found it easy to keep herself more than busy with the studies she was constantly taking up. It had been easy to fall into a routine, especially with her mother falling sick and needing so much care this year. Somehow though, her death and Rose's sudden move had shifted her own perspective quickly. Things were not seeming the way they did a few short months ago, and though she hadn't put words or definite thoughts to anything yet, a sense of questioning had come over her. It was strange that Philip had shown up right when he did.

She decided on a loose, flowing red dress, with white, black and green worked into floral designs throughout the fabric, along with some nearly-flat brown leather shoes, with a slight heel, a closed toe and a strap reaching over to a buckle. After she did her hair, she sat on the bed with a thick hardcover book on her lap, though she didn't get to reading it, being lost in thought. She was happy to have had Philip at the restaurant over the week, it was good to have his help, and his thoughts on the all the problems that came up. He didn't know anything about restaurants, but he had a viewpoint coming from his own range of experiences that she found interesting.

He was probably more quiet than her. She could tell he was enjoying having a small role in the restaurant, learning their methods and techniques, joking a little with the two young assistants. It wasn't his business and he was on a break from his work, so he could afford to be more easy going than Katerina, but it had lightened the mood and made the first week without Rose bearable. She had no idea what she owed him at this point, she hadn't settled up for the repairs, and she guessed they were still working under the pretense that he was just around because he was interested in restaurants. She didn't have the social skills to try to clarify the odd situation either. She didn't want to offer to pay him again, sensing that a transfer of money might be insulting and maybe bring to an end whatever was developing between them, dispersing the spell that had come over the restaurant that week. She was glad that he had asked her to join him at the return festival, him expressing interest in her directly brought a little clarity into the situation.

Philip rapped on the window below, and Katerina came around back to the dock. She looked at Philip on the sidewalk through the fence. He had cleaned up nicely, he must have given the deeply tanned skin on his face, his hands and forearms a hard scrubbing. His beard had was trimmed, and he was wearing a new navy denim collared work-shirt, the sleeves rolled up into light-coloured cuffs just below his elbows, with some dark denim pants and black leather shoes. She came through the gate and joined him, and they took off walking towards Osborne Street.

Over the evening, they really didn't discuss anything from the previous week, and just let themselves have fun at the various attractions that had been had been set up along the the avenue, lit by the wavering flames of torches posted along the way. They sat and listened to some country music, and got some kettle corn and some roasted and spiced peanuts. They stopped at a bench to watch a play that was being performed several times over the evening. It was short, and the focus seemed to be more on the artistry of the costumes and the brilliantly coloured paper-mache masks than on the plot, a comedy about a greedy figure who tries manipulate all the characters around him, whose house of lies comes down around him in spectacular fashion.

Late in the evening, Philip walked Katerina back to the restaurant, and after they unlocked and opened the gate, she leaned over and placed a kiss on his cheek. He pulled the gate closed again and clicked the lock, before heading back to his apartment, entirely elated.

THE FEELING REMAINED AS Philip made the walk over to the union compound in the early morning. He hadn't been sleeping much since he'd come back to the city, only a few days ago: he was full of energy, his perspective was overturned, all of the sudden everything seemed new again. His mind was streaming with plans of how his life might work together with hers, though he hadn't mentioned any of this to Katerina, and was trying to suppress these thoughts somewhat, afraid of being disappointed. Light poured down from the high windows in the old brick building that had been retrofitted to house the union's shops and storerooms. Philip saw a broad wooden cart and wheeled back to get his crates of tools and equipment out of his storage locker.

The restaurant being closed today, he thought he'd at least spend the morning in the shops. It was probably best to give Katerina a little space, though he was debating if he should stop by later in the day, once she'd be finished her preparations for the upcoming week. For a few hours though anyway, Philip wanted to get ready for his own upcoming work, it was only a few days until the union was to meet to make arrangements for the fall schedule. The morning after the first return parties, the union buildings were likely to be fairly empty and quiet.

Philip stopped his cart at the storerooms related to his work, and looked through the piles of cast iron and steel pipe, the bins of threaded fittings, the bricks of plumbers' lead, the bags of mortar, clay and crushed char. Only a few member in each division of the union, usually the most well-established and their helpers, stayed in the city for the summer, to watch over the union compound and take care of urgent jobs. Some were fairly conscientious, and others not so much, but if they were overwhelmed at all Philip knew that their storerooms wouldn't be in the best order. He figured that after the union meeting, and after Alex and himself had time to get set up at whatever job he took on, they'd probably be back to work in around fifteen days. If there was any glaring deficiencies in their stock, he wanted to get an order placed soon, so that when work resumed, the supplies could at least be loaded and on their way, possibly, by boat or by train.

The Maintenance Union took care of purchasing and storing materials for the members, who paid the union back for what they used from what they earned on their jobs. Constant disruptions of supplies and the near impossibility of getting credit had made this model, where the members pooled their resources to maintain the stock they drew from, pretty much essential for anyone who wanted to work in the various trades. The Central Maintenance Union had slowly evolved out of frequent and repeating cycles of economic dislocation. Carbon rations and then fuel shortages began to limit how far crews were being sent to jobsites, and firms began to limit the areas they worked within, even more as suburbs began to break away from the city, forming their own municipalities.

Depressions and bankruptcies pushed many owners and suppliers out of business, and sometimes workers would group together to buy what was left of these companies, to keep themselves working in times where there were few jobs to be had. As times got even worse, and workers in city departments had not been paid for months, the city negotiated an arrangement with the Maintenance Union where the city workers would be taken on as full union members. The union would acquire a lot of city assets, buildings and machinery, in return for providing the city with certain services. When the city's finances improved, the union would again be paid for the contracts they had with the city.

So while the Central Maintenance Union was an independent organization, owned and controlled by its members, it was closely connected to the city government and was subject to the council's legislation. The union also dealt closely with the city's few industrialists, who employed it for larger commercial and industrial projects, though there were definite tensions between the independent tradespeople who formed the whole of the membership, and these wealthy and demanding patrons. The members were a closely knit and in-

41

sular group, and though they were responsible for their own jobs and incomes, they also formed a mutual aid society, collecting dues to provide for illnesses and injuries, storing food to provide the members at least basic rations and regular community meals.

Philip emptied the crates on to the long table in the machine shop, mostly keeping the groupings he'd used when he put them away in the spring. Hammers and mallets, chisels, screwdrivers, pipe wrenches, trowels, a hand saw, a hacksaw, a torch, a pipe cutter and a pipe threader were among the tools he laid out to inspect, sharpen, oil, and repair as needed. As he worked his way down the line, taking a break to brew a small pot of tea to bring back to the shop, his thoughts drifted between his work and Katerina. Once the stretches of long days resumed, he wouldn't have the time to stop by the restaurant for anything like he'd been this unusual harvest week. Whatever it was that was developing with Katerina, could he keep that going or was that going to fade away as his old routine took over his days? He poured another cup and leaned back on the stool to look out at the sky through the high windows.

When the tools and materials were ready to be packed, Philip got up to get his trailer from the other side of the compound, emptied of the food and gardening tools they'd brought back from the farm. Passing through the hallway, a voice called him over to the offices. He took a detour over to and up a staircase to Andrews, a union representative, who was getting up from his desk.

"Yeah?"

"Ah, have you heard what happened to Alex?"

"No," he said, growing worried, "what is it?"

"He was arrested, a bunch of them, a crackdown from those councillors from the rich districts. I'm not sure of the charges, or even if they were caught really doing anything."

"It's political stuff?" Philip asked. "He hasn't been involved with any of that since he's been working with me, I'm sure."

"Well, it's gotten more serious recently," Andrews replied. "They're pushing back against all the complaints and the unrest, they're making a statement before the upcoming session. They've got to have some judges and who knows who else on their side, I think the mayor is pretty much with them too. Anyways, I just thought I'd let you know, if you didn't already."

"Alright, thank you," Philip said, reeling. He walked over to an empty dorm and sat on the cot, trying to collect his thoughts. He really had no idea how to deal with this, but he felt responsible. He had never dealt with the legal system, his father's advice for staying out of trouble was always to be useful to his union and to steer clear of the law. Defending yourself wasn't easy if you wound up dealing with a corrupt officer or judge, best to stay out of their sight entirely. If Alex's father was still alive, Philip would've let him handle the case, but from what he knew of Alex's mother, she wasn't the person to deal with this competently.

He thought the matter over, at a loss for what to do, while he distractedly loaded the trailer. Once he pulled it back again into the garage, he packed a bag of clothes and a little bit of food into the cargo tricycle, and headed off for the house of Alex's family.

KATERINA HAD SPENT HER second day off getting the restaurant ready for the second week that she would operate it. She was still buzzing from the evening before, she hadn't had a carefree evening like that for as long as she could remember. She was uneasy at moments throughout the day, when Philip didn't stop by, she wanted some sort of confirmation that he'd felt the same way she did about the evening. But, she thought, they hadn't made any plans, and the restaurant was closed today, maybe he was thinking of coming by tomorrow like he had been last week? Well, she hadn't even known him the last time the restaurant was closed, how could she know what the routine might be? She smiled at the absurdity of it.

She was looking over a book by a candle at her kitchen table in the early evening, when she heard knocking at the restaurant window coverings below. She looked out her second floor window, and saw Philip below, his cargo bike in the middle of the street.

"Hey Philip," she called down, waving. "Did you want to come in?"

"Yeah, please."

She carried the candle down, and set it on the docks when she went to unlock the gate for him.

He looked distraught, and she wasn't sure why he was here.

"Is something the matter?"

"Yeah, it's my apprentice, that I had mentioned, he's in some trouble."

She tried to catch his down-turned eyes. "Hey, come sit down. I'll get some tea." He paced a bit on the dock while she went back up to the apartment for the kettle, and came back down with it and two small cups in the other hand. "Hey, come sit down," she said, setting the kettle down by the candle on the ledge. "What happened?"

He relayed what he had gathered of the details. "I'm not sure what to do. We can't afford a lawyer, and I'm not sure that would help anyway. We're supposed to be starting back at work later in the week, he's supposed to be working with me for the winter. And it's not that so much, it's more that I'm kind of responsible for him, he's living by me, he's under my watch, to some degree anyways."

44

"Do you know what he did?"

"You know, I'm not sure he did anything, but he was part of some political actions last year, on the side of those councillors that got arrested. I think it's that, but maybe he did get involved something over the last week in town, I really don't know."

He paused. "As I'm thinking on it, I'm wondering if him getting in trouble with those political types last year, then joining a union right away, if that didn't set off an alarm in somebody's head. That he'd be spreading politics in the Maintenance Union."

Katerina was aware of the politicians he was probably referring to. She read the daily papers closely, and she'd seen a lot of politicians and government officials in the restaurant over the years. They sat in thought for a moment, looking in the direction of the nearby law courts. The jail cells where Alex likely was being detained were in a building just beyond that.

Katerina reached her arm around his back, and placed her other hand on his shoulder, giving it a rub.

"Hey, we'll figure something out, we will."

DAVID RENCIT WAS SITTING at his desk, reading through some letters, when he came on envelope with a typewritten address, from a Kyle Chulnak, Attorney at Law. The return address was a post-office box in Charleswood. He didn't think he'd come across this lawyer before, which was a little unusual.

Dear Mr. Rencit, I'm writing to you on behalf of my client, Alex Roche, who you may be aware is currently in detention, possibly in relation to some political agitation he was believed to be party to.

First, I want to assure you with all sincerity, that the details of this letter have been shared with no one, and have been kept in confidence between myself and my client.

That said, my client does have information related to some plans of yours, that may be of interest to you. He knows about the plans for the union mergers, the changes to the ownership legislation for union projects, as well as the names of specific firms and individuals who have a stake in these plans.

The letter laid out a list of names and the details of their alleged business and political plans. It was not entirely accurate, and there didn't seem to be any evidence behind these claims, but it was close enough to get Rencit's heart pounding. How would anyone have known about this? Alex Roche—this was a relative of Bill Roche? Hadn't he been gone for over a year now, and how would anyone in his old office have known about any of this anyways? Whenever Rencit had met with anyone to discuss this in public, and even at home for that matter, he'd always made sure to be vague and to speak pretty much in code. He didn't think they had left any sort of paper trail either, it had all been face-to-face meetings, away from their offices.

I want to stress that my client has no interest in releasing any of this information, or in having any further involvement in political action. He has been employed learning a trade for almost a year now, and would like to continue along that path. Your help in securing his release, so that he could continue his work in his union would be greatly appreciated.

David folded the letter. This wasn't the only leak he was trying to contain, and once all the deals were made, they'd be on safer ground. The danger was in being derailed by the public before the arrangements were completed. He sighed. It was so much trouble to manage all this, but in the end, this had to be how the city was going to stay afloat. It was about investment and not about playing with new distribution schemes. The best the communal types could hope for was getting fair shares from a disappearing pie. Without opening some new industries, all the activity was going move up north. Times were changing, and the city had to find some new niches in which to compete.

David calmed himself and considered the letter. Maybe it wasn't that bad, they did not seem eager to go to the papers with this. He appreciated the tone, their deference and their tact.

IN MID-DECEMBER, ON THE edges of a crowd gathering at the markets, shipping yards and docks where the Red River and the Assiniboine met, Alex and Katerina were setting up a concession stand. It had become a ritual in the city for people to see off the last shipping boat of the season, before the rivers froze over for the winter. Things quieted down a little after that, with far less people and goods coming and going from the city. After the solstice, people and their families tended to turn inwards for a time, keeping to indoor work, focusing on keeping their buildings warm for the cold spells.

Katerina and Alex attached some metal legs to an iron channel, which they filled with pieces of charcoal and then set to light. They rested skewers across the channel, over the hot charcoal, a few pieces of meat alternating with vegetables, onto which they sprinkled some minced preserved lemon, some chili flakes and salt. Their younger helper got their booth ready to take orders and payment, and folded some newspaper sheets to hand out to their customers with the skewers, to catch any wayward pieces. After helping their older assistant carry over the crates of skewers, a layer of ice at the base of each, Philip took a seat on a nearby short brick wall that held a hill back from the pathway, watching the people in the crowds.

Since his release, Philip had kept Alex's name off of union paperwork as a precaution, and Alex made himself scarce at the union compound. He'd been spending some time working at the restaurant, learning all the prep tasks and how to cook at the woks. Philip wasn't sure of the wisdom of this, as Alex would be seen by many more politicians and officials than he ever would working in the union. But he also didn't think that anyone was that likely to make the connection here, if anyone was still interested in Alex's case at all. For the most part, it seemed like people assumed that Alex was some relative of Katerina's, come in to help out after Rose's sudden departure. And, if there were going to be more reprisals, it was going to be something to do with unrest in the unions and the new laws and regulations being put through by city council.

Alex still came out to work sites as needed, Philip still planned on seeing Alex through his apprenticeship, whatever the difficulties. Philip had started to organize a shop in one of the vacant spaces in the buildings surrounding the restaurant's courtyard, coming and going through the gate that the deliveries were made and received. He'd started making some of the deliveries himself, an with himself and Alex working at the restaurant, he was able to be more discerning with the maintenance jobs he took on, which were growing a little scarce anyways. He was also thinking of asking the boy helping in the kitchen if he'd like to start helping out with maintenance work as well, that way Alex could stay in the kitchen if needed, they would all have more options to handle whatever jobs they were able to get.

This also let Katerina resume something more like her old schedule, watching over their accounts and the correspondences with suppliers from her table at the side of the restaurant, and dealing with the bookstore and the requests of her clients. Philip was thinking, if Alex could learn enough of the restaurant by spring, maybe he wouldn't have to spend the whole summer out at the union farm, perhaps Katerina could spend some of the summer in the country with him and they could leave Alex to manage the restaurant for stretches? It could give Alex more of a chance to stay connected to his band and his friends.

The uncertain mood in the city had Philip thinking over all manner of ideas for how they might make ends meet, maybe setting up a repair shop, or starting to deal in scrap metal. And if none of it worked out, maybe they'd all leave together and try their luck up north, under Rose's wing.

The young girl unpacked some tongs, a long fork and some clean rags, and hung them from the hooks on the grooved brackets jutting out from the side of the channel, into which Alex was fitting a oiled wooden plank to use as a cutting block and working surface for the afternoon. Katerina left Alex to deal with the cooking and the crowd, and in the light winter snowfall, went to sit beside Philip. She leaned on to his shoulder, he placed a kiss on her head.

Neighborhood Watch

Marcus Tremain

n an age of hard times my father was a hard man. His muscles and sinew were taught with not an ounce of fat on his wiry form. His face chiseled by the winds, his eyes deep set in his skull were dark and joyless and no matter how often he shaved there always seemed to be the suggestion of a five o'clock shadow permanently etched upon his jowls. He had not always been like this though it was hard now to conjure the memories of his warmth and laughter. Something had broken inside him when mother had died.

Once I asked my father what had truly changed from his life before the war. I expected him to talk about the lack of running water, heating, sewage or the many comforts of my early youth. For instance young though I was, I still remember piping hot water flowing into steaming baths and the warmth that seemed to penetrate your very bones. He stopped and looked through the open window pausing in concentrated thought.

"Listen what do you hear?"

Somewhat puzzled I answered "Nothing, what do you mean?"

"Listen again." This time I remained motionless letting the stillness wash over me. I heard bird song, then from a great distance a dog barking intermittently and finally the hum of insects each separate sound clear and distinct as I plucked them from the rhythm of the environment outside.

He lent back into the well-worn leather of his armchair.

"What I notice now is the silence. I never realized until it was gone how deafening the old world was."

I wondered if it wasn't only the absence of the cars, planes, leaf blowers and the deafening cacophony of noise from all the machines of that age that he was referring to or if the silence was also due to the passing of mother.

I left the house at first light and headed towards the old golf club and father called out "Mind where you step son" as he always did. It was a bit of an in joke between us something we shared in a relationship of mostly nonverbal communication. The street where we lived was essentially abandoned. Several houses were already partially collapsed rubble and debris spilled onto the front yards now entangled with thorn bushes and weeds. I watched carefully for movement there were a lot of squirrels in the trees here and they made for good eating. That wasn't my target today though I had sweeter things in mind.

I soon approached the old school on my right where the town major now lived. The old golf course sat behind a tall metal fence now completely covered by vines and topped by taller trees and bushes. I needed to follow the bend for some distance before I found the gap and squeezed through like I had done a thousand times before. I put my backpack on the ground and pulled out the .22 revolver that father had given me for hunting. I lay down flat on my stomach and waited. I had been there motionless not less than thirty minutes when I saw the ears of the first rabbit come into view. The distance was not great and ammunition was a precious commodity in the community our defactocurrency in fact so I hesitated and suddenly it was gone. I sighed and sat up, sometimes you could just feel it would not be your day I was thinking of switching my target back to easier game in the form of squirrels when I saw her.

I don't think I will ever forget the moment, there was an almost dream like quality to her movement as she seemed to glide towards me. She was blond and tanned in the manner of most who spend their time in the California sun. She looked near my age possibly nineteen at the most, but it was her smile that caught me and demanded all of my attention. Onward she strode with a confidence I had rarely seen in one her age. She held out her hand.

"I'm Daisy" Her nose creased in apparent annoyance "You do speak don't you?" Her voice broke the spell long enough for me to reply "Sorry I'm John I don't think I've seen you around before".

"No I'm just passing through" She smiled somewhat mischievously this time.

"Passing through?" I asked somewhat incredulously.

"I'm here with my father for the market tomorrow he's a trader from up north."

I gave a half smile of comprehension.

"You must have traveled a long way." I said weakly. She appeared to be aware of the effect she was having on me and smiled again this time with the hint of a pout.

"You been far?"

"When I was very young with my father, but I can't say I remember too much about it now."

"What do you remember?"

"Been down to the beach and along the coast. Up Topanga canyon there's a guy who's got an off grid place and we all go up there a couple of times a year to listen to the radio." I seemed to have caught her interest.

"What news did you hear?"

"Well it was a while ago now, but I hear that there's a new President. Says he's going to reunite the states bring back power and water to every home in the country"

She snorted "They all say that, but not one of them has made a move out of Washington since the war, a lot of hot air if you ask me." I didn't know what to say to that.

"I suppose you're right, the old timers say much the same."

"Well they're right about something then." And she laughed. It is a sound I can still hear when I close my eyes, a sound bereft of malice the closest thing to innocence in this changed world.

"Nice meeting you, but I've gotta go help father, see you around."

I waved at her retreating form still slightly in shock, watching her graceful movements as she drifted away. It was sometime before I finally stood up and made my way back home.

As the sun set I looked down the street at two old cars crouched like giant insects as the last rays of sun hit their rusted hoods touching them with fire, but for a brief moment in time seemingly alive and watchful before receding into darkness. I always marveled at the thought that these metal beasts once moved at speed through the shining highways of my childhood. The last vehicle I had seen was nearly ten years ago and was part of a long military convoy heading north from refueling at the Long beach refinery to the border of the Republic of Northern California as it was now called. It had been a few years since I had seen a plane either and that too was military and as I gazed at its sleek silhouette I found myself wondering whether father had worked on that very plane during his days as an engineer at Lockheed Martin. Although unlikely everything seemed possible now. That was the most unexpected lesson that love had taught me that everything either was or could be connected. The random nature of the universe was at last defied and all things were joined by a silver thread. But for a series of unlikely events that caused a man and his daughter to travel a thousand miles or more to this little insignificant speck in the abandoned metropolis that was once Los Angeles I might never have known her. The wonder of that was akin to a spiritual revelation in my young mind.

MY FATHER WAS IN the kitchen sharpening a row of knives on the counter top. His movements were precise almost robotic. Without looking up he said matter-of-factly

"No Rabbits today?"

"Only saw one, the range wasn't right."

"Squirrel stew again then it is," he said with the suggestion of a smile the closest he ever got to laughter these days.

I lay there that night thinking of her drinking in every fleeting memory. At least I knew her name and that she would likely be at the market the next day. I reached under the bed and pulled out the old tin where I kept my valuables such as they were. Thirty rounds of .22 ammunition and another ten rounds of various calibers I had collected in trade over the years. A couple of furs from some coyotes that I had shot a few years back not much even for those sparse times, but likely enough to make a few trades and hopefully enough to make an impression on Daisy's father. In the morning I waited for father to finish breakfast going to the Sunday market was one of our weekly rituals, but he waved me on "Got a few things to take care of this morning I'll catch up later, if you see a good hammer though reserve it for me." I couldn't wait to get out the door and before it slammed he called out again.

"Don't let those traders fleece you son, especially the northern ones".

"I won't dad" I called back.

I couldn't believe my luck not having him tag along would make things so much easier. The closer I got the more nervous I was. I was almost at the old school house that faced onto the farmers market when I hesitated and then froze. Somehow I could not summon the will to move forward. Straining my eyes I could not see Daisy and guessed her stall must be somewhere near the end.

I don't recall at the time what I bought or even what I paid. I put the purchases in my bag feeling somewhat pleased with myself when I felt a tug on my arm I looked behind and there was father staring at me.

"Come with me now" he said his voice barely a whisper. I was about to argue, but one look at his face stopped me. His visage was dark with anger and with an intensity that I had never seen in him before. He didn't wait for my reaction before striding purposely away.

I glanced at Daisy and she shot me back a puzzled look. I gestured an apology with my hands and turned to look at father, but he had already gone.

I was angry at father I knew how he had suffered over the years, but I had never wanted anything like this before. As I hurried home that anger intensified into a fury. He at least owed me an explanation. I flung open the front door and slammed it behind me. It took five minutes or so before I realized the house was empty. My father didn't socialize. Oh he nodded to the neighbors and made small talk in between jobs, but never spent longer than he needed to appear polite. It didn't take long to figure out where he had gone and somewhat calmer now I went to see if my hunch was right.

I stood at the corner and looked down Wilshire in the direction of the sea. Once a mighty road that lead into the heart of what had been one of the greatest examples of urban sprawl was now a carpet of green punctuated with slivers of dark asphalt and strewn with the rusting hulks of abandoned vehicles. I strained my neck and stared upwards at the steel tower before me wrapped with vines, green growth exuding from the gaping holes that had once held giant sheets of glass. A bird flew out of a six story window and a squirrel leapt lithely onto a ledge a floor below.

A few blocks down there was the bar. That's what everyone called it not the Phoenix as the owner had proudly named it. I saw him sitting at the bar a lone figure staring into his drink. This is where he would always disappear once a year and like most things though we never discussed it. I'd worked out that was when mother had passed. That wasn't today though and it was another indication that whatever was eating him up was serious. I ordered an ale and sat two stools down from him. Not wanting to break the silence so soon I inspected my glass the dark amber liquid was heavy with sediment then stared at the fading murals on the wall opposite the only sign that the establishment had once been a classic Tex-Mex. We both sat for maybe ten minutes neither of us directly acknowledging each other's presence. Then he turned his head and spoke to me.

"Son I want to tell you a story." his words were ever so slightly slurred. I rarely saw him even close to being drunk. He always drank alone at night long after I had gone to bed.

"Many years ago now." he waved his drink in my direction.

"When you were still in nappies." he gave a half smile then carried on.

"I was driving to work. I remember that it was a beautiful day, as perfect as it gets in this part of the world. I had the window down, the radio on and the music was playing. I was cruising along, I was in the zone." He paused a moment then looked back at me.

"Of course you don't know what I mean because that was then and this is now and now is a very different world son. Still you can understand at least that it was a moment when things felt so good that you were untouchable, just riding a sweet wave. I passed an intersection and all I could hear was some arsehole tooting his horn. I don't know if I had cut him off or what he was shouting about. I do remember I shouted something back as he accelerated past and gave me the finger. So I got into work trying to reclaim my mood, then I saw his car, a brand new BMW parked in the lot. I was at my desk most of the day then I saw him come out of the conference room. He looked straight at me with the biggest smirk on his face. I'll never forget that expression until the day I die. Next day I'm told I'm being made redundant. My boss didn't even have the balls to say it to my face. Twenty years at the same company then they throw me on the scrap heap. The next part of the story you know all too well. We had taken on a lot of debt and your mother had quit her job a year before to be a full time mum to you. We had no choice, but to move to that shitty apartment downtown. Then she got sick."

He slammed his glass down on the counter.

"One moment in time and everything changes and suddenly your whole world spins on a dime."

It took a while for me to gather my thoughts. I'd always been hungry for knowledge about the family and the past. This though wasn't the time I wanted to hear it.

"Why now dad? Why tell me now? What possible connection does this have to anything that's going on now? Why did you have to embarrass me in front of Daisy?

He looked at me solemnly.

"You love her don't you?"

"Yes I think I do." I said with some force. He turned away again and gestured at the barman for another drink. I waited sometime for him to continue until I realized that I was now dismissed in his eyes.

"I've tried Dad I've really tried." I got up quickly as I felt tears welling up in my eyes and I didn't want to give him the satisfaction of seeing me like that.

ALTHOUGH MY MIND WAS in turmoil thoughts of her gave me clarity and purpose and I slept deeply that night.

As soon as it was light I snuck out of the house. I took care to bring my usual canvas bag with the revolver so that it would look like I had gone hunting when father found me gone. Perhaps in a way I was hunting I smiled to myself. I don't know what had gotten into father, something had triggered him, but I couldn't figure out what. Most likely he was sleeping it off and wouldn't be awake for some time. When I got there I could see that the wagons were still unhitched from the horses. Two of them were almost brand new with freshly painted wood, but several of them were old trucks their original wheels substituted for wooden wagon wheels, their engine blocks removed and their metal chassis stripped down to minimize the weight.

The traders were just emerging from their wagons and stretching in the cool morning air. There was no sign of Daisy though. I felt momentary panic until I saw her father his distinct bald patch marking him out from behind. The curtains were drawn at the front of their truck, but there was no sign of her there either. I didn't feel comfortable asking her Dad and I couldn't just stand there loitering either. I don't know why, but driven more by instinct than logic I made my way through the gap in the fence and into the open field in the old golf course and then I spotted her. She smiled as I approached.

"Thought I might find you here" she said still smiling, "But what's up with your Dad?"

"Damned if I know never seen him like that before"

"Sign of the times, parents tend to get a bit protective these days I guess". I didn't reply just smiled sheepishly back at her.

"I always wonder how places like this survived; I mean what keeps people here when everyone else left?"

Suddenly I felt I was in comfortable territory as I replied.

"Same as everywhere else I guess. Water. There are underground springs which bubble up into a small creek near the old golf Club. When it comes down to it that's the only real essential."

"So how did you end up here anyway?" She asked keeping her eyes unnervingly focused on mine.

"My uncle left for Australia just as things were getting bad and he gave his house to my dad for safekeeping. That was a few years back now and we've not heard from him since."

"And your Mum?"

"My Dad lost his job and we had to move to another part of town. Turns out it was the epicenter of the epidemic. It was all we could afford then. She didn't last long once it took hold." She nodded sadly, but didn't seem surprised and waited for me to continue.

Then partly to change the subject I asked her "And your mother is she back home in northern California?"

"Oh I've no idea where she is. She ran off with some guy before things fell apart. She could see the writing on the wall long before anyone else I'll give her that. I doubt she even cared for him he was just a convenient way out. I'm sure she is still alive somewhere she was always pretty good at taking care of herself."

"Tough on your dad."

"I'll be honest with you I think it hurt his pride more than anything else. Sure he loved her in his way, but he was married to his job and back then no one seemed to stop and think about the here and now everyone was just chasing a dream."

"Never thought about it like that before. If it weren't for mother passing I sometimes wonder if dad might not have preferred this life."

"We were both too young to remember much, but I like the life on the road. I think I might have been bored living back then." I looked at her longingly and she pretended not to notice.

"I wish I could join you, nothing really changes here."

She smiled that smile of hers again and softly stroked my cheek.

"Then why don't you?"

"I couldn't just up and leave Dad."

"He's old enough to look after himself isn't he? Besides it wouldn't be forever. Take the route up north stay a while then come right back when the next traders go south." She saw my look of doubt then said, "Hey think about it OK. This girl doesn't make offers like this every day. I'm leaving in around two hours. Meet me by the school if you decide you want to come. Either way no hard feelings."

She took my hand gently for just a moment then leaned forward and kissed me softly on the lips before walking slowly away. I was physically stunned and it took me a while before I could move again. If ever I had any doubts about what I was about to do they vanished in that moment.

When she picked me up in the wagon I was surprised to see that it was another trader's until she explained that her father Jason had to take care of some business first. He would travel separately and we would all meet up at a small town just before the great Bakersfield desert.

I soon fell into the rhythm of the journey. Daisy taught me how to care for the horses and how to load and unload the wagons as we stopped at several small towns on our slow journey to San Joaquin Valley. We waited a long time for her father to re-join in the end we had to wave goodbye to the traders who carried on north. Not that I minded we made love every night under the stars and woke to the cold desert morning wrapped in the cocoon of our love.

IT WAS A LONG time after, maybe three months before I happened upon a trader who had passed through Brentwood. I was sitting at the bar when he came in, it was fortunate that Daisy was away that evening. At first he didn't know either Jason or my father by name, but he did know that a trade wagon had been found abandoned on the road its owner nowhere to be found. The strange thing was that apart from a missing horse all the goods had been left untouched. Around the same time a local had up and left some say he was looking for his missing son.

Some weeks after that I had been out hunting and it was getting late.I could barely see anything outside of the immediate glow of the campfire, but I knew it was him even before he stepped into the circle of light.

"Dad?" He didn't reply just sat down watching me wearily. I sighed and looked back at him watching the firelight reflected in his eyes. I wanted to hug him then, wanted to cry ask him why he did it. Still I did none of those things just sat silently on the cold hard ground and waited.

"I had to do what I did."

"But why?" I asked with all of the desperation and pain filling my voice.

"Things have come full circle son. He was there for a reason ... I ... you were there for a reason." He wanted to go on fighting an internal struggle that had begun when my mother lay dead on a dirty mattress on the wrong side of the tracks and had not ended more than a decade later.

"When I first saw him I knew immediately. It's almost like

he had not changed at all, but you know what hurt the most?" he didn't wait for a reply, but rambled on.

"That he didn't know me probably doesn't even remember what he did. Like swatting a fly that lands on your wrist. That he could end my life on a whim, destroy the only person that I ever cared about and then know nothing of it. Without you, son, I wouldn't have made it through. There's a part of her in you then he was going to take that from me too… "

I knew who he meant of course all the pieces of the puzzle were starting to come together, his conversation with me in the Phoenix and his strange behavior before that.

"Dad it's not like that.." He couldn't stop now too many years holding it in and so I let him carry on.

"It's not that I ever stopped thinking about your mother, every night and every day she's with me, but with time it fades, the numbness spreads and the pain becomes bearable. The day I saw him the wound was ripped open and it felt fresh almost like the first time."

There were tears in his eyes now I don't think I ever remember him crying not on the outside anyway.

"I suppose I should almost thank him for that. She was there with me again. I remembered her face, her hair, her voice. Your mother always had a beautiful voice even near the end.

"There are just some things you can't walk away from son. I won't say what I did was right I can't say he even deserved it." He was quiet again seemingly reflective.

"Back in those days you'd hear about these things in the news and shake your head. Another crazy who just couldn't live with the world anymore, one more homicide statistic. These times are forged anew and people now find their own sense of justice. I'm not proud of what I've done I just did what I had to do."

"You killed him then?"

He was silent for a moment. "It was dark, but I'm pretty

sure I got him."

He started coughing in a prolonged fit that ended with him spitting blood into the dust. It was then that I noticed how pale he was, his skin waxen and drained of blood. He sat awkwardly against the flatbed truck one shoulder was secured with a makeshift bandage of torn cloth. It was as if he had given everything of himself to get here and tell me this and now the strength was flowing rapidly out of him. I reached forward to hold him and he fell into my arms, limp and almost weightless. I felt the wetness of his blood soaked shoulder as he shivered one last time before the life left him. I don't know how long I held him in my arms sobbing, but it must have been some hours later when Daisy arrived with a blanket and wrapped it around me. We buried him that night in silence the stars bearing mute witness to our efforts.

We didn't speak the next day, but she held my hand whenever we were close squeezing it gently to let me know she was there. I looked into her beautiful grey eyes and the look of pity and concern I saw there melted my heart. I don't think I could have loved her more in that moment. She must have wondered what had happened to Jason and one day I would have to tell her, one day, but not today.

The Winged Promise

Catherine Trouth

The winged metal rusting at prairie's edge
Towering still, after years of neglect.
Whispering, "Offer the world as your pledge
What the beloved could never reject.

Bring fair precious stones from far away mines,
Unseasonal food in winter's deep want,
From a thousand miles away clothes so fine,
Then your lover can your devotion flaunt.

Think on limitless riches from afar,
Don't think of outsized use or unseen loss.
Fill her desires, true costs are no bar."
So was all else but dreams treated as dross.

I'll make my love's ring of scraps from this plane;
A promise that such thoughts will be our bane.

Shacked Up

Justin Patrick Moore

Their bodies entwined together as the rain from the latest thunderstorm pelted the leaking roof of the squat. The smell of old wet carpet, and the cardboard they'd lain over top of it was heavy in the air, as were other scents, their skin, their sweat. The smell of damp soil from underneath the understory of honeysuckle in the patch of woods where they had suckled each other on the herb gathering trip earlier in the day still clung to them, and they were making the room ripe with their perfumes once again.

Theirs was a new love and a young love and they were enthusiastic in sharing their passions with each other.

"I'm gonna miss this tomorrer," he whispered in the aftermath, after he had taken her a second time.

His fingers interlaced with his girlfriend's fingers. She laid her head on his chest, placed her hand along the outline of his scrawny ribs and sunken stomach. They sat up and rolled cigarettes out of butts they'd scrounged from the ashtrays outside the restaurants on Ludlow Hill where the bougie ate. They scavenged as much as they could, and hitting up ashtrays was part of the routine when they made a dumpster diving run as part of their work in the Sprout House Collective.

Wyatt rested in the memory of the first run they had made together, soon after Magdalena had showed up on their doorstep, looking for shelter and protection. They were rooting for anything edible in the slop buckets behind the Lamplight Tavern and they'd filled up a bag of used rib bones to boil down into pork broth and gravy. When the kitchen boy came out with another haul of scraps, he'd caught them and started shooting rocks at them with his slingshot. He saw her smile as they started to run and noticed how her hips moved as they hopped over the fence and started to fall in love. When they were far enough away, when they recovered their breath, they shared their breath, and their spit, and their lips as they leaned against the columns of Unity Lodge. They held hands in quiet night as they walked back down to Camp Washington, the tough neighborhood wedged between the rail yard, the Mill creek and the remains of I-75.

"You don't gotta go." She exhaled the smoke into the air. It mingled with the steam from their love making and the steam from the ramen soup they'd brought up from the kitchen. Syd had been able to trade some seeds for forty-eight packs of stale dehydrated noodle soup.

"I do gotta go. I need to do this, I gotta at least try to find my brother and make amends, otherwise it's gonna be like Marvin says, I'm gonna be haunted by what I shoulda of done, and that's gonna make it harder for me to keep clean."

She turned her head and met his eyes in what remained of the LED lights glow. The batteries had started to fade and would have to be put back on the solar trickle charge again tomorrow, which wouldn't do much good if the sun didn't come out. "Then will ya take me with ya? I know I ain't supposed to ask, that this is your bidness more than mine and all, but, it's just that…" she wanted to say, I'm afraid, to lose ya because I lost too many damn people already, I need ya and I can't bear to risk ya. She did say it with her brown eyes, with a look of loss that spoke without speaking. Everyone they knew had lost someone, and since neither of them knew anyone bougie neither of them knew a family who had been spared the tragic blows dealt by drugs, tornadoes, influenza.

"You'll be alright," he tried to reassure her. "I won't take long. Juss a day, two at most. You can hang with Syd and Iz, and Marv. There's always's work to do, specially with spring here. And when I gets myself back we'll keep trying to make that baby, start our family." Since they'd first made love it had been a possibility, one they both accepted. It's not like they'd ever used protection. Condoms had become a high ticket item during the trade wars, and medical procedures were only available to the bougie, or to those who saved enough to pay up at a clinic. For most folks being broke meant it was too expensive to not have kids.

She pulled her bottom lip up between her teeth. "If it's a girl I wanna name her Polly."

"After my sister?"

Her smile was his answer, and he couldn't find it within himself to argue. He would give her anything she desired. Their pit bull Ziggy got up and moved in closer with them, laid down in a heap. Wyatt soaked in the feeling of safety and warmth. He had lived on the memory of how soft her skin felt against his, of the fullness of her lips.

"Then, we name him Alejandro if it's a boy."

Magdalena had protested. "No. Any old thing but that."

"Why not? If you'd use my sis's name for a girl ain't it a bit hippiecrit to not use your brother's for a boy?"

"I don't wanna get into it right now."

There were still so many things about her he didn't know, so much about her he desired to learn. He needed to know every inch of her, her whole story, leading up to the time when she first stumbled into the squat two months ago.

"Still, I'm going with ya," she said, "Whether ya like it or no and no matter what we name the bay, if and when it comes."

He sighed in defeat, unable to make a comeback. He knew it was pointless trying to get her to change her mind once she'd made a decision. Her stubborn persistence was one of the things he admired about her.

"Besides, I wanna see the hood ya grew up in."

"Okay," he said, "It ain't much, but okay. It ain't safe over there for me now, that's kinda why I didn't want ya to go. Lil Dem and the Ratboy's don't take kindly to deserters. I can't ken what they'll do when I show up on their turf. There's a reason I ain't been back, and I don't want you getting hurt."

"But you'll protect me right?" She squeezed his biceps. For a nineteen year old who didn't always get enough to eat he was strong. He had gotten stronger since Marvin had helped sober him up, since he'd started doing some meaningful work with the Sprout House crew.

"Sure will, Maggie."

She buried her head into his chest and pulled the covers up over the frayed sleeping bag. They snuggled together in a tight knot until dawn. Ziggy kept their feet warm.

He woke up hard in the morning, and he woke her up with his kisses, as he pressed his hardness against her thigh.

"You're mine, Wyatt. For real and for true. Promise?"

"I promise."

As he ravished her body with his, he had never felt so sure of anything else in his life.

THE NEXT MORNING WYATT went back to his own room to put some things in his leather hip pack. They still hadn't moved into the same room together, but he thought they would, soon. They were getting serious. Space was at a premium in the squat and the collective could always use more hands to make light work. If he knocked her up as they both hoped, they'd be sharing a lot more. He hoped to borrow a ladder somehow so he could climb up on the roof and patch the leak, so their digs wouldn't be so damp.

After they ate some more ramen with a couple scrambled eggs from the chickens out back and asked Joan if she would mind the dog while they were gone. Syd and Iz were out fishing in the Mill Creek, Marvin was on one of his mysterious jaunts looking for the useful kit he always seemed to find and bring back, and the rest of the crew were about some chore or other.

"No problem," Joan said. "I'll be working out back getting the beds ready for the seeds we started. I hope y'all can make it back for the gig. *Terpsi-Core* is in town from Cleveland, and it's sure to be a full house."

"Damn, I forgot about that." Wyatt muttered.

The Sprout House served as one of many homes around the region for the ad hoc folk-punk music circuit. The gigs often doubled as a potlatch between squat houses and sometimes after the shows Marvin would hole up in the second floor library with other members of what he called the *Arachnet* or sometimes the *League*. Wyatt wasn't sure if they were the same thing or different, all he was able to gather so far is that they were a secretive group who were organizing around several agendas. Politics had never been his thing and he was only now learning to read a little better, with the help of Joan and some of the others. Marvin had promised he'd learn more in time, but his first task was staying sober, and that meant attempting to heal the rift with his brother.

"If we get back tonight it'll be late. I ain't know how long things'll take with Brett. We might be out overnight."

"It's all good," Joan said. "There'll be other shows. *Terpsi-Core* usually comes down at least once a year. May the gods bless and keep you both, and your brother."

They were about to head out when Wyatt had a funny feeling in his gut. "Hold on, I feel like I'm leaving something behind. Back in a sec." He ran up to his room and grabbed the banjo from the wall where it hung.

"Yer lookin' like a regler old troubadour," Magdalena said when he returned, pointing to the way the instrument was strapped over his back.

"That's what I was thinkin'. It might help to have some tunes on the way"

"Well be careful you bring it back in one piece," Joan said. Marvin had given it to him as a first year sobriety present.

He tapped the back of the banjo with his thumb. It had a painting of a turtle shell on the back. "Having this makes me feel better already."

GOING FROM CAMP WASHINGTON to River Rat Row was a six mile slog across town, up the hill from the valley, then back down the other side to the community on the river. The city was bustling and alive, but within the throng and crush of moving people, they felt a sense of privacy sometimes absent in Sprout House and they talked over the course of the three hour walk.

"What was growing up in the Row like?" she asked.

"It weren't all bad," he said. Each hood had its gang, but the Ratboys were known as some of the fiercest, with intimate connections to the drug trade along the inland waterways due to their turf along the docks. The Row had a reputation for hard living, fighting, and dying.

"We used to play tag around the houseboats at Mariner's Landing, or we'd sneak onto Branson's farm to steal some veg or whatevs. One time he caught me and Brett and put us to work. But there weren't nothing to be done. It was either work or take the belt, so we worked. Then he sent us home with a basket. After that I'd go sometimes go over there to help out and he'd give us some food. His farm used to be a park. Mom said her old man played baseball on them fields. Branson's farm was extra ripe cause the floods during the winter rain put down new soil every year."

"Furreal?" she said. "I used to help out the nun's up at St. Theresa's up in Westwood. They used an old baseball field for their garden too, and fed a lot of the church."

"The church down here got taken out by a landslide."

Wyatt wasn't prepared for her next question. "So, did you have any girlfriends?"

He thought it was a no brainer. He was good looking and had been a member of the gang, so had his pick of the Rat-girls; but girl's whether Rats or not, always seemed to want to know these things.

"Yeah, I had a girl. Carly. We grew up together. She was friend's with Polly." He was hoping they wouldn't run in to her. Or Lil Dem.

"What was she like?"

"She's a redhead. About five feet tall. Liked looking at comic books when she could get em."

Magdalena frowned, got quiet. Wyatt felt a sinking feeling in his stomach. *Had he just said the wrong thing?* he wondered. Surely she hadn't expected him to not have been with anybody else before her.

She ran her fingers through her braided black hair with all their beads, bolts, shells and feathers tied in. "I thought you liked Latinas?!"

"I do. I like you!"

"I never heard of a Latina girl with red hair. Not unless she died it. So was it like the color of a beet or a rose?"

Wyatt did'n't know what to say. He hadn't encountered this side of her before. All he could think of was, "You must'a had a boyfriend too. It's ain't like you were inexperienced."

Uh oh, he thought. *I done blown it now.*

They kept walking in an oppressive silence. After awhile he started to pick a tune on the banjo to try to lighten the mood. She glared at him. His playing wasn't the best. He'd only just started to learn a few months ago. He tried playing a song they'd both heard at a gig at the Phoenix Asch House Collective. It was a simple number, and he had been working on playing the tune himself, though he still didn't have the chords down quite right.

"Our house, in the middle of our street... our house. I remember way back then when everything was true and when, we would have such a very good time, such a fine time, such a happy time, and I remember how we'd play, simply waste the day away, then we'd say nothing would come between us... two dreamers. Our house..."

"Yeah, I had a beau," she conceded, lightening up the mood.

Magdalena told him about Max. He'd been a member of the Westworld Locos, succumbed to the drug nepenthe as so many had, and after two years on it, no longer recognized her anymore. Her trust in him had disintegrated just as Max's memory had. Not that she'd been drug free. Just nepenthe free.

He told her how he snuck Carly into the upper floors of old brick homes in the intertidal, whose first floors were underwater, parking a borrowed canoe in the living.

They were quiet again until they reached the top of the hill and could see the Ohio river stretched below them, the docks of River Rat Row on its banks, and the hustle and bustle of vessels in the brown water.

"I hope Brett's down there," he said. "He probably still works for Lil Dem. I did too. We all did. Anyone who was a Ratboy worked for him. I don't wanna run into Carly or them. That was my old life. But I've kicked nepenthe and am getting my memory back, getting my life back. That was my old life, I don't wanna shut the door on it, but I want you to know I ain't gonna re-embrace it neither. You the only thing I'm gonna embrace now."

Up on the top of Walnut Hill the city lay sprawled all around them, from what remained of the skyscrapers downtown to the redlight district in Kentucky on the other side of the river, Cincinnati's Southside. They took in the view. They took each other all in, their past lives, loves and whatever future lay ahead. He brought her close into him and kissed her in the cold spring sun as the wind blew through his blonde hair.

Holding hands they descended down the potted and crumbled asphalt gravel road to the valley below.

BACK IN THE DAY River Rat Row had once been known as the East End. Except for a brief splurge by the bougie when it poshed out and money flowed in and condos were built in a rebranding effort, it had always been a working class hood. It had slid back down to its original status as a place for the stiffs when a series of landslides from the constant rain spilled onto the condos that had been built on the bottom of the hill. At the same time the banks of the Ohio started creeping up over the roads, and anyone who still had a dime to their name bolted for higher ground. It was a pattern replicated all across the seven hills of the Queen City. Those who could afford it moved to the top and those who couldn't slid into the many valleys and hollers of the region.

Coming back down to the grounds he had stomped as a child and young man, after being gone for almost two years, filled Wyatt with fear and a sudden riotous longing for his old way of life. The excitement of the violence and the oblivion of the drugs and the interpersonal drama within the gang all called out to him as the ramshackle collection of houses, sheds, shacks, chicken coops, garages, tents, yurts and junk cabins came into view. All of these were built up around the long warehouses close to the docks where goods flowed into and out of the city.

Magdalena could tell Wyatt was agitated. "Take a deep breath," she said.

He inhaled through his nose and imagined a spark of fire within him, radiating stillness and serenity as Marvin had taught him.

When they stepped over Columbia Parkway they became trespassers on the Ratboy's turf.

"Just cause I quit the game ain't mean the Rats will see it ataways. Far as they care I ain't rat no more, but a mouse."

"You're no mouse to me. It'll work out, you'll see. Will ya show me the house you grew up in?"

He sighed and said, "Might as well."

As they walked he saw a group of ten year old boys and girls headed down to the river with their fishing poles and pails. "On the happy days, that's what it was like," he told her, pointing to the kids. "I do miss livin' by the river. Fishin' the Mill Creek ain't near enough the same as fishin' the Ohio. Sure, you got mostly carp in either stream, but down here there's something 'bout watching the barges, sailboats and canoes on the big water that juss set's me right. Even if there's a bunch drama going down, or whatever, standing at the docks in the morning or at night, or down at some of the other holes, it's just peaceful."

"You good at fishing? Round Westwood people spent more time trying to shoot geese or hunt deer."

Wyatt looked at her. "You kiddin'? I can fish the hell out of this river. Give me a gun or a slingshot and I'll get a goose from Christmas dinner, you juss wait 'n see. You won't starve with me. Not if I can help it."

They passed the five and dime on the corner of his old street. Tobe was still sitting out front under the awning with his peg leg, courtesy of a barge accident, propped up on a plastic bucket. Mothers and their broods were hanging laundry on the lines that crisscrossed between the buildings and shacks. Wyatt recognized some of them and felt a trickle of adrenaline, and the uptick of his heart. It was only a matter of time before he ran into a banger.

They came to the house he'd grown up in. Smoke wisps blew out the chimney, and shouting, just as it ever had, drifted out the windows sheeted by plastic and duct tape. Fading graffiti spoke in rude idioms across the brick.

"There it is," he said. "I can't say I miss it. It ain't like a whole lotta good ever happened there."

She could tell his mood had slumped. "Hey Wy, it's all good. If we were up in my hood looking at all the different camps and flops my padre dragged us through, I'd feel about the same. But I do like you showin' me."

"I know ya like it when I show ya," a small smile cracked his lips. "But yeah, this house, it don't hold any memories I like to dwell on. A few weeks after I got jumped into the Ratters, Polly ran away and I ain't seen her since. Mom lost it bad after that. I came home after a run on a warehouse for Lil Dem and found her dead. Empty nep baggies were all over the bed."

"Hell, I'm sorry, I shoulda known better than to ask you take me to this place, stirring things up."

"Don't worry bay, we got this." Wyatt squeezed Magdalena's hand.

"My padre done got himself hanged because of nep," Magdalena said. "He shot a man in the back for a fix, and then the Locos came down on him, 'cause the man he killed was one of them. So they caught him, and noosed him up in a tree for everyone to see. I wanted to cut him down and bury him but Max wouldn't let me. After that, I hated Max, and Max started losing his memory from the drug, and I couldn't deal with all that drama. Then my drinking got worse."

Nobody knew who'd brewed up the first batch of nepenthe. Some speculated it was the Chinese, or the Russians adding fuel to the fentanyl flames in a plan to further deteriorate and demoralize the American republic. People in politics still blamed Islamic terrorist cells, or on the troops who'd brought it home from the Middle East and formed gangs to distribute it when they couldn't adapt to realities at home in the fading empire. Others said it came from a big pharma lab up in Canada, that it had been part of an Alzheimer's cure when the recipe got leaked onto what remained of the dark net.

After an intense bout of pain numbing euphoria, nepenthe reworked the memory circuits of the brain resetting the short term, so the person who took it couldn't recall they had taken it. It pulled the blackout curtain down over what they'd done while under its influence. The fact that it was highly addictive made it a royal pain to get off of because they hardly remembered taking it in the first place. For those who got hooked long term memories disintegrated over time into nothing until they ambled around the world like someone with dementia.

"We stopped staying here after mom died and went to live in the Rathaus. Brett's a bit schizo, has these super hyper moods, and then he can't get out of bed for days. It got worse when he got jumped in. He got tight with some of the upper crew and didn't listen to me much after that.

"It weren't long after that when I caught Carly sneakin' behind my back with Lil Dem. I got so jealous I couldn't take orders from the bastard. Brett didn't need me, and I hated myself for giving him his first dose of nep so I took myself down to the tracks hoping to end it all."

"And that's when Marvin found you?"

"Yup. He jumped off a box car and tackled me when he saw what I was gonna do. Talked to me all night, then convinced to go to the Sprout House, get clean. I'm finally starting to get my memory back. Seems like I'm only now kennin' who and what I am. Maybe if I'd never taken nep or joined the Rats I'd be workin' on the river now."

"So where do we go now? The Rathaus?"

Wyatt was nervous and wanted to stall. "We could go to the biergarten first. Can I buy ya lunch?" The walk had burned off the ramen and he had a bit of coin from doing odd jobs Marvin found for him.

"Sure."

The biergarten was next to the docks and served the men and stout, butch women who were unloading goods from the boats, zipping two-wheelers loaded with boxes down the gangplanks and into large warehouses.

Long rows of picnic tables under an open shelter made up the biergarten. Food shacks were set up between towering cottonwoods and sycamores, serving up gumbo and chili potatoes. It was a Saturday and people were getting off work early, and the boats-men were starting in on the beer.

He got a large bowl of carp, catfish, and mussel gumbo with chunks of cornbread from one of the stands and they sat down at table as far away as they could get from the others who were chowing down.

"Ya know what?" she asked. He shook his head. "This is our first date."

He laughed. "Some kind of date I've taken you on," and then then spooned a scoop into her open mouth.

He remembered Marvin's advice on eating regular meals when they could be had. They were an antidote against slipping back into old patterns, and if he wasn't hungry, he'd be less irritable, discontent, better able to do what he had to do.

The meal took the edge off of his nerves.

As they ate a man wearing a frayed seersucker suit jumped up on a table and began to address the gathered crowd with a bullhorn. He rattled off a scurrilous screed marking him as a member of the New American Syndicate. Members of the Waterways Union were starting to salute the speaker with sloshing steins of ale.

"Let's get outta here before these folks get all riled up."

They slipped past the tables and the warehouses and were almost in among the rowbo shacks and drug dens that huddled around the protection of the Rathaus when he spotted Carly walking towards them. She was wearing the blue bandanna of the gang tight around her tangled red hair. Carly saw Wyatt at the same time and he could feel tension in the air rippling off of Magdalena who already had her hand clenched in a fist.

As Carly walked up to them he saw she had a fresh black eye and a bruise on her cheek. *Lil Dem*, he thought. He'd seen the chief lose his temper before. It could've been a fight with another gang, but it was probably Lil Dem. Wyatt never could kill his conscience enough to treat the women the way some of the other guys in the gang did.

He could tell she was seething from the way she hotboxed her cigarette. Some drama must have just gone down and he found himself relieved he didn't have to live like that anymore.

"You come back to get your ass killed?" she said, flicking the cig onto the dirt trail.

"'Course not. I came to talk to Brett. Is he around?"

She huffed and looked over her shoulder. Then she nodded her head over to a side trail through the brush along the river where they went to be out of view.

Carly sized Magdalena up. "I'm guessing you with him?"

"That's right. He's my beau and I'm his girl."

"Well ain't you lucky. Me and him had some fun together, but in the end, he wouldn't ever been able to take care of me, or my needs. I hope it's better for you."

Magdalena and Wyatt both knew her hardness was a front, but it didn't make them any less uncomfortable. Magdalena had her guard up, but was trying to stay cool, reasonable.

"He'd doing just fine. I'm lucky to have him."

"We heard you was living in some kind of hippie-punk commune, is that so?"

Before she knew what she had done Magdalena let it slip, "yeah, the Sprout House Collective." Wyatt glared at her, and Carly's lip curled in a slight grimace of a smile.

"Carly, I'm not here to stir up any other shit," Wyatt said. "I'm not in any other gang. I just need to talk to my brother, Brett."

"Yer brother ain't yer brother anymore, he belongs to the Rats, just like your ass does if any of 'em spot ya out here. Me I'm givin' you a pass because yer sister was my girl, and I know how it is to lose the only blood you got left."

Carly's brother, her last blood family, had been in the gang. Now he was on the bottom of the river. He'd had an unfortunate run in with the 100 Proofers.

"So where is he?"

"He's across the river. He ain't been around for two days. We sent him over to Bobbie's Honky-Tonk on a job and he ain't made it back. Lil Dem's startin' to worry."

"Why'd you send him there!?"

"Bidness, just like usual."

"You sure that's where he went?"

Carly lit another cigarette and nodded.

"Come on Maggie, we gotta go."

Running to the ferry landing Wyatt felt even more guilt for his brother's fate than he had before.

THE FERRY RIDE ACROSS the Ohio to Southside Cincy's redlight district was quick. Dirty biodiesel fumes spilled into the air. A worried grandma in her forties with a couple of scared toddlers in tow looked over the rails into water chopped by the wind. The ferry passed between the columns of an exhausted bridge. Wyatt and Magdalena held hands as they looked up through the gaps where concrete had fallen away from the rebar. The sun was in the west and the clouds glowed with pink phosphorescence.

Wyatt rubbed the coarse stubble above his lip. "You've heard the rumors about Bobbie's, right?"

"Never even heard of the place."

"Really? I thought everyone kenned the honky-tank. People tell all these stories 'bout it, 'bout how the owner Bobbie never ages but looks the same year after year. But what's more, supposedly down in the basement, there's a gateway to the underworld. To the land of the dead, or the fairies, some say both. They say that's where Bobbie comes from and gets her power from."

Magdalena had been raised on tales of miracles performed by the saints, and honored the dead on Dios de los Muertos, but even with all her Catholic folk belief it still sounded preposterous. "You juss messin' right?"

"Naw, I'm furreal. At least that's what the stories say. I only went once before, Lil Dem dragged me up there with him, and I never saw Bobbie, so I don't know. But the place felt weird. I felt real tired after leaving, like something'd been sapped from me."

As they traveled downriver they passed a long stretch of rowbo jungles along both banks. A grizzled old man tended a cauldron of mulligan stew over a fire, and others passed around mugs of dandelion coffee and jars of moonshine. Cincinnati had some of the biggest rowbo camps outside Cairo, Illinois where the Ohio met the Mississippi as itinerant workers canoed, kayaked, and rowed up and down the rivers of the country looking for work. The one along Cincy's Southside was a real popular jungle due to its proximity to the brothels, hookah lounges and nep dens.

"My mom told me my dad was rowbo," Wyatt said. "Maybe he's in that camp now. Or some other camp down on the Mississippi. If he ain't dead, if he ain't drowned himself in liquor or the river itself."

Magdalena raised her eyebrow, gave him a look. Wyatt went on.

"He was working down on the docks when they met. He spent a couple years with us. I still remember his mustache. They was always partying and always fighting, but then they had a real big fight. Mom said he'd grown restless for the rowbo life, so he left and went to stick his rod somewhere else. I kinda wonder how many other bro's and sis's I got out there."

"It'll be different for our kids," Magdalena said. "They'll know the both of us and know each other."

"It'd be good if they ken their uncle. I wish Polly'd stuck around too."

The ferry docked on the other side of the city and they started to walk towards the Licking River, a north flowing tributary that wound its way through the hills and hollers of Kentucky until it bisected the Southside of Cincinnati and poured into the Ohio.

"Bobbie's Honky Tonk is a couple more miles up the Licking. Let's get walkin'."

The streets were jammed with pedestrians, bicycle rickshaws, horses and buggies. Beer and bourbon flowed in the bars, money was being lost and won in the gambling holes, and male and female prostitutes of every stripe and persuasion plied their ancient trade. There was something to be had for whatever price point fit the budget. The wealth that flowed into the district kept the streets and buildings there in better repair than some of the other neighborhoods, but underneath it all was a sense of something of rotting.

AN HOUR LATER THEY were at the entrance of Bobbie's Honky-Tonk. Surrounding the building proper was a small compound of shipping containers serving as hookup pads for the customers who came looking to pay for sex. Men and women ranging from their teens to their thirties stood outside or milled about on the patio, smoking cigarettes, drinking, flaunting their wares. Magdalena kept her eye on Wyatt's eye, making sure he didn't look overlong at any of the women who were dressed to sell.

Wyatt looked her in the eye, "None of these have anything on you, girl. Besides, life's best things are free."

She smiled.

Hanging electric lights flickered above the patio as the sun set lending the place a touch of class. The power came from a generator in the watercourse. The entire area the nightclub was situated on was verdant and full of life. Having stepped onto the property they both felt a sense that the rest of world was dull. There was a sense of being more alive and it made them both wary, as if something had been overlaid on top of them.

Inside the clientele was a mix. Not just dockworkers, buggy drivers, and hard labor, but wealthy farmers in fancy duds, bourbon and horse barons entertaining potential business partners, and some bespectacled clerks and suited newspapermen who milled about the bar ordering drinks. A crowd gathered in front of the stage where a real live electric billyrap band was tuning up to play. Lots of women mingled, and not just Bobbie's employees. They'd come to slake their thirst for whisky, music, men, or women. Bobbie's had a reputation, not just for the strange stories, but as a place anybody could come to forget their cares. The one thing the visitors all had in common was an enchanted sparkle in their eyes.

The smell of the battered fish and chips wasn't bad either. Servers carried platters to the tables. Wyatt's stomach rumbled. All through the winter he'd struggled to get enough calories.

There were upstairs rooms for various entertainments and rumors of other pleasures downstairs below.

"You see your brother?"

"No. Let's ask." He waved down a waiter, and slipped him all but the remaining coins he'd need to get back over the river. The band had started to play and he had to shout into the guy's ear.

Magdalena noticed another room off the main hall. A taxidermied deer head and large snake were mounted above the entrance and a leather clad bouncer guarded the door.

"He's in there," Wyatt said. "VIP only. I don't ken how we'll get past him."

They felt odd standing around, without drinks, the only two sober people in the place, so they sauntered up to the bar, ordered ginger sodas, and formulated a plan. The house band started in on a version of the *Knoxville Girl*. Wyatt knew the murder ballad and it filled him with a sense of dread.

"I took her by her golden curls and I drug her round and around, throwing her into the river that flows through Knoxville town" the band rapped.

Magdalena got up and walked over to the bouncer. She gave him a distressed look and then started raging at him, then pointed at an unsuspecting man watching the band. The bouncer went over to talk to the guy, thinking he'd done something to her, and she dipped out the door to a meeting place down the road.

Wyatt slipped into the vacated door and headed down the stairs to the basement, and into another world.

THE SMELL OF THE river permeated the porous rock of the basement. Another smell of honey, milk, and the nectar of fresh cut flowers floated on top of it. There was an orange oscillating light coming in from the room, low voices, giggles, and sighs.

Wyatt stepped into a love nest. Soft pillows covered the floor and silk hangings adorned the walls. Vases with exotic flowers were set on stands and oil lamps scented with fragrant perfumes intoxicated the air. A multi-stemmed hookah was in the center of the room, it's drifting smoke adding to the haze of unreality he started to feel. Underneath it all was a slick smell of sex, a throbbing heat, and the wetness of the previous night's rain seeping through the foundations.

Brett was there and the elfin Bobbie tangled up with him, her cream white buttocks bare in the glow, covering Brett's more private parts. She was as young looking as the stories told, a lady in her early twenties. Yet how could it be she looked so young when she had owned the honky-tonk for over fifty years? Some said she'd owned it longer. Her jet black hair fell to her shoulders. She turned to look at the interloper and the room grew cold with her gaze, the lighting dimmed, shivers ran up Wyatt's spine.

In the corner of the room he noticed a cellar door with a heavy lock. A skeleton key hung around Bobbie's neck. She held one hand on the key and another clutched Brett's neck. "How did you get past my guard?"

"I didn't see nobody." He looked at his pale, spent brother. "I didn't mean to interrupt yer fun, but Brett, I gotta talk to ya!" Bobbie kept her long green painted fingernails wrapped around his neck.

"What the hell..?" His brother looked as if he was coming up for air after a deep dive.

"You always said I had bad timing." Wyatt adjusted the banjo strapped to his back.

"You can put that down," she said in a commanding hypnotic voice. "I can see you've been carrying it awhile and the burden must be getting to you."

No one stood between Wyatt and his banjo. All he could do was shake his head.

Brett tried to talk but he was so high and sexed up all he could do was a mumble.

"Maybe you'd like to join us, then" she said with a greedy hunger and bewitching resonance in her voice. "Come sit down here and smoke and play with us. You don't mind sharing me, do you, Brett? You never did before."

A strong arousal started building in Wyatt's blood despite the fact that Bobbie wasn't his type. She was way too pale for his taste, but he got the feeling that his response wasn't of his own volition. It took every effort of his will to resist the urges she was casting into him.

Images of the girl he loved ran through his mind.

"Come on, Magdalena won't mind."

"How'd you know..." *The stories must be true.* He shuddered.

His brother sat up. His hazel eyes were bloodshot and rheumy. He wiped his nose on his arm, reached for the stem of the hookah and took a long puff, then directed the stem towards his brother. He could smell hash interlaced with nepenthe. Wyatt noticed Bobbie wasn't smoking the stuff herself.

"Naw, brother. I gave it up. That's why I've come looking for you. I need to tell you I'm sorry."

His brother fell into a coughing fit. "For what?"

"For giving you the stuff in the first place. And for all that's happened between us since mom died."

Brett looked dislocated, as if some memory had just dropped into his skull offering a new temporal view. A small tear, glistened in the corner of his eye, close to the tattooed tear from the Rats he wore so proud.

"I got this girl Brett, and me and her are bound to have some kids soon, from the way were going at it. I want you to meet her, you could come live with us, and we could help get you clean."

"You're a grown man," Bobbie said to Brett before he could reply. "You don't need a big brother to baby you. Look how long it's taken him to come back to you anyway."

" Bobbie, shut up! Aren't you getting enough of me? What's the harm in talking? "

"I missed you bro, all our adventures, the good times, the craziness…"

"Why'd you ditch me, man?"

"I lost my fracking head." Wyatt said. "I was going to kill myself, and then I was stopped by this man. Then I was saved again when I met Maggie. I been meaning to come see you, but…it's been hard to come back, I didn't wanna risk what I'm starting to build, but I got to this point where I couldn't go on unless I came back…"

"I apprish ya coming back Wy. I do. But down here," he looked at Bobbie, "I never felt so good in my life."

"I ken ya do right now. But there's so much more than the game. And after a few months off the drugs, life does get better."

"I don't ken man. I think this the best it'll ever get for me."

Wyatt's heart was breaking. Then he heard an old tune they'd both known calling in his soul. Something mom had sung to them all those years ago. He thought maybe if he could play it, he'd have a chance of getting through to him.

He started banging out the tune, clawhammer style, rapping the words in an incantatory cadence that came from a secret place he hadn't kenned was inside him.

As he played the milk and honey and nectar which had covered Brett's eyes started to dissipate and Bobbie's heart softened for a moment from the sound of Wyatt's playing and she let go of the clutch and glamour she held on her boy toy. The light was coming back into Brett. He rose unsteadily to his feet and shambled towards his brother.

Now was his chance.

"Let's go" Wyatt turned to go upstairs, in a hurry to get his brother back to the land of the living. It felt like he was climbing up a mountain. Each step was an effort to take and when he reached the top he looked back down to see if Brett was still with him. To his dismay Brett was once again entangled in Bobbie's lair.

Brett called up to his brother, "Give my love to the bay when you have one, and please, name her Polly."

"Are you crazy Brett?"

"Maybe I am, maybe I am. Be seeing you bro."

Wyatt let out a horrified moan of despair and he ran to find Magdalena, letting his brother go.

WYATT KEPT TO THE shadows on his way to the docks where Magdalena was waiting for them, the ferryman ready to take them back across the Ohio. This time they were dropped off downtown, closer to Camp Washington.

It was still a long walk back and Wyatt was lead-footed in silence on the way home. He didn't want to let her see him cry, and he didn't want her to see him fly off into a rage. He craved the false comfort of nepenthe, and he craved anything that would obliterate the pain of loss that burned inside. He tried to recapture the divine spark of the void, the stillness within him, but it was elusive.

Then he looked at Maggie and knew she was enough.

As they got closer to their block the smell of fire lay heavy on the air. It wasn't just

cook fires, trash fires, bon fires, or stove fires. This was house fire, plastic fire, burning furniture and timber down to the foundations fire. Both were all too familiar with the smell. They could hear it too, the cries, the crackle, the chaos.

"Come one," she yelled, and they mustered a third wind of energy in the late night to make a final mad dash to the grand old building that had once been Sprout House. Flames spit out the window that had once been their room. Marvin, Syd, Iz and a crowd of people they didn't ken were doing their best to fight the conflagration. It was to no avail.

Joan came up to them crying with Ziggy in tow. Joan leaned into Magdalena.

"What happened?" Magdalena asked.

"Don't worry Wy," Joan said. "It's not your fault. At the gig tonight... some different folks than usual came in. We thought they were bangers and had our people check them out, but we couldn't be sure, so they came in. The girl, she was all bruised up, and we thought she needed shelter, and in the middle of the gig between songs, she lit a Molotov, and said 'this is for harboring a Rat' and threw it into a bookshelf. Another was with her and threw one in the stairwell."

Wyatt looked at Maggie who was pulling her hair in anguish. She had mentioned the Sprout House to Carly. "It's my fault... I let slip where we live."

"It ain't your fault bay," Wyatt said, taking her in his arms. "I take the blame, look at all this trouble I brought on us all. It was too risky going back. I shoulda let my brother go a long time ago."

"No, you did what you needed to do," Joan said through tears. "You can't be responsible for her actions. All we can do now is try and rebuild. And it's a good thing you took that banjo with you, otherwise it'd be up there burning."

(Two months later)

THE MEMBERS OF THE Phoneix Asch House had helped put some of the Sprouts up as they began the process of scouting out a new squat, but their space was cramped and some folks decided to build a temporary camp in a field along the banks of the Mill Creek.

Wyatt was putting the last nail into a shack he'd improvised and Ziggy was already sacked out inside when Magdalena came over to him and said. "It looks awesome! And I've got something to tell ya."

He grinned. "What, you pregnant already?"

She nodded. "I am. I ain't had a period since just about a week after the fire."

"I guess now that you's knocked up, think it's time we shacked up?!"

"You ken it! Only promise me one thing."

"What's that?"

"That you'll be mine, forever."

"I will girl, I will. Always and forever. For real and for true.

on. "You know," she said, "if you don't mind, I'd rather stay."

Courting Songs

Tanya Hobbs

This is VK4Red, VK4Red, VK4Red calling VK2Gutenberg, VK2Gutenberg, VK2Gutenberg, over."

"VK2Gutenberg to VK4Red, receiving you 5/9, over."

"Righty-oh VK2Gutenberg. Ya be pleased to know your advice fixed our antenna problem. VK4Red is now six hours out with 120 grumpy camels. Should be in Canyon for dinner tomorrow night. Over."

"VK4Red, acknowledged."

After a pause, "Johannes, have ya told anyone I'm coming yet?"

"No?"

"Johannes, you invited me specially to meet your sister. I've brought two skins of wine and a round of her favourite cheese 18 days through the desert. In Mama's Name, let her know we're arriving for dinner tomorrow night.

A further pause…

"She might not like you. Or like you too much, she gets tetchy when men refuse her. Mam listens to her."

"I'm the Master Trader, let me worry about how to sell

the goods. You go and tell yer sister now."

"Acknowledged. VK2Gutenberg is over and out."

"HERE," THE TALL, SLIGHTLY stoop shouldered man turned and pushed the heavy hide door aside, leading the way through the rocky entrance passage.

As the small party passed the kitchen alcove, the man grunted to the apprentice leaning over a large pot, "Traders, dish three more". Then he gestured towards a shadowed doorway off the main living chamber, "Guest chamber, Canyon 1's finest".

He watched, lantern held high, as the three travellers unslung their packs onto the floor of the rocky chamber and washed their hands and faces from the water jug provided. Then he led the group to join the two journeymakers and Master already sitting at the dining table.

"Bess," he nodded acknowledgement to his fellow Master, "Red," gesturing to the first traveller, and folded his long legs under the low table with a grunt. The traders followed suit while Bess murmured a greeting. The apprentice reappeared, serving out bowls of acorn and three bean casserole fragrant with sage and saltbush, before sitting down himself. The tall man mumbled thanks to Mama Earth and the Ancestors and everyone tucked in with the silence of good appetite.

With his first hunger sated, the leader of the traders sat back and grinned at the tall man, "Well, Johannes, good to see ya ain't become over talkative in your old age. I were worried. That last broadcast ya did must of had a good thousand words altogether. I were dead sure you'd run dry before ya could spit them all out."

Johannes's journeymakers exchanged knowing grins. Johannes rolled his eyes, "Real funny, Red. Radio's faster than Trader post for organising."

"Yah, never thought the Long Dry would come to this, though. It were one thing when a few remote Canyons back of the Never Never were shuttered but Canyon 1's oldest of all."

Johannes shrugged, "Mama wrote the message clear in the sky last fifty odd years. Wise man don't stay on country without welcome."

Bess added, "We've twice eaten well into our drought buffer since I received my apprentice's apron and the catchments stopped refilling in the rain years.

"The Ancestors' Rules are clear, too," she sighed. "We knew it was our time to leave when we finished our ten year drought store at the fire solstice. After all, not like we'll run out of welcoming desert country anytime soon, the way those Coasters farm."

"Are yer transitioning the Canyon altogether, or did ya end up all split?"

"About a quarter of the Canyon went to family in other Canyons, too old or set in their rounds for such a dramatic change in tempo. Of the rest, most left immediately to start the courtship when we heard of a new canyon with a potentially harmonious spirit from you traders.

Red said, "I heard there was nice soaks in the country round about, and the Coasters twenty years gone, so good light grazing. Yer herders must be right pleased, at least. Got any idea how much longer ye'll be here?"

"We think, about six months. We still need to disperse excess copies and archive the core Library and Canyon records. It also depends on how many traders turn up to help. Then, we'll hold a farewell smudging ceremony, mud up the entrances and set off to greet the new canyon.

She smiled sadly, "Canyon 1 will become an occasional rest stop for you traders and sink back into the Dreamtime for everyone else."

"Have ya had contact with any Firsters, told 'em about the shuttering? Though, I'd guess they know alright from their song-lines."

"It's been too dry for good hunting around here lately so we don't see many, but three Wadigali walked out of the deep desert the day before the fire solstice feast. Their medicine man agreed they would smoke out the bunyips and visit with the Canyon and Ancestor spirits while hunting here in future. Our Elders let them know when to expect acorn fall, for as long as the trees hold out, and showed them where to dip water from the cisterns."

Red sighed, "Ah, well, one day Mama will change her moods and then we'll be out and about waking all these canyons again."

Breaking the melancholy mood, Bess leaned forward to ask, "How is your family, anyway? Johannes has mentioned you but never seems to get around to asking about your family during your radio nets."

Red brightened, "We was worried about my nephew for ages but he's come real good now. Only four and still small but already a sharp eye and quick hand for a rabbit. My sister, well, she's only just caught again. After all the trouble with her first little tacker coming so early, the family and me Mam got permission to swap herd duties. They're doing their six months herding now with the Master Healer. Then they'll all sit together tight as a tick in canyon quarters for the last two months.

"While I were there in Canyon 3 with them, I picked up your 'cast about needing traders to haul stores and the books that you're sending to other Branches. I thought I'd do my big brother bit by nipping 'round, see if ya got anything rare on midwifry the healers might like. Thought I could take 'em back along with a train load of whatever Library copies ya want to send the Branches out our way and top up my trading stocks of personal copies all at the same time."

"Canyon 3 ... the Master Healer is Salvation Jane, right?" said Bess.

"Yah."

"Aw, your sister will be fine then. Mam always says Jane's Master Named her well, she's the best baby whisperer around and then she can turn around and curse Death himself if need be."

Johannes stroked his beard, "Midwifing? Got a couple copies in store, suit even Salvation Jane. Late pulled journey-maker prints, not Library copies, but readable."

"I got some corkers for yer personal shelves and 30 spare camels ya can load up with Library copies for the other Branches," promised Red.

"Morning, then. Bring your request lists and promise chits, we'll fill your train."

Red nodded, reached for the jug of dark brew on the table, and started a tall tale about his last trip with the Coasters up North. Bess responded with a tale of her own, while a journeymaker took down a lap dulcimer and picked out a tune. Eventually, Red brought out his wineskins and the cheese, and a long and lively night followed.

NEXT MORNING BESS AND her apprentice bustled around, talking in low voices, as Red stepped into the main chamber. "That kang bed were right nice last night, think my journey-makers appreciated the ease too," said Red. "Sorry if we took yer place."

At a gesture from Bess he sat at the dining table. Bess paused in her preparations to bring him a bowl of soaked grains and settled down with the tea tray and her apprentice to join him. She shook back her hair and smiled at him, "The kitchen chimney does do a good job of heating the kang but I find a hot brick from the stove keeps my futon warm enough at night."

"Camel will keep ya warm at night too, but they don't smell nice as fresh woven reed mat what's been laid over warm bricks," he said. "Got any big plans for today?"

Bess smiled again, "Cotton here has a handle on his flora, inks and papers so he'll be mixing gel trays. Not much call for new printing at the moment but, if he practices, his gels should be smooth enough to try pulling a few prints by the time we get to the new canyon. Might be able to get started on his apprentice pieces and get Named early."

At this praise, young Cotton flushed bright enough to blot out his freckles and lowered his eyes modestly.

"Johannes has worn his sheets beyond darning or turning so I'll be spending the morning digging out some new ones from the extra stores Mam and Da left in the lower caves." Bess lightly touched Red's arm, "You'll be sore from your trip. You know, we still have one small steam cave set up, a bit of eucalyptus helps ease muscles..."

At that point Johannes shuffled out of the gloom of the inner chambers, paused to scowl at the kitchen counter, picked up a steaming mug of pure liquid darkness, and continued out the door. Bess watched, then turned back and quirked her mouth. "Might be best to give him an hour or so before you bring around your lists."

Red grinned and nodded, "Thanks for breakfast, and for the tips. Think I'll leave ya now, though, I've got to check on the camels. Apprentices and journeymakers should have them set to rights but there's two what picked up nasty abcesses in the spinifex country. I want to keep my eye on 'em, maybe mix a poultice to draw the poisons." He nodded again and left.

JOHANNES ROSE FROM HIS desk with two texts in hand as Red strolled through the Library entrance mid-morning. "For Aunty Jane: detailed colour anatomical, hard to reproduce, and diary of some Ancestor healer. Birthing babies on country in bad conditions hasn't changed much."

Red checked the bindings and nodded. "I brought ya Donne and the Amateur Radio Handbook, the gen-u-ine '95 edition. Also a pretty Weavers' Flora for your Mam, next time ya see her," handing over a bundle.

Johannes hastily pulled on cotton gloves, before he slid each text gently from the wrapper and onto his desk. Turning the pages he checked the bindings and print quality. Frowning, he flipped to check the print number on the Flora. "Very high print number for such bright colours," he sniffed.

Red rolled his eyes, "Ya know the Elders approved the fire rock inks ten years ago because the old inks were eating through pages and books needing remaking every 50 years ain't good neither. If them pine tar inks ya trying last 200 years, we can stop again. Anyways, taint hardly counts when ya just scooping old mine seepage out of waste pits. Not like we're burning them fire rocks."

Johannes pursed his lips, then snorted and shook his head. "Quality binding, Mam'll like it. I'll sacrifice a few months to Mama, work off the debt." He held out his hand, "Requests, hand 'em over."

Red smirked and thrust a thick sheaf into his hand.

Johannes squinted at the closely spaced list, fanned through a few double sided pages, and grunted, "Don't ask much, do you?" Sitting, he pulled out his copy catalogue and ran a charstick down the request list as he compared the two and started making annotations. Every now and again his other hand drifted out to touch the little stack of new books beside him. After five minutes he looked up and growled, "Off, this'll take days to glean."

99

Red grinned and strode off. A Branch closure were pretty rare. No chance of Library Grade copies, of course, they would all go to other Branches. Still, it were a good time to prise a decent stock of personal use prints out of the tight fisted Archivers Guild. He had a second 30 camels for those. If he traded well, it would set up his Caravan for their next five years book trading with the Coaster lords. Might even find some in Asean script. And, to return the balance, his trading chits represented resources to nourish the new Canyon during its difficult rooting phase.

All in all, things was lookin' good. Time to find the lovely Bess.

RED STEPPED THROUGH A deep slit in the canyon wall to find Bess digging through a pile of wrapped bundles near the front of a large cavern that smelled of centuries of warm sand and the sweetness of dry sun-cured hay. As he adjusted to the gloom and flickering lantern light, he eyed the impressive number of packets and bundles stacked more or less neatly in the cave. His trader instincts couldn't resist the chance to poke and prod a few of the odder shapes.

"This isn't all our stuff," Bess sounded vaguely embarrassed. "This cave is now temporary storage for everyone who travels with our quarter of the herds."

Red nodded absently, more interested in scrambling up and then balancing on a convenient wooden frame to examine a fleck of yellow that had caught his eye high on the wall. After a bit of gentle easing some yellowed paper fell out of a crevice into his hand and turned out to be a small paper wrapped cylinder, covered in some gritty, slimy substance.

After climbing down he looked the grimy cylinder over, then shrugged and chucked it over his shoulder.

There was a very loud, flat, CRACK!

As Red and Bess jumped and spun around, the entrance pillar gave a couple of deep retorts of its own. As one, Red and Bess dived into a deep alcove along the side of the cavern. A thunderous BOOM from the entrance rumbled on and on for several seconds, a massive dust cloud billowing past in the wildly swaying lantern light.

Coughing, Red picked himself out of Bess' arms and stumbled around the corner of the alcove. "Cripes!" His mouth fell open. Boulders and rubble now completely blocked the narrow cavern entrance, some of which spilled past the alcove.

Bess stepped around the corner herself, then turned on Red. "Cripes?" she shrieked. "Cripes! You complete and utter fracker! We coulda been killed!" She kicked his ankle, then turned away, waving her arms, striding deeper into the cave.

Red blinked several times, then followed sheepishly behind, unhooking the lantern as he went. "I reckon it were a bodgie build, it were just waiting to fall. Could have happened to anyone."

Bess snorted expressively.

"We still mates?" he inquired meekly, as he peered over her shoulder while she poked through a new area of cloth wrapped bundles.

Bess straightened slowly and glared at him, "Why do you care?"

"Well, yer a right lovely lass ..." he replied weakly.

Bess raised a deeply sceptical eyebrow.

"... with an older brother what can pinpoint electrical interference sources by ear as well as being yer Canyon's Master Archiver," Red finished. "We've been chewing rag when the bounce were good on my trips the past few years. Anyways, I thought it were time to see if he'd be up for something more."

"Johannes, my brother," Bess said dubiously. "The man who spends his sun hours locked in the library lab concocting toxic brews from pine trees; his nights hidden in the back stacks reading prints so ancient they're from the Dreamtime. The man who refuses to speak three words a week to his family?"

"I trade with Coasters and Aseans for months each trip. Sure he don't talk much sometimes but it were comforting to have some familiar static in my ear to talk at. Reunions might be nice, too," Red said wistfully, "my sister's busy with babies and me Mam don't leave her herds much.

"You know he's well respected in the Canyon? It's been a massive work, bedding down the Canyon and closing the Library Branch. Johannes has orchestrated much of it. Our Councils trusted him to orchestrate it, despite being young. Traders are fun for a laugh but you're also a twisty lot, not exactly reliable."

"Well, I reckon that were between him and me. He's interesting with his discoveries and competent at what he does, which is refreshin' after a trading day with the Coasters. Feels awful like I'm cheating meself when half the time I'm stuck making both sides of a deal.

"And, there's all those old books still lying around in Coaster attics and barns. 'Cept the lords, taint hardly any Coasters out there what can read no more. Seems a shame not to bring 'em to you and yer brother for winnowing."

Bess narrowed her eyes at Red, then selected a long pry bar from the bundle next to her and shoved it into his chest. "You prove your charm and competence by digging us out of here and I'll consider putting in a good word for you with our Mam. She's the one you'll need to convince and you've just been dancing around on her second favourite loom frame."

Red strode over to the base of the rubble and poked the pry bar warily at one of the larger boulders. The whole stack of boulders groaned alarmingly and some smaller rocks rolled down towards him. Skipping neatly out of the way, Red turned to Bess and shook his head. "There's a breeze round about, making the lantern flicker. But, 'less we can prop those boulders, digging will just bring the whole show down on me head.

Bess rubbed her chin, then exchanged the pry bar for a pick and led him to the alcove they had sheltered in and pointed at the rear wall. "This is the deepest alcove. The next cave is only half a meter away through that wall. It's soft rock. Get picking, no bludging," she commanded.

Red groaned but started swinging the pick as Bess brought over a shovel to move the mess away as it built up.

THEY SLUMPED AGAINST THE wall for their third break some interminable time later. "I think ya were wrong about that soft rock," Red picked morosely at the blisters on his hands. "I got calluses from the reins, ya'd think they'd be enough but I'm bleeding out like a new aproned apprentice."

Bess looked over, "They're in the wrong spots. You Traders don't spend six months a year growing food and tending swales like we Canyoners do so your hands aren't shaped to pick and shovel."

"I can't rightly picture yer brother with a pick."

"True, he's not Plantfellas Guild like our Da but he keeps Mama's Balance the same as anyone. Six months on country with the herds like everyone else and growing duties while he's in canyon.

"Of course, he tends to spend more time prodding the paper mulberries' bark than mulching the melons growing between them, but he does his bit. He says plants and sheep are easier to work with than apprentices, anyway."

Red nodded, "I can see that. I likes me camels, now. Lots of people say they're right cranky beggars but really they're just smart. Treat 'em respectful and they're willing enough but they don't forgive nastiness.

"So, you says yer Da is a plantfella, is yer Mam Weavers Guild then?"

"Yes, and you've already met Mam's sister, Aunty Jane, Salvation Jane. They were both born Coasters, you know, then sold as children. It's not that they dislike all Traders, you realise, it just made them a bit ambiguous about Traders generally. Grateful not to have ended up slaves, of course. But they saw all the adults in the slave caravan killed, even the slavers' servants, and it's not like you Traders give the children you 'salvage' any choice about joining a Canyon."

"There's good reasons for that, you know. For starters, most don't even have a family to return to. Or their family were the ones that first sold them."

"Of course, but still. Anyway, Mam is a lot less angry about it than Aunty Jane. But then, Mam says Aunty Jane likes to get angry about a lot of things."

"Yer Aunty Jane sure were an impressive lady."

"Ah, typical Trader Diplomacy. Though, I've noticed your cant slips a bit sometimes."

"Yah, I blames them Coasters, addled on plastic fumes. Me Trader Art's wasted on 'em, leads to sloppy habits.

Bess shifted, "so, I've been curious, is Red a nickname or your Name?"

"Me Master said he'd never had such an apprentice for twisting orders and digging under peoples' skin with questions. He said giving me my apron were like bedding down overnight in Red Stipa grass, so that's what he Named me at the end of my apprenticeship.

"Mind, that were after seven years of saving his drunk hide with the Coasters and twice with Asean slavers. I were careful not to give the old beggar the satisfaction of thinking I cared. Anyways, could have been worse, one of the healers in Canyon 8? He were Named Devil's Claw."

"What did he—" Bess heard a faint ringing sound coming from the alcove. Yelling, she ran over to its back wall. Red pushed past her and returned to picking. Sure enough, a small hole opened up and slowly enlarged.

Eventually, Johannes' familiar scowl appeared. He thrust a skin of water and several pieces of acorn bread through the hole, then raised an eyebrow at Bess. "Heard a bang. Saw the rubble. Thought you were after sheets, not doing remodelling."

"I love you too," said Bess, "but get me out of here now or you can change your own fracking sheets."

Johannes smirked, "Settle, Cotton's here." Then he stepped back and he and Red carefully widened the hole enough to allow Bess to wriggle through.

"Oof, I'm off for a steam and some sleep," said Bess, standing. "He's alright, so you know, for a Trader," flung over her shoulder as she walked off past a grinning Cotton.

Johannes stared after her in confusion, then turned to help Red lever himself up and through the hole.

"Good?"

"Yeah," said Red, "thought for a mo' that Mama Earth decided to collect early for your book debt but then your sister kicked me ankle and set me straight."

Johannes nodded seriously.

"Hey, I got something to show ya once we can get a ladder through that hole," said Red, as he finished brushing himself off. The two men wandered off together through the deep dusk of the canyon evening: two Masters sharing the flow of discovery, sure in the knowledge that dinner was the apprentice's problem.

A FEW MORNINGS LATER, Bess marched back to the scene of the rock fall, looking for Cotton and drawn by the sound of voices and whistles. Seemed like nearly every person left in quarters had gathered to watch Red swing a pick to widen the hole between the two alcoves, opening the blocked cave. She had to admit the sight repaid the seeing. Red had, quite unnecessarily she felt, stripped to his unders and the warm lantern light gilded ropy muscles as he laboured. Dozens of long, thin white scars slashed across his left side and shoulder and wound through the hair of his forearm.

Adding to the entertainment, two journeymakers and Cotton had started a freestyle call and response chant on the familiar theme of peacocking, lazy, lying traders, as they shovelled Red's debris clear of the cave. Between swings, Red's harmonious tenor contributed responses on the subject of smelly, inbred Canyoners who were selfish slackers in bed. The audience was adding impromptu suggestions and whistling its appreciation of particularly finely honed lyrics. Only her brother was missing from the small crowd. Oblivious as usual, she thought, smugly.

Red caught sight of Bess as he levered the last of the rock out from the hole. He smirked, adjusted the cloth strips wrapping his hands, and gestured to his gleaming chest. "Didn't want to get me clothes dusty," he said.

She sniffed but, before she could speak, she heard Johannes' deep growl from inside the cave.

"Fascinating, partly natural but striations evidence mechanical digging, cylinder description matches expired dynamite from my reference. Controversial. Elders won't like it: can't have hypocritical Ancients, makes their Rules look bad. Still, explosions! ... very dissonant with the Canyon's spirit," rumbled her brother as he stepped through the hole.

"Anyways," he continued, "trading to do, ya bludger. I've gleaned you a mighty stack of books."

Bess gaped as her brother flung his arm around the slighter man's shoulders and led him off, hopefully to clean up, before they set a bad example to her apprentice by dirtying the books.

She turned to the alcove again, flicking her braid over her shoulder. She did have an appreciation for fine standing timber but perhaps a turn too twisty for comfort in this case. Pity. Mam would sort them out though, she knew, and she still had those twice-fracked sheets to find and now a hole in their main storage cave to secure. She held no hope of Johannes nor Red remembering to come back and do it. Men!

COTTON WHOOPED. A SMALL broken column of blue smoke were rising from behind a distant mountain cob, clear against the bold pink and bronze streaks of another of Mama's fine dawns. He jumped down to the faint track tracing the side of the new Canyon 56. He counted six months since they'd arrived and he could already run the steep descent in the dark, at least until the Masters had put a stop to the apprentices' nightly dares.

Leaping from rock to rock, Cotton made his way to a shallow hollow, the beginning of the new Library Branch complex. "They're 'ere! I see'd a smoke coming over the cob," he panted.

Johannes grunted acknowledgement and turned from roughing out the entrance to the new stacks. "Mam."

Cotton dashed off to report.

Once Cotton passed out of sight, Johannes paused to glare thoughtfully at his pick. He was looking forward to an interval with his promised. Following two trading trips and the successful birth of his niece, Red had returned to help with Canyon 1's finale and haul stores, accompanying Johannes on the month long trek to the new canyon. Mam had been tickled to see her second best loom frame emerge, newly polished, from Red's camel packs.

It hadn't taken Mam long to divine his understanding with Red, either. Johannes knew she'd been getting impatient with Bess and himself, both still unwed as Masters when most married at journeymaker. Johannes guessed Red had done a decent job of sweetening her up, maybe too much. Apparently, Red had been trading through the Coaster area where Mam was born, even meeting several people she had known as a child. Red took to sitting beside her loom sharing the news he'd picked up while showing surprising proficiency with a drop spindle. Eventually, Mam made Johannes answer a few searching, deeply uncomfortable questions. Then she kicked him off his own radio and out of the cave, to spend long hours chin wagging with Red's folks.

Upshot was, Johannes found himself promised to Red. Their Mams had arranged things with the Elders. Their wedding would be held as an auspicious prelude to the ceremony celebrating the new Canyon's Name. Johannes felt grateful he hadn't had to do all that talking and arranging himself but Mam had seemed to be acting a mite hasty.

Still, Red seemed happy enough and he did do the asking, using a ring of camel hair he'd plaited himself, following the deepest and oldest tradition. Supplementing tradition, he had also presented Johannes with a pendant pouch of softest rooskin so he could bear to wear the scratchy thing against his skin.

This past three months, though, Red had been off on one last trip before their wedding. Sent by the Council of Elders to trade with some of the Asean mine superintendents. Always a tricky business, an outsider trading with slave takers and the radio sprites had not been kind during the journey. The bands closed down and he'd been lucky to catch Red's signal once a week and even then generally too weak for a proper rag chewing session.

Gathering himself up, Johannes returned to swinging his pick. Red was still half a day away, the library stacks weren't going to dig themselves out, and it was still two days until his wedding.

At the End of
the Gravel Road

Ben Johnson

I

Lana's feet tingled, gravel crunching with each step. Her
stomach rumbled. She felt it may fold in on itself. She shook
her head. The tight curls of her dark hair today swung limply
around her hollow cheeks. Flies buzzed around her face then
surfed away on the waves of shimmering hot air. An old man
walking in front of her staggered away from the column of
prisoners and collapsed into a drainage ditch that ran alongside the gravel road. Lana did not look back when she heard
the shot.

The sun began to set over eastern Iowa. Their column
inched along eight hours, until they reached a row of dilapi-
dated mobile homes lining each side of the gravel road. The
six guards escorting the soon-to-be-inmates prodded them
into a single file line. A woman wearing a white lab coat
swiped a thermometer across each of their foreheads. Occasionally, she would prod a person with a gloved hand. A tall
white man wearing scrubs and carrying a baton followed her.
He pushed the captives to the right or left side of the road at
her instruction.

The woman in the lab coat swiped Lana's forehead and looked her up and down. Lana did not flinch when the doctor grabbed her breasts and squeezed. She stared straight ahead. The doctor squeezed again, then looked over her shoulder at the tall man. She grinned and informed informing him that she didn't feel any lumps. The tall man suggested maybe he should perform the exam. The woman in the lab coat pointed to the left side of the road. The tall man pushed Lana to the left and moved along behind the lab coat.

She shuffled to the middle of the group. Finally, the separation examinations finished, the guards prodded the group that contained Lana towards a cattle gate adorned with barbed wire. A uniformed man pushed the gate open and they shambled through it. The guards herded away the group on the right side of the road. Ten minutes later, a hundred shots pierced the simmering July evening.

II

PETE SAT IN THE shade of an old semi-tractor's hood, propped up by scrap PVC. He passed a canteen of lukewarm water to Zenobia, a broad-shouldered woman in her late twenties. She took a drink and passed it to an skinny teen named Jamal. Pete scratched at the two-week-old stubble clinging to his chin. He kept it trimmed as close as a dull pair of children's safety scissors allowed. He looked across the packed ground in the middle of the cluster of lean-tos and crudely constructed shacks at the new arrivals. Each new inmate carried a thin plastic bag stuffed with a gray burlap uniform to replace their clothes, which had half rotted off from overuse and exposure,

"Outside must be getting worse," Pete mused. Zenobia grunted and crossed her arms. Jamal volunteered to pull one of the newbies aside and ask about it. Pete nodded. Jamal trotted over to the crowd. They had coalesced around an old school bus roof hoisted up on six-foot-long two-by-fours, listening to a lithe young man shout at them about the rules of the camp. The observant newbies clung to the shade of the big oak tree growing near the entrance. Jamal walked back with a new arrival. The middle aged man looked worried as Jamal led him over to Pete and Zenobia.

"What's going on out there?" Pete asked the man.

"Well, the Hudson Bay Buccaneers won Super Bowl 100," the man said. His nervous voice croaked through cracked, dry lips. Pete poured some water in the cap of the canteen and handed it to him, admonishing him to drink slow. The man complied, then continued, "if you believe the news net, we glassed the Persian Gulf again, so Russia and China glassed Venezuela. Ah, yeah, President Lopez annexed Quebec for good this time. The news nets refers to the Red River as the southern border, not the Brazos anymore. Oh, and Lopez announced that he isn't calling a Congress this year either. There were protests about it. I got caught in Jefferson City, now here I am…"

Pete thanked the man for his time and took back the canteen. The man reluctantly handed it over. With slumped shoulders, he walked slowly back to the other new inmates.

A trim, muscled man in his early twenties with light brown hair to match his cafe-au-lait skin, sauntered towards Pete, Zenobia. Jamal slunk away from their shelter and the man approached. He'd finished his welcoming speech and left the shade of the school bus shelter. His eyes darted quickly, in contrast to his casual stride. He stopped in front of them and put out his hand. Pete and Zenobia looked at each other, then, at his open palm. Zenobia sighed and held out the canteen. The man wrapped his long fingers around it, lifted it to his lips, and drank. He swished the water around in his mouth, then, spat it on the ground near them. He handed the canteen back, turned, and strolled back towards the bus roof shelter.

"Good talk Twan!" Zenobia shouted after him. He did not acknowledge her.

"How many of the noobs do you think he'll want?" Pete said, frowning.

"Mmmm... One or two of the men look like they might survive initiation. I'm sure a few of the younger women will get passed around," she said. She shook her head in frustration. She continued, "at some point, he'll have more toughs than we do. Looks like I"m going to have to round up some of the fightier inmates, and do something about him."

"You'll make a benevolent dictator, I'm sure," Pete said, nodding in Twan's direction. Zenobia smiled, and, punched his shoulder.

Jamal returned with a blond girl and a boy in his early teens with black hair. The three of them flopped down in front of Pete and Zenobia. They young ones talked about pulling ear worms off the corn growing in the internment camp's north field. They speculated on what type of flour would make the best breading in which to fry them. Jamal remarked that ear worms were not the only bits of flesh people pulled out in the cornfield. The younger inmates laughed, while Pete and Zenobia silently smiled. They passed around the canteen of water, followed by a small jar of fermented honey water. The sun set beyond the barbed wire.

III

LANA LAID ON HER back. She watched a security drone buzz above the camp in the early morning sky. The night temperature barely dipped to eighty degrees. The purple glow on the horizon promised another sweltering day. She barely slept for the rumbling in her stomach and the aching in her joints.

Gradually, sunlight welled up over the horizon. A guard wearing tan BDUs covered in patches to mend holes in the fabric, walked from inmate to inmate. He kicked them in the ribs if they did note rise to be counted. Lana sat up before he could deliver her wakeup call. The guard told them to get in line for oatmeal. He admonished them to sleep inside the shelters. The new inmates waited with watering mouths as the senior inmates ate first.

After breakfast, the senior inmate with the poorly trimmed beard and the ebony skinned woman, assigned the new inmates to work details. They Lana assigned to the okra plot on the west side of the camp. She spent the morning working Bermuda grass out of the dusty soil.

Lana wiped sweat from her brow after tossing a handful of weeds into an old plastic bucket. She caught the eye of the older man holding the bucket. Before she could ask her question, he grumbled that if she needed water, she could drink from the canteen, otherwise, she needed to get back to weeding.

She sat down on the north side of the plants. At four feet tall, the plants offered a small sliver of shade from the intensifying sun. She smirked at a senior inmate, an older woman with silver hair, working a few feet away.

"What's funny?" the older woman asked.

"The okra leaves kinda look like mary-juana," Lana said, her voice flat.

"You wish they were!" the older woman said. She adjusted her long silver hair from her left shoulder to her right. She told Lana that if she wanted weed, she would have to get cozy with Twan and his gang. The woman frowned as she finished the thought. Lana looked down at the dirt, then back up at the her.

"So, I guess that Twan guy runs this place when the guards ain't looking?" she asked.

"Sort of. They have a, for lack of a better term, gentleman's agreement, with the guards. Twan's crew keeps order inside the fence, so the guards generally keep out," the older woman stopped weeding and sat up. Several of the new inmates stopped weeding to listen. She introduced herself to Lana, saying her name was Sherri.

"Lana," the twenty two year old replied. She paused. The other newbies looked at her. She spoke again, "so, what Twan said when we showed up, he was serious?"

Sherri paused. She opened her mouth to speak but went back to digging at the dirt. She spoke softly, her face towards the ground, "if he said it, he meant it."

They worked in silence for some time. The other newbies went back to pulling weeds. A breeze pushed the stalks of okra back and forth above her head.

"So, what about that guy that everyone takes orders from, and the black woman, they part of Twan's crew?" Lana asked.

"He is not," she said. Sherri stopped weeding. She brushed straw and strips of cardboard back over where she had been working.

"So, what's his deal? People sure jump for him," Lana continued.

"Well he's not like Twan," Sherri said curtly. She softened her tone, "four years ago, when this camp got set up, none of us knew what to do. The guards staked out the barbed wire and left us to die. Pete told everyone to start pooping in old kitty litter boxes we'd found around the old mobile home. He said we could to avoid getting cholera or dysentery if we composted it. People stopped getting sick, at least stopped getting sick from that, so we started listening to him more often. He and Twan talked the guards into bringing in seed. They convinced the guards that giving us a way to help feed ourselves would keep us busy, would cause less trouble for them. So now, they, mostly leave us alone. The guards, that is.

Twan got twisted by this place. Said he was too good for yard work. Anyway, we composted the poop in the litter boxes and used it for fertilizer."

"So I'm digging in four years of composted shit? Wonderful," Lana said. She stuck out her tongue and shook her head. Sherri simply nodded in reply and continued pulling weeds. Lana recalled watching raw sewage seep up out of broken sewer lines in the back yards of her neighborhood when she was ten. The lines never got fixed, and everyone in the neighborhood got sick more often. She bit her lip, and got back to pulling weeds.

Lana's work detail labored away in the okra plot as July flowed into August. Every morning she watched as the same half dozen inmates crowded around Pete for instructions. She never saw him hit any of them, she never saw him berate any of them. She rarely saw him get visibly angry. The stout black woman with cropped hair and the skinny teen with a deep tan always seemed to be near him. Lana asked one of the senior inmates of her work detail if Pete and Zenobia were involved. They simply laughed.

One day in mid-August, Lana finally asked Sherri a question about the plot, for which the older woman did not have an easy answer. Sherri said she would raise the issue with Pete. Lana quickly volunteered to ask him and walked away. She found Pete and Zenobia, dripping water at the base of the melons planted on the east side of the internment camp. It had not rained much lately, and rain barrels were running low. Lana stopped a few feet from them and cleared her throat.

"Ah, Mr. Pete, we have a question from over in the okra patch," she said. Her head spun, but with excitement instead of hunger. She balanced on her tip toes, enjoying a sensation she rarely felt over her twenty years. Pete set down the red plastic cup of water. He turned slowly. She noticed he had green eyes.

115

"What question could not wait for the evening meeting?" he asked. He neither raised, nor lowered, his voice. He scratched at the shaggy beginning of a beard under his chin. He looked her in the eyes, rather than from head to toe. She returned his gaze but did not speak.

"You deaf, dumb, or both, girl?" Zenobia asked sharply. Lana jumped at the volume of her voice, but did not look away from Pete.

"Well, um, cover, Mr. Pete. Don't we need to start planting cover soon? What seeds will we need?" she asked. She racked her brain as she spoke, searching for the right words. She stumbled through her question,.

"We will have to look into what we have. Don't need to worry about that just now. Its only August," he said. He dismissed her with a wave of his hand. She did not turn to leave. She lower her eyes and looked down at her bare feet.

Pete stood very slowly and took three halting steps towards her. He pushed off the top of his knees so his legs straightened out. He noticed her staring has his hands massaged his thigh muscles.

"it is good to think ahead. And yes, I'm not near old enough to have such bad knees, but that is a story for another time." he said softly. Lana reached her left had out towards him briefly, then pulled it back quickly. She looked at his face. He did not smile; he did not frown. She discerned little emotion from his taut cheeks and chapped lips. His eyelids drooped slightly, then, world lift, when he spoke. They stood face-to-face, his green eyes looking back into her brown eyes. Zenobia cleared her throat, telling Lana to hustle back to the okra.

Lana allowed her lips to tick up slightly at the ends, then, turned and walked away. She stepped lightly as she headed back towards the patch. She took a shorter route from the gardens on the east side of the camp. Instead of passing be-

116

tween the barbed wire of the south perimeter, she passed by the school bus roof shelter in the middle of the shacks. A burly man with huge fists stepped out from under the shelter and grabbed her arm. She yelped. He pulled her over a bench cobbled together with seats from the bus. Twan reclined on one of them, his head propped up in his right hand. He grinned. The burly man released Lana's arm.

"Hey there, girl," Twan spoke slowly. Two of his crew sat across from him on another bench. One, a skinny white man missing teeth, the other dark skinned boy several years younger than her. The pair chuckled. Lana said nothing. She crossed her arms. He pressed her to respond; "You gonna say something?"

She shook her head. Twan raised his left arm, flicking his hand over once the arm fully extended. The burly man stepped forward and grabbed the hem of her gray shirt. Lana yelled at the man and grabbed at the fabric with both hands. She tried to keep him from pulling the loose fitting shirt over her head. Twan laughed as she struggled, assuring her they just wanted to take a peek at the goods.

Lana jumped and turned away from the shelter, trying to get away from the burly man's iron grip. She fell over backwards, frantically pulling the shirt back down with one hand. Her other held onto knot tying together the cord running through the waistband of her pants. The burly man did not pursue her. Lana looked up.

Zenobia stood behind her, just outside the shelter, her hands on her hips. The burly man did not move forward. Zenobia clinched a metal spade in her left hand. Lana crawled backward on her elbows, keeping her eyes on her tormentors. Twan smirked at her.

"Put some meat on those bones. You make a good replacement girl," Twan said. He smiled slightly, his thin lips quivering after he spoke. He looked at Zenobia. He said "I

117

know you into girls Zenobia. You can get a piece of her when we done."

Zenobia spat on the ground. Lana crawled behind the other woman's stout legs. Twan's crew stood up and stepped towards them. The four of them walked to the edge of the shade of the shelter. Lana looked around for a weapon. Finding none, she filled her hands with dust and pebbles. Zenobia whistled. Half a dozen inmates stopped work in the fields and gardens around the shacks. They began walking slowly towards the shelter carrying their farming implements with them. Twan and his crew remained under the shelter. Zenobia told Lana to get back to the okra patch.

IV

"Can we avoid blood?" Pete asked. Passed since the confrontation. He knelt in the melon patch. He poured an ounce of water at the base of vine, then moved to the next plant. He did not make eye contact with Zenobia.

"When I fought off one of his crew, when I first got here, they said they'd get me one day. That was three years ago. Every day since, they watch me. Waiting for me to let down my guard. Good thing I'm used to it. But you, Pete? Well, when they come for me, they'll come for you, too. You should have killed that pretend protest boy when he first got here," Zenobia said. She moved along the row of melon vines that ran parallel to the ones he watered. She splashed water at the plants' bases. She did not measure, she did not conserve.

"Well, I hope you learn from my mistakes, cause apparently I don't," Pete said. He shook his head. He tossed the rest of the water in his plastic cup at the plant he knelt closest too. He stood slowly, and walked away, back straight, knees almost buckling under. He left the melon patch, remembering the sack of skin and bones that Twan had been four years ago. Pete remembered the day Twan had bounced up to him, proudly displaying the spades and trowels the guards allowed into the camp. Buoyed by the guard's perceived benevolence, Pete spoke to everyone about what they could all accomplish if they would just work together.

He walked to the okra patch and conversed briefly with Sherri. Several inmates laid on their backs on the north edge of the patch, sweating and attempting to sleep in the shade of the okra stalks. The plants stood over six feet tall, white flowers with purple starbursts at their centers bloomed from every stem. Bees from the camp's hives buzzed from flower to flower. A lone figure knelt in the middle of the stalks, unbothered by the pollinators.

Pete stepped around eight thick stalks to reach Lana. She pushed scraps of cardboard away from the base of the plants, pulled weeds, them covered the tall stock's roots back up. She stood up and turned around. Pete watched the limp curls of her dark hair stick with sweat to her sallow cheeks. Dark rings marred the caramel skin under her hazel eyes. The new arrivals put on at least some weight after arrival. None still showed such obvious signs of malnutrition. She stood only a few inches shorter than Pete's five foot eight, but he reckoned she weighed no more than one hundred pounds. He reached for one of her left hand, to inspect nail beds. She pulled her hand away.

"I'm sorry to startle you. I just wanted to check your nails, to, ahh, you know... Are you feeling ill?" he spoke softly. She placed her left hand in his, relaxing slightly. She watched him as he inspected her fingernails. A bee buzzed busily between them

"I... I haven't eaten much lately." she said, hesitating. His palm warmed her hand, even in the heat of the summer sun.

"How come? The food isn't that bad," he said, He twitched the edge of his mouth upwards a bit.

A tear ran down her cheek. She wiped it away with her free hand, leaving her left hand in his. She swallowed and pressed her palm hard against her face, trying to slow the tears.

"Did a bee sting you?" Pete asked, his voice wavered. Unsure of how to proceed, he frowned. He opened he mouth to speak again.

"No," she pulled her hand away from his and sat on the ground. She buried her face in both palms. Pete sat down across from her, folding his knees slowly. They sat in silence for some time. A bee landed on Pete's forearm. He watched it clean it's antennae. He looked up at Lana. Her hands in her lap, she watched the bee as well.

"I do feel ill," she said, her voice hummed like a taut cord in the wind, "not from food or disease. I'm sick from all the meanness. I'm sick of all of them, pushing the rest of us around every day. I want to eat; I just can't. Every time I try to put food in my mouth, I hear his voice. This guy, Jack, a ration distributor back where I'm from. I hear him saying 'Yeah, you eat it. Put it all in your mouth girl,' Over and over again," she paused, then, went on; "I had to feed my little brother. I had to feed my little sister. I had to. Jack had food. I didn't. He fed us. I got pregnant; I lost the baby. He stopped feeding us. We hid with the other orphans. My brother disappeared. My little sister moved in with a police lieutenant. She cleans his house and watches his kids. She got a job and a roof, but all I got was anger. And sickness. I was so sick of it all. I joined a protest. We got rounded up, beaten. Now, I'm here. And even here, there's men wanting to push everyone else around."

They sat in silence long enough for the shadows from the okra to move with the arc of the sun. The jagged shadows of the leaves slashed slowly across their faces. For four years, Pete spent all his time solving problems of food, fuel, sanitation, and shelter.

"I wish," he began. Lana looked up at him, her eyes bloodshot. He stopped, took a breath, spoke, "Lana, I wish... I wish that sickness was of flesh and bone. We could splint it, maybe, apply a salve, but, to the heart, to the mind..."

"I want to be free," Lana said, interrupting him, "I want to be free to eat, free to breath. To not feel a squeezing fist around my heart. I don't even care about escape. I just want to be free from all the Twans and Jacks in the world."

Lana grabbed his left hand and squeezed. Pete placed his other hand atop hers. He watched the splashes of light move back and forth across her face as the hot breeze blew the plants above them. He held her hand in his. An idea bounced off the inside of his skull.

"The old man who looked after our bees died shortly before you arrived. You don't seem bothered by them. Sherry has his notes down about them. Would like to take care of our little helpers?" he said. "they might keep the sickness away."

Pete stood slowly, unsteady for the fiery pain in his knees. A recollection of the interrogator flared back into his thoughts. The man's shouts, his spit, the stink of bodily fluids splattered on his BDUs. Pete blinked back tears. He struggled briefly to maintain his balance on knees that had never been given time to heal. He kept ahold of Lana's hand, and she steadied him as he straightened up. He held steady as she held his hands, pulling herself to her feet. Pete mumbled about being thirty three and having such weak knees.

"I would like to look after the bees," she said.

V

THE BEE HIVES CIRCLED a willow tree in the far southwest corner of the internment camp. The hive furthest west stood between the willow tree and the barbed wire that marked the edge of the inmates' world. No one bothered her while she tended the bees. As the weeks wore on, Lana rarely left the hives, even sleeping under the cascading branches of the willow tree. Pete and sometimes Sherri would visit her. When she was not tending the hives, she made sure that she was around the other new inmates and far away from Twan and his crew.

Lana stood under the willow tree, watching the shadows of the barbed wire fence form grids on the weathered plywood sides of the hives. The bees worked later than usual, as the sun turned the late August evening sky to hues of ochre and scarlet. She looked up from to see Pete approaching. She noticed he held something behind his back.

"It's been a few weeks. Are you still liking the job?" he asked. Several bees guarding the entrance of the nearest hive buzzed close to him, then ,return to their positions.

"I'm not liking the stings, but I suppose that's what I get for breaking into their homes and stealing their hard work," she brushed curly strands of hair from her face. She stepped towards him, holding up her palms to show off a few welts. She turned her hands prone, then wiggled her fingers, pointing at what Pete held behind his back. Pete looked about, to either side of her, up into the dangling green branches of the willow tree. He looked anywhere except at her pointer fingers. Then he broke into a full-toothed grin.

"Well, I wanted to give you this," Pete said. He swung his hands from behind his back. In them, he held a broad brimmed hat with mosquito netting stitched to the edges of the brim.

"It's for beekeeping!" he said proudly, puffing out his chest a bit. She lifted the hat from his hands.

"That's wonderful! I get nervous when they really get in my face!" she exclaimed, setting the hat on her head. It was slightly large for her, and the mosquito netting tugged down the brim, obscuring her face. She reached out and took his hands in hers and pulled him closer to her. "It's very thoughtful, but, uh, I really needed it earlier…"

Pete frowned, then raised an eyebrow. She threw her head back to flip up the brim, wearing a broad grin. She squeezed his hands. Pete exhaled. He drew in a deep breath and stepped towards her. Her grin turned into a full smile, and she stepped back.

"Look how busy they still are, even this late in the day. It's odd," she said. She let go of his hands and gestured at the activity around the hives. Pete looked around for a minute and shrugged.

"Maybe they just feel industrious. After all, they have to work hard, with you stealing from them all the time." he said. He actually pointed an accusing finger at her. Lana grinned again and grabbed at it. He pulled his hand away just before she reached it.

As they walked back towards the sleeping shacks, Pete told her he recalled the old beekeeper saying they work harder before the rain. He hoped openly for some water to fall from the sky. The sun sank below the horizon. The wind picked up speed and changed direction after midnight. None stirred in the camp as their blanket of stars winked out one by one.

A rumble of thunder woke Lana. She sat up and looked around the dim confines of the shotgun shack. Only one other woman woke to the bass roll. Lana tiptoed over the other women and stepped outside of the shack. She looked west at a flash of lightening. Jagged lines of electricity darted back and forth from cloud-to-cloud and cloud-to-ground. Clouds boiled up and tumbled over themselves and rolled towards her from the southwest. Her heart caught in her throat as she looked up and up and up, trying to locate the top of the thundering anvil above her, and seeing only turbulent water and lightening moving towards the camp. Thunderclaps rattled the thin walls of the shack behind her.

The branches of the oak and willow trees groaned from gusts that bent them back and forth. Cold air whipped the edges of her baggy, ill-fitting prison garb against her legs and arms. Another bolt of lightening struck something just west of the camp. Lana jumped as the peal of thunder rattled her ribs as much as the wooden frame of the shack. Other women stuck their heads and hands out the windows, closing them with shutters fashioned from old road signs.

Pete, Zenobia, and Jamal darted around the compound, checking that the doors of the seed shack and tool shed. The branches of the willow caught her attention twisting in circles before the onslaught. She took off running towards the tree as fat drops of rain bounced off the dry ground underfoot. The hives stood on wooden frames of two by fours, and Lana feared the wind would blow them over, or a branch would fall from the tree and smash them. She dug rocks the size of her first from the soil around the base of the tree, and put them on the frames under the hives.

The rain and wind picked up. Willow branches lashed her face and back. She worked feverishly, ignoring them. The rain fell in sheets now. She looked up briefly. The top of the tree ceased blowing back and forth; instead the limbs swirled in the maelstrom. A hand grabbed her left arm. She turned, lifting the rock in her right hand. Pete's face appeared out of the pouring rain, half a foot from her face,

"Are you trying to get struck by lightening? Get out from under this tree!" he shouted.

"But the hives might blow over!" she shouted back.

"The bees will be fine! C'mon!" he tugged on her arm. They ran past the okra patch and back towards the shacks. The wind and rain stopped. Lana's ears popped. Pete threw her on the ground and fell on top of her. She yelped.

"If you pray, now would be the time!" he shouted and

pointed up. A low roar emanated from the clouds above them. Lana looked up. Flashes of electric fire in the sky illuminated low clouds pinwheeling above the camp. The roar turned to a deafening whoosh. Grey tendrils coiled and swirled over them, reaching down towards the earth. The wind, still a moment before, picked up speed, rapidly shifting from north to west to south to east. Twigs and small branches separated from the tops of trees, and cartwheeled above them on currents in the sky.

The wind shifted out of the west again. The roaring whirlpool of clouds swirled away from them. Pete and Lana sat up and looked east. Flashes of light backlit a twisting column of dirt and debris plowing across the soybean field east of the camp. It disappeared into a writhing cloak of rain and vanished into the night. Soon, they could no longer even hear its roar over the background symphony of slashing rain and crashing lightening. They hugged each other and laughed with joy.

VI

HOURS LATER, PETE AND Zenobia stood by the fence, surveying the damage inside of it. The funnel cloud blew limbs out of the tops of the trees but reached the ground outside the perimeter. Zenobia lamented that fact to the guard on the other side. The guard laughed and remarked that if the inmates escaped, he would have to get a real job. Zenobia offered to run the camp, so the guards could take an extended vacation. The guard said he would run the idea up the chain of command, then, walked away, crushing uprooted bean bushes under foot.

"Speaking of thinking they run this place," Zenobia nodded at the guard's back once he was out of earshot, "you seen Twan or his crew this morning?"

"Of course not," Pete grumbled, "you know they get scarce when real work needs to happen."

Zenobia and he checked in with those working the melon patch. They reported only minor damage to the plants from the hail. Pete and Zenobia moved on to the outhouses. The wind removed the roof, fashioned from the side of a 54 foot trailer, and tossed it into the branches of the big oak tree near the main gate. Inmates swarmed through the canopy of the tree trying to remove it without too much damage to the siding or the tree.

As Pete and Zenobia watched them work, one of Twan's crew ran up to the group, waving his hands and shouting. The other inmates stopped working, trying to make sense of the skinny man's shouting. They calmed the man down. He blubbered that something bad happened to Twan.

Zenobia looked at Pete, who nodded. He knelt and urged the skinny man to do so too. As soon as he did so, Zenobia wedged the man's neck in the crook of her left elbow. She gripped her other arm with her left hand, and pushed froward hard on the back of his head with her right. The skinny man flailed about as she increased the pressure. He slapped at her arms, trying to put his hands between his throat and her muscles and bone. The inmates looked at Pete, who crossed his arms and turned his back on the scene. Others followed suit, forming a ring around Zenobia and the skinny man. The rest of them carried on with the repairs.

VII

LANA WOKE UP A few hours after the storm passed. She ate another a breakfast of oats with the other women in the shack. Afterwards, she picked up her netted hat and strolled towards the willow tree. Other inmates pitched in to clean up from the storm. A few offered her help with the hives, but Lana. She told them she did not want any jittery inmates around the hives in case the bees felt rowdy after rough night.

She passed between the barbed wire and the okra patch, which appeared undamaged and thus devoid of other inmates. Lana stared out wistfully beyond the gridded barbed wire. A pair of figures moved parallel with her on the other side of the tall plants. At the west side of the patch, she almost ran into Twan and one of his crew, a skinny white man with no front teeth. Twan grabbed her arm and pulled her towards him.

"It's time girl. Lets get you out to the cornfield," Than said. He grinned and pulled her along. The skinny man cackled and followed.

Lana pulled her arm out of his grip when he relaxed after a few paces. She took off running towards the willow tree. Twan trotted after her, treating the pursuit as a game.

"Oh, I like a chase, girl!" he said, not raising his voice. He loped only a few paces behind her. The skinny man picked up the pace, trying to get in front of her. Lana sprinted towards the willow tree.

She saw that one of the hives lay on its side. She darted past the grasping fingers of the skinny man and ran around the hive, putting it and ten 10,000 upset bees between her and the pursuers. Twan and the skinny man stopped about five yards away, pacing back and forth, taunting her with lewd insults. Twan told her they were not going to leave. He said that it would only be worse for her if she made him work for it. The skinny man used less subtle language, but neither of them came any closer.

Bees swirled around the damaged hive, a cyclone of yellow and black stripes. Lana abstractly assessed the damage to the hive. Two U-shaped frames lay on the ground, dislodged from the rest of the hive. The lid of the hive lay flipped over next to it. She put on the hat and pulled down the setting in front of her face.

"You want it so bad, come and get it!" she shouted at them. The skinny man looked at Twan, then, at the bees, but neither of them stepped forward. She pulled off her pants and worked the legs of the pants up her arms, balling the cuffs of the legs in her palms.

Twan licked his lips and took a step forward. His skinny accomplice did the same. Lana taunted them, saying she was so good, they wouldn't last a minute. She tuned as she spoke and bent over, hoping she looked seductive. She put her hands on her knees and looked back at them. They advanced on her. The skinny man grabbed at his crotch, swatting at the dozen bees flying around his face.

Lana spun around and sprang forward. With her hands gloved by the pant legs, she snatched up the frame closest to her. Bees bounced off the netting around her face and tried to sting her through the think burlap pants. A few stung her bare feet. She hardly felt the pain through the surge of adrenaline pumping through her veins. The swirling cloud of angry bees almost obscured her view of her assailants, but she heard both Twan and the skinny man shouting in alarm. The yellow and black cyclone expanded in size and fury.

She swung the frame at the skinny man. It cracked on the side of his head. He staggered backwards, turned, and ran. A hundred bees chased after him. She saw Twan backpedaling from her and the hive. She lunged at him. He held up his hands to defend himself, but, they went through the honeycomb. She let go of the frame, backing away from him and the storm of tiny wings.

He shouted in alarm and frantically tried to push the frame off his arms. The bees converged on the wreckage of frame, defending a part of their hive. Lana took a few more steps back. She could barely see Twan flailing about in the midst of the furious bees. She reached the edge of the willow branches, shook out her pants, and put them back on.

The bees around her did not attempted to sting her. Twan collapsed on the ground, grabbing at his throat, each breath he took more labored than the last. She stood still, watching until he stopped moving at all. After a few minutes, the bees stopped swarming around him and returned to the hive. Hundreds of their tiny corpses littered the ground. Lana knelt and picked up a twitching, stinger-less bee. She cradled it in her palm until the bee's legs stopped kicking.

VIII

LANA LIMPED TOWARDS THE shacks, shelter and kitchen. Zenobia and a dozen other inmates had rounded up the rest of Twan's crew. Lana saw the body of the skinny man. The men of his crew slumped their shoulders; their eyes darted from one another to the grim faces of the other inmates. The guards at the main gate looked in at the commotion but did not enter.

Pete walked over to her. She sat down, exhausted from the fight. He knelt next to her, inspecting the welts on her feet. Sherri handed him the camp's small jar of rubbing alcohol. He dabbed it onto the sites of the stings.

Behind them, at the middle of the inmates, Zenobia shouted about administering justice to the members of Twan's crew. The crowd collectively growled and closed in around those who had tormented them for three years. Pete glanced over his shoulder once or twice but focused his attention to Lana's wounds. After cleaning them, he applied a balm of crushed lavender and honey and wrapped her feet with strips of cloth.

Eventually, the guards opened the gate and shoved their way into the crowd. They pulled four badly beaten men out of the camp. They ordered a dozen inmates to pull Twan and three other bodies out beyond the fence. Four of the guards remained in the camp, making various threats should any more rioting break out.

Suddenly, a guard and two prisoners began shouting at each other and pointing up. Pete and Lana shielded their eyes from the noon sun and saw three white, feathery lines racing from west to north just above the horizon.

"What is that?" Jamal shouted at Pete. The teenager looked terrified.

""Contrails," an old man standing next to Jamal and Sherri answered, "I haven't seen civil jets that big in 20 years. Must be bombers. Even Air Force don't fly transports any more"

"Why? Where are they going?" Sherri asked him, placing a hand on his arm.

"Fuel's too expensive to fly for fun. I don't know. Only thing to the north is the Arctic. Then, Russia," the old man's voice trailed off. A hush fell over the inmates and the guards alike.

"How long until their bombers arrive?" Pete spoke.

"When I was in the Air Force, NORAD said a few hours. I worked dismantling our missiles. They said the Russians did the same," he said.

"You think the Russians will bomb here?" Jamal's girlfriend asked the old man. She looked frantically around the camp, possibly for a place to hide.

"Kid, they don't even know we are here," the old man said. He laughed.

No one worked for the rest of the day. Every few minutes, someone would look north. The guards disappeared into the mobile homes by the entrance of the camp. They passed on no information to the inmates. A few whispered that now may be the time to make an escape.

Shortly after dinner, a shout of alarm ran through the camp. A second sun lit up the eastern sky. Soon, they saw the top of a flat cloud rise up over the horizon. The cloud glowed red and flashed green. Some inmates said it was Milwaukee, most that it must be Chicago. Those with relatives in either city wept.

Lana and Pete watched for a few more minutes, then, sat back down under the oak tree, watching the setting sun. They spoke in low whispers, ignoring the conflagration behind them. The sunlight drained from the western sky, stars winked to life above them. The mushroom cloud dissipated, disappearing into the gathering dark. Some of the inmates drifted to the shacks; others laid down to sleep in the open air.

Abruptly, Lana stood, tested her weight on her feet. She told Pete the stings no longer hurt. She motioned him to stand. He did. She grabbed his left hand, turned, and led him north, towards the cornfield. They stopped at the edge of the stalks. Lana turned, threw her arms over Pete's shoulders, and kissed him. His beard tickled her chin. She giggled and broke the kiss.

"I try to keep it trimmed," Pete said, looking sheepish. She removed her arms from his shoulders, ran her hand down his chest, then took his hands in hers. She stepped backwards between rows of corn. He hesitated.

"Are you sure? I mean, with what's happened today? Twan? Chicago?" he asked.

She took another step backwards, pulling him forward with her into the cornfield. She answered, "they're gone Pete, but we are still here. Forget the old world. Let's make a new one."

The Doctor and
the Priestess

Violet Bertelsen

My family is of old healing stock. We are many generations of doctors that endured and survived the Backlash of the last century. As the times mellowed, my father began practicing medicine openly again and training me in the afternoons and evenings after I labored until lunchtime at the Baker's farm. Anna and Brian Baker had the land in their family since the early twentieth century, and their only child Cynthia also worked the farm. Anna and Brian were, being of an old academic family, more sympathetic to our people. And so they let me work a mere six hours a day and study for another six with my father, Marcus Cohen. They also had him do veterinary work for their cattle, and in exchange they gave us a full grain share. Alexandra and Maria worked there as well. And Jimi too, of course, with his pale skin, black hair, and baleful eyes.

It was in March of the blistering heat of the bad drought year that Emil arrived and joined the crew one morning, looking dazed, sharpening his hoe in the dust, and talking quietly with Jimi, who looked similar enough to Emil to be his brother. Emil seemed to be in his mid forties and Jimi was about thirty-five at the time. Jimi was smoking a cigarette, holding it between his pinky and ring finger so his face was veiled by smoke and his hand.

"Came from the East?" said Jimi, "heard that things have been heating up there."

"Barely escaped with my skin," said Emil, carefully filing with the angle of the hoe's blade, "some folks found out who my father is. Had to leave real fast. I'm real glad to be sleeping in the hay loft for now."

Jimi nodded his face wreathed in smoke, "An ecologist, right? I think I've read some of his work."

Emil looked up with eyes cold and hard as steel, and nodded

"Thank the gods you managed to make it here."

Emil stopped sharpening his hoe, "I am an atheist. Fanatics killed my parents before my eyes. No gods for me, thanks."

Jimi took a long drag on his cigarette, and then dropped and crushed it under heel, "time to get to work," he said coolly.

We walked out to the fields, joining Cynthia, Alexandra and Maria. A few months earlier Maria and I had been fast friends, spending long hours staring up into the night sky, identifying planets and constellations, smoking cigarettes, discussing her work as an apprentice priestess and mine as an apprentice doctor. That was before things got fraught. Maria and my eyes met. She gave me a pained look, and I blushed and turned away.

We worked until the sun was overhead, hoeing down the beds, weeding peas, carrot and beets, Alexandra belted out "St. James Infirmary Blues" in her gravelly voice, Maria hoed across from her and I glared at Jimi, who worked across from me.

"When's the next time we'll see each other?" I asked.

He stopped, rolled a smoke, striking a match and lighting the cigarette in one fluid movement.

"I told you from the beginning that I won't be tied down," he said passing me the cigarette which I took and inhaled, leaning against my hoe as Alexandra kept on singing and moving further down the row.

"But Maria?" I protested, handing the cigarette back.

"I don't know what happened, but, sure." shrugged Jimi, veiling his face in smoke, "we'll meet up tomorrow. Like old times."

He handed me the cigarette and I took it, my hand cold and trembling. We worked the next few hours until lunch in silence.

At lunch that day, Farmer Brian stared out the window, "you guys know Rachel Kramer?" he asked.

Jimi struck a match and lit a cigarette, "the entomologist? Right? Studied native pollinators and did a lot of work designing bee gardens?"

Brian nodded, "yep, that one. She's dead. Her house burned down. No one's sure if it was arson or a candle fell or she fell asleep with a cigarette in her hand. Either way, she and her house and her family are now ashes."

There was a long moment of silence as we finished our meal, now tasteless and difficult to eat. Afterwards I left and went home where my dad drilled me on human anatomy, pulse diagnosis, and the organ affinities of herbs. He seemed annoyed that I was distracted as we studied, thinking about the news that Emil had brought from the East, Rachel Kramer's ugly death, and especially Jimi and Maria and me.

THAT SATURDAY, JIMI AND I walked together through what used to be a town but now was a mess of old ruined buildings, ailanthus trees, and singing birds.

"No one lives here but bears and wasps," said Jimi, "all these houses are abandoned. No one lives here... the vibe, it's off?"

"I don't like it, it feels like bad things would happen here, like the beginning of a ghost story."

Jimi gave me a strange look, "here ghosts reign, and not just the little ghosts of little people with their little lives, but the ghosts of dreams, shared dreams. Look at that church. People used to pray there to their god. A few years ago I snuck inside and saw that there are nothing there but yellow jackets and snakes, got stung real bad."

"Well, the good news it that soon enough it will be dirt and a farmer will be grateful to have such fertile land so close to the river."

Jimi lit a cigarette, "fair enough," he said through the smoke, "but it's hard for me to share your optimism. Instead, I am lonely and bored. Those are my two demons, that forever bay me forward. This is our inheritance, Claire. These ruins that now lay rotting, already stripped of anything that may be of value. Just bad memories."

"I guess."

"Bad memories of bad people who did bad things. I guess I can't blame them, people are little better than animals, all things considered."

"Let's get out of here Jimmy, I hate it here."

We started walking through the woods and towards the river. Jimi looked me dead in the eyes, "we live in the ruins of the old world. The ruins of a sick and dying world. It eats me, Claire. My ancestors were chemists, you know. When I cared for the Henderson twins a few years ago when they died of cancer I couldn't stop thinking about what my grandparents did while working for pharmaceutical companies. Sometimes I can't sleep so I come here to pray and ask forgiveness. Sometimes, I have visions beautiful visions that once these ruins are destroyed, then and only then, will we be free to make the sort of world that is worth living in."

We reached a shaded spot by Connecticut river, which was the lowest I'd ever seen it. Jimi dropped his cigarette on the ground and crushed it underfoot. Jimi touched my face and brought me to his lips, and in a flash everything else dissolved in the heat of passion. I took hold of his hair greedily, jealously. His hands wound to my back, pulling my shirt off and with a little growl he pushed me the ground. I gasped and my eyes rolled into my head, while I grabbed his back, fingernails scratching into his skin, both of us, laughing, sneering and biting as we made love while the sun went down.

ON SUNDAY, WE ALL met up around noon at a house in the woods, an old house in good condition about five miles from town that Jimi had found while spending a week alone eating psychedelic mushrooms and wandering though the forests.

When I arrived along the secret trail my head was heavy with dark thoughts of jealously and the Backlash. When I arrived, Maria was there smoking a big marijuana cigarette, laughing at something Alexandra had said, they smiled at me, and said practically in unison "Hi Claire!" and offered me the joint. Smoking it, my dark feelings receded for a moment and I began to relax. Alexandra began strumming her banjo and singing an old murder ballad.

Maria forced a smile, "Claire, we're celebrating my induction into priesshood, I finished all of the work and last night and the Moon applied conjunction to my natal Moon and the High Priestess conferred the initiation."

"Congratulations," I forced myself to say and shook her hand, "I wish I had known earlier, I would have brought a gift."

Maria frowned and blushed, "I'm just glad you're here..."

Just then Jimi entered, "Claire!" he said with a mischievous smile, "so good to see you!" He offered me a cigarette and stepped outside to stand by a few peach trees he had planted on the south side of his house, "they're going to make fruit this year" he said, "I carried them five miles from the Baker's and now they're going to make fruit in a few months. When they do you know what I'm going to do? Make a whole mess of peach wine."

"That's nice," I said, numbly taking the cigarette to my mouth, still shaken that Maria was there, wondering how many times they'd had sex in the house, wondering if Jimi made the same faces with her as he did with me.

"I owe it to the trees," he continued, "gods know that they've done a lot more work than I have, but there's something else I want to show you." And he led me up into his attic. I followed with my heart in my throat, hoping that we'd make love right, loudly, so Maria would hear and leave.

"Books," he said as my face fell, "found boxes and boxes of books in one of the old houses in really good condition. Feel free to take any that you want..."

Just then, Maria and Alexandra entered laughing. Jimi smiled at both of them and taking a jug he poured all four of us blackberry wine from last year. We drank it, Alexandra singing with her banjo, and Jimi trying to make the best of an audience comprised almost entirely of his love triangle. After a few hours, Jimi made a big show of yawning, and said "got to hit the hay, kids, see you Monday."

Alexandra, Maria and I walked down the stairs into the night. Alexandra slipped off to the North. Maria and I realized that we had a long walk ahead of us all the way to Northampton, three long miles along a deer path. For a good while we walked, in an ugly silence, Maria looking more and more forlorn.

"May I have some water?" she asked, "I forgot to take

any with me and didn't drink any while I was at Jimi's."

I handed her a gourd and we both stood there drinking for a few minutes, she looked at me with her big luminous eyes and said "thank you." I offered her a cigarette and she nodded and we both lit them on the same match.

"I don't want to be enemies, Claire," she said, "I really don't. I treasure our friendship. Star gazing with you was something that I profoundly enjoyed. I know things are messed up and I'm sorry, I don't know how it happened..."

The moon rose ahead, "Oh Maria, I'm sorry. I feel torn... but...let's not be enemies. I don't know quite what that will look like. But...I'm...I'm open."

She smiled at me and we walked the few miles through the woods in a companionable silence until we reached the fork and went our separate ways.

EMIL TOOK THE SPRING tomatoes in his strong pale hand and placed it on the cutting board, slicing it into quarters and tossing it into a great pot. I did likewise, and when it was about three-quarters full Cynthia took it and brought it the big woodstove. Every few hours Alexandra would bring a wagon with another couple of bushels.

Now it was about seven in the morning and just starting to get hot when I asked,

"Where are you from Emil?" as I cut a tomato into quarters.

"Well, my family lived in Boston for generations but with the waters rising and the last hurricane about fifteen years ago, I had to wander."

I nodded, and fell silent cutting out the core and slicing into another tomato.

"The thing is… well…things must have not gotten as bad here as they did back east. My parents were murdered by a roaming mob during the food riots when I was nine. My cousins at that point had already left to live with my aunt in Argentina, but I didn't have the money to go with them."

Cynthia came and placed another pot for us and she began pouring the sauce into jars which she then plunged into boiling water.

"There is an irony to the story as well," said Emil, "a bitter irony. My father was an ecologist, and a very harsh critic of the hubris of science. His vehemence was at times nearly equal to the crowd who tore him into bloody pieces." he stopped cutting for a moment with a bitter look.

After a beat I said, "Well, Emil, I'm glad that you've made it here."

Emil seemed to return into himself and almost smiling said, "Me too. Thank you Claire, me too."

THE HOUR GREW LATE, and so I excused myself with a nod to Cynthia, washed up and then walked to my father's house. When I arrived he was putting together his satchel in a rush, he looked up at me, his face grave and pale; "I just got a radio message a few minutes ago that there was another stabbing, Claire. We got to go down to the Henderson farm house immediately and talk with the sheriff and be prepared for the worst."

My heart rang in my ears as I raced out, stumbling to the barn to harness the horses.

My dad came in wearing his clean, black shirt and trousers with his blond moustache and fedora, he looked at the horses and looked at me and then we got into the carriage and we headed towards the Henderson's ill-fated house, about three miles away.

When we arrived, the Sheriff was on the scene, smoking a big cigar and making jokes with the deputy. We got out of the carriage and I hitched the horses to a tree.

The Sheriff was a big pot-bellied man with salt and pepper hair and a twinkle in his eyes. He nodded to Marcus and me, "domestic disturbance gone all to Hell. Craig Henderson comes home, drunk on cheap rotgut, finds his wife in bed with another man. Craig gets his shotgun and Mrs. Henderson and her backdoor man each receive a shot in the face."

"Any survivors?" asked Marcus.

"Eldest son Danny and five-year-old Lula, they're on their way down the river to a cousin's house."

"Anyone needs care?"

"Yessir; Craig, the murder. Tried to slash his own throat, but missed."

I averted my eyes from his and nodded.

"Where is he?" asked Marcus.

"Over this way," motioned the Sheriff.

We walked into the barn where Craig was tied to a beam, he smelled of rotgut and vomit, caked blood covered his face where he'd managed to miss his throat, his half open eyes stared fixedly at some distant point.

My dad and I cleaned up the gash on his face, packing it with honey, applying some butterfly bandages. Craig screamed and cried. We gave him laudanum and he grew quiet.

After we finished, Marcus gave a few words to the Sheriff and then Craig was hauled off to jail to be hung in the very next day. Marcus signed a few papers and then that was that.

We arrived home around 10 pm. I put away the horses, took a shower and fell into a deep dreamless sleep as soon as I tumbled into bed.

AT DUSK SATURDAY, I walked to the secret house and found Alexandra, Maria and Emil sitting around the kitchen table.

Jimi wasn't there, but Emil was offering shots from a nice bottle of whiskey. Alexandra lit some of the lanterns, they cast their eerie light, and she strummed a minor key folk song on her banjo in the dimness while humming a ghostly melody.

Maria looked at me, "the Baker's told us that this is going to be your last season."

"It's true. I'm about ready to enter practice. Eventually, I'll have to take over for my dad if this town is going to have a doctor, period. The Sheriff prefers working with folks that have proper training, and he pays in sterling silver rather than grain shares."

"You share the feast you share the fate!'" boomed Jimi from the doorway, smoking his cigarette. Emil nodded at Jimi, and poured him a shot of whiskey which Jimmy slammed back.

"Hi Jimi," I said, "did you hear about the Henderson's?

Jimi took a long drag from his cigarette, "Yep. Yep; sure did. And I can't help but wonder how did they get so desperate? And I just keep on coming back that it's because of what our ancestors did and failed to do." Emil poured some more shots and we sat in silence drinking them.

Maria shut her eyes and swallowed, "Please be gentle with yourself, Jimi."

Jimi shook his head, "our ancestors, our specific ancestors caused tremendous suffering. What should we do about it? I can't just sit with this and not do something."

For a long while Jimi sat silent and then laughed eerily and took some playing cards and shuffled them and we played a few hands of cards and we spoke of only pleasant things. Maria looked directly into my eyes. I shifted uncomfortably and looked away and then back. She raised her eyebrow and smiled, motioning towards the door, I nodded once and we both left at the same time. Emil stayed behind and dealing out another hand.

The moon was rising in the eastern horizon. Maria touched my hand, "follow me," she said as she led me towards the river. Annoyed, I followed sullenly her for half an hour in the bright moonlight. "Jimi and I broke up," she said as we approached the smooth river stones and we both sat down and looked at the moon. She took a flask and offered it to me, I drank the rotgut, and offered her a cigarette, and we began to laugh. Harder and harder as the moon rose higher and higher and I could almost see every detail of her face as she smiled and touched my hair, "hey," she said, "hey you," and she put her other hand in my hair and laughed and said, "I always wanted to..." and then she kissed me. She brought her her head back and regarded me in the moonlight and stroked my hair again smiling. She kissed me again and I kissed her back, as a roaring, buzzing, hungry silence descended upon us. She panted and fumbled with my belt and I took it off and in a moment later we were both naked, making love loudly, almost explosively, on the smooth river stones still warm from the sun. I must have drunk more rotgut, because the next thing I remember we were asleep in my bed, wrapped in each other's arms.

MY DAD FRANTICALLY WOKE us before sunrise, "we need to go into town immediately," he stammered, and rushed out to prepare the carriage. A few minutes later we got into the carriage already, hitched. Outside a red glow came from the center of town and embers rained down. When we arrived the Sheriff was covered in soot and shaking his head, dazed.

"Someone set fire to the abandoned houses by the old airport. As the police and firefighters went down to put that out, someone threw a Molotov cocktail into the windows of the public library."

"Anyone see him?" I asked.

"He got away for now; tell everyone that we're offering $5000 bounty, in gold" replied the Sheriff.

"How many wounded?"

"About two dozen, maybe half will make it through the other half are going to need serious support. Our guys keep on pulling more out, we're lucky most of the building in the area are brick, otherwise..." the Sheriff, shuddered.

Marcus sighed, his face gray, "We're going to need to employ triage; those who can be saved will be worked on, those who are not seriously wounded will be left to their own devices and we'll some laudanum to those who are too far gone. You, Maria, help Claire with the infection control."

For the next few hours my dad, Maria and I worked on dozens of folks. The ones who were experiencing respiratory failure or had burns over more than half their bodies we could do nothing to help. The others, we gave nettles to support kidney function, smeared honey and St. John's Wort on their wounds to help them heal and resist infection, and gave water and laudanum as needed to all.

ABOUT EIGHT HOURS LATER things were mostly under control, so I took Maria to the store and bought milkshakes for the two of us. We sat outside on the table, and Maria took my hands.

"Claire, do you think..."

"That this is another Backlash?"

She nodded, her lips drawn downward.

I sighed, "I guess I do. I don't want to think about it too much because it terrifies me, but yeah, these attacks seem directed specifically against intellectuals and the like."

"You mean people like us." she whispered.

For a long moment we sat in silence thinking, "I don't know, I haven't thought about it much." We drank our milkshakes. I took Maria's hand. "What are we doing?"

"I don't know." she said, "I don't know. What are you doing with Jimi?"

"I don't know anymore. I don't know what game I'm playing, or who's playing who."

"Well, I'm not playing anyone." said Maria, taking her hand back and running both of her hands through her long blonde hair, "I'm sorry Claire, I'm freaking out right now with all the fire and death and can't handle more love drama now," her voice broke and tears began to roll down her face, "this has all been really hard for me, you know, for months. And know, I feel...I feel, I care, I mean...about you a lot. This is hard, I guess...you know; let me know, please, when you figure things out." she got up and walked away, I wanted to chase after her, to call her name and stroke her and let her know everything would be alright, but instead I lit a cigarette with cold, trembling hands and ordered another beer.

JIMI WAS PACING AROUND the attic of his house, books and ashes and crumpled papers strewn all about. Emil was there with a bottle of whiskey dangling from his fingers, Maria nowhere to be seen. Jimi was smoking and looking out the window, a line of sweat on his forehead, Alexandra played blues licks on her banjo, cigarette between her lips, singing in a throaty forlorn voice about a lover who had gone forever.

"Imagine," Jimi said, "imagine that you could kill one person and in killing that person you could redeem the world. Okay, now imagine you could kill ten people and redeem the world. Literally, after you kill those ten people the evil our ancestors did never would occur. Alright, but what if the number then goes to a hundred people? a thousand? a million? How many people would you kill?"

"Would it even matter if you became a worse person?" I asked.

145

Jimi smoked his cigarette and nodded, sweat pouring down his face, his eyes cold and lifeless like fish, "what if a god told you that you needed to start killing people, then what?"

"Is that any god you'd want to follow?" I shot back.

"There are no gods," said Emil slamming his fist on the table his face red, "we only have human reason. That's it. Now, it being the case that there are now more humans living than the earth can possibly support, a good argument can be made to reduce the surplus population logically, rather than haphazardly."

Jimi smiled darkly, and spoke slowly, "So you're suggesting eugenics?"

Emil took another drink, "that's not what I said!"

"That is exactly what you said. Perhaps you don't think deeply about the implications of the sort of world you create with your ideas, but if you permit yourself further consideration you'll see that I'm neither exaggerating nor caricaturing your view."

Emil began to protest, but Jimi shot him a look, "we may agree that many people have to die, and indeed should disagree vehemently about who those people would be. You think we must make an idol of reason, whereas my hope is rather to remove the taint of this evil civilization."

Emil started to protest, but I interrupted him, "let's change the subject Jimi, this is getting ugly."

Jimi nodded his and lit another cigarette. I stood up and looked at Jimmy grimacing in his smoke and Emil fuming, said goodnight and left into the gloaming heading back home.

THE NEXT MORNING EMIL WEEDED a carrot bed with me. He had a black eye, "Jimi and I got into a fistfight last night after you left, Jimi kept rambling about killing people, and I got drunk and the next think I know he'd punched me in the face, broke a bottle on his table and threatened to cut my face unless I got out immediately. So Alexandra and I left."

The hair on the back of my neck raised, something clearly had gone very wrong.

Emil stopped and looked dead at me, "There's something else though; Jimi threatened to burn me, I think he's been starting the fires. At lunch I'm going down to tell the Sheriff, it wouldn't be right to sit back and let him kill any more people."

"Please stop, this is too much for me right now," I said as a cold sweat pricked my skin and I felt something tear in my heart.

Emil frowned and we worked together in a tense silence until lunchtime when I left for home. I tried to study, but my head swam and heart beat loudly so I stopped and stared at my ceiling for a long while trying not to think. A radio transmission come through and a moment later my dad ran up the stairs, and opened my door, "Claire, there's another fire in near downtown, almost certainly arson. We need to leave immediately."

Marcus clutched the reins and the carriage raced towards town, as we approached we saw a strange scene. Most of the townsfolk stood around as buildings burned, while the fire brigaded carried water in a line. The High Priestess of the Lunar Temple stood on a platform, speaking a foreign tongue and waving an oaken wand. As she did so clouds began to grow darker and darker. Maria and a dozen other priestesses stood on the ground below her, chanting in time at odd points, throwing incense in unison on four censers, and pouring wine onto the ground in time with other words. The old woman's voice rose upwards in a singsong voice with the smoke in the censers. The words stopped and quiet descended with only the gusts of flames heard and firemen's curses in the distance.

All eyes were on the High Priestesses and then, with a little flick of her wand, there was a loud peal of thunder. Heavy rains began to fall, the first in months. Everyone looked up into the nearly black sky as our clothing become instantly soaked threw and the fires raging downtown died out. Maria saw me, and walked over and I let a little cry out of my throat and we held each other and sobbed right there in the storm. And then she took my hand and came with me.

As LUCK WOULD HAVE it, hardly anyone was injured in the fires, and so my dad hosted something of a little festivity at our house, to celebrate the rains. Maria was there, and Emil who had been looking for the Sheriff managed to arrive just in time for a front row seat to the rain miracle, was there as well, appearing to be in something close to shock. Alexandra strummed on her banjo, singing an old blues song.

Marcus poured brandy and offered a toast, "to rain" he said and as he spoke lighting illuminated the entire inside of the house. We drank and sat down.

Marcus sighed, "this has been quite the week, quite the week. And perhaps this will just keep on going and going," he looked up a little mischievously in the candle light, "but now we are alive and we shall celebrate." So we feasted on salt pork, rice and a whole mess of collard greens and fell asleep sated and relaxed.

EARLY NEXT MORNING THE Sheriff came, "I'm looking for Emil," he said a strange look on his face, "caught Jimi last night in the rain, with a candle trying to set the old Episcopalian church on fire, crazy look in his eyes, covered in soot. Shot him dead right there. Couldn't have found him without your help," he tossed Emil a heavy bag. "Something else you all should know; you all may want to leave town. Many folks aren't to taking kindly to any association with Jimi, especially given the old Backlash. We don't yet know who did it, but the Baker's farmhouse got burned down. Several hours after Jimi died, that is. They died in their sleep. Wouldn't want the same thing to happen to you."

Emil paced around and finally said, "we're leaving tonight. We're going to board a ship and proceed to the Atlantic, there I'll pay for passage to South America. I have family there and we can make accommodations when we get there. I'm not going to leave you guys here like I got left."

Marcus nodded, a glimmer in his eye, "You make me feel young again Emil, I'll gather my things and we'll leave tonight."

The Sheriff whistled, "you've been real kind to me throughout the years; I'll help you too."

For the next six hours we all ran about gathering our things, sowing valuables into blankets selecting which books to take and which to leave and then when the moon rose the Sheriff came in his carriage and brought us to his boat on the Connecticut river.

He and Emil rowed, Maria and I held each other, and Alexandra clutched her legs against her chest. Marcus looked around with a dazed expression. When we reached Holyoke, the Sheriff said "Go with God," and then with a grunt turned the boat back towards Northampton

It took us a week walking overland to reach Hartford where Emil managed to bribe the notary to call his aunt, who was overjoyed that he was still alive and welcomed us all to live in her attic. We spent three ghastly nights on the docks before the boat left to Havana, and from there to Rio Plata. As we boarded the ship Emil said, "we've had a lot of disagreements but nonetheless at this point we are, I think, something like family. I hope you can accept my friendship."

Marcus smiled and shook his hand, tears in his eyes and Maria gave him a hug, and I squeezed his shoulders and kissed him on the cheek. Emil sighed, "Well, it's going to be a lot. We'll all probably be sharing a tiny garret in Córdoba, at least when we first arrive."

My dad put his hand on Emil's shoulder, "which is so much better than sharing a tiny grave below the earth."

Alexandra and Emil talked softly, and Marcus studied his Spanish grammar book. Maria and I stood right next to each to other by the prow. Wordlessly, I put my hand on hers and she turned to me and touched my hair and smiled, tears running down her face. We kissed sweetly and laughed and kissed some more through our tears as the ship pulled out of Havana, the prow cutting through the blue-green waves, as the thin sliver of the waxing moon rose in the East.

A Nuclear Story

Ron Mucklestone

F inally, the rain had come in late August, in answer to everyone's prayers, and just in time. It had been such a long, dry summer that all the farmers feared that the rice and sugarcane fields would be so badly stunted that if there was one more rainless week, they would have to burn the fields and hope for a fall crop of buckwheat—if enough rain came after the burning. Now it looked like there would be a harvest after all, although a meagre one.

Carrie stepped out of her family's cabin and relished the feel of the soft, warm rain soaking her hair and face and clothes. She could stand out there all day—if her mother permitted it.

"Carrie!" came the familiar, stern, voice of her mother, Agnes, "what do you think you are doing out there? This isn't the time for lazing about in the rain. Hurry and bring the cows home before the crick floods the back fields!"

Heaving a sigh of exasperation, Carrie headed down the footpath to Wilson Creek to bring the two Jersey cows home. But she hardly had to: the cows were already walking back by themselves. They knew well enough that heavy rains would soon flood the only green pasture left on the property. How Carrie hated those cows, along with the fields and the split-rail fences and the barn and the cabin. How she hated her life of dreary toil all 19 years of her life.

But Carrie stopped herself. "Count your blessings, girl," she said to herself, reciting what her mother always said to her, but she knew it was true, "think of all those starving 'Mericans dying while trying to cross the Niagara River or cross Lake Ontario in their home-made rafts, and those few who make it across bringing with them nothing but empty bellies crying to be filled. At least you have a roof over your head and some decent land to farm." Her mother was right, of course. She was always right. People still talk about the 'Great Hunger of 2101' when the Canadian Army destroyed all bridges to the USA because the flood of starving refugees was more than Ontario could handle. Still, two years later, desperate refugee families regularly show up in nearby Have-lock hoping that the village will tolerate their presence and relieve them of hunger even for a short while. But, of course, two years can make a big difference. Now there is no more USA; now there is no more Canada. With the Great Hunger came the Great Riots. Horrific stories about the streets of New York and Washington and Chicago and Toronto and Ottawa running red with rioters' and rival gangs' blood as well as the blood of many assassinated politicians. Far better to be safe out in the country where 'boring as Hell' is actually a good thing, especially if you are lucky enough to have a farm.

Carrie hurried back home. She knew Mother would be impatiently waiting for her to help dress the chicken and peel potatoes for dinner.

AFTER DINNER, THE RAIN stopped, but the clouds were still low and dark. Carrie's friend, Sushmita, showed up at the doorstep and encouraged Carrie to go walking with her. Mother was in a good mood by this time, with a full stomach and relieved that the rains will save the rice fields, so she let Carrie go under the condition that she returned by sunset.

Sushmita and Carrie had been friends for as long as they could remember. Sushmita's grandparents had been among the last Indian immigrants to the region, and when the climate changed dramatically hotter in the 2060s, her grandparents taught the local farmers how to grow rice and sugar cane and mango trees. The region had prospered greatly as a result. Consequently, Sushmita's grandfather had been elected Mayor of Havelock and upon his death, her father had been elected Mayor and had now continuously held that position for 15 years.

Sushmita liked to give Carrie treats that only the Mayor and the richest people in the region could afford—like maple sugar. Carrie appreciated that. But more importantly, Carrie appreciated Sushmita's sense of adventure. Their favourite 'forbidden' activity was to visit Blake, the local hermit, who lived in a shack in the woods to the north. Sushmita's father said that Blake was labelled 'bad' by the local doctors because he was bad for their business. Blake had been living in the woods as long as anyone could remember, and it was commonly believed that he must be over 90 years old.

The two girls liked Blake because of the strange stories he would tell about the 'old days' when people drove cars and flew in airplanes, and how he could predict the future by use of geomancy. People would secretly visit Blake for him to locate lost items or identify a thief and predict the year's harvest. But Carrie and Sushmita asked Blake about prospective boyfriends, when they would marry and how many children they would have.

Carrie and Sushmita walked to a big rope-and-tire swing

that hung from the limb of a large oak tree in the back of Carrie's field. They took turns pushing each other on the swing and recalled some of Blake's stories about life when every farm had electricity and a diesel-powered tractor, and how Blake had surprisingly told Carrie that her next boyfriend would be a 'dangerous stranger'. They parted at sundown and promised to meet again the day after tomorrow.

ONE EVENING ABOUT A week later, Carrie was walking with Sushmita alongside Wilson Creek about two kilometers upstream from her home, when they saw what looked like a heap of dirty clothes on the opposite bank about one metre from the water. A goat was grazing the shrubs near the clothes.

'What are clothes doing here?" enquired Carrie, turning to Sushmita in wonder, "there's nothing upstream here but the woods—and nobody lives there except Blake. And these are definitely not Blake's clothes! Look, under all that mud, they are an ugly yellow colour."

Sensing an adventure, the two girls edged closer to the heap. Now they were directly opposite it. The creek was about three metres wide at this point. "If you look closely", observed Sushmita, "the clothes are almost the shape of a man curled up on his side. See—there's the torso, and the legs, and… oh my God, I think I see a head!" Carrie followed Sushmita's guiding and confirmed what Sushmita said. Both girls screamed simultaneously out of fright. There was nobody near to hear them.

"I had hoped to never see another dead man on Wilson Creek, but now I have. Let's go!" stated Carrie as soon as she regained her senses enough to talk. She took Sushmita's hand in hers and pulled her away from the scene.

But Sushmita dug in her heels. "Well, if he's dead, then

he can't harm us, can he?" retorted Sushmita in a surprisingly brave voice. Both girls had seen dead people before: small children in the wake of measles and scarlet fever outbreaks, women who died during childbirth, and the large number of adults in their prime (including Carrie's father and Sushmita's mother) during the Great Flu of 2094—and worst of all, the corpses of the American refugees in 2101 and the starving thousands who fled Toronto when the power stopped and never came back in 2097. The last thing they ever wanted to see for the rest of their lives was another corpse.

As the rush of shock subsided, Carrie calmed down and then curiosity returned to her. "What should we do now?" she asked her friend.

"Let's just take a closer look, so that I can tell Father", said Sushmita. "He needs to know these things and then he can call the Sherriff." Carrie nodded in mute agreement, still a bit jittery.

They left their canvas shoes on the bank of the river and waded in the tepid water up to their thighs. The lower parts of their knee-length hemp dresses soon soaked up the water. A moment later they were standing on the far bank, looking down on a wretched-looking, bedraggled young man. His dark hair was cropped very short, with bald patches, and he had a sparse beard of the same length. He was thin but muscular. His feet were bare. But the thing that attracted the girls' attention the most was the blotched look of the skin on his face and arms.

Suddenly, the man moaned. The two girls jumped in surprise.

"Holy shit, Sushmita, he's alive. What are we going to do now? We can't just leave him here. The coyotes will get him for sure overnight."

"We can't carry him and besides the road is at least 500 metres from here. We need to get help."

"Hey, here's an idea", Carrie pondered, "my brother Seth should be coming home from the market along the road soon. Seth's as strong as an ox; he can carry this guy easily. And he'll have a waggon with him."

Carrie walked along the creek up to the road where a small wooden bridge crossed over and waited there for about ten minutes. Soon Seth arrived in a two-wheeled waggon drawn by a horse.

"Seth, I need you to park the waggon here and come with me down the crick. I've found a man there and he seems to be wounded or badly hurt or something, and there's nobody else to help."

"And then what are we supposed to do with him, little sister? Take him home? Can't take him to a doctor 'cause we can't afford one."

"I've been thinking about that, Seth. What if we take him to Blake? That way nobody else gets involved and nobody even needs to know! Blake likes me and he seems to know a lot about healing people."

"That crazy old coot? How many times have we told you not to go to Blake? The guy gives me the creeps. People say he consorts with the Devil!" And with that, Seth gave the slack reins a flick and the horse started to walk.

"Now hold on, Seth. Just 'cause you don't like Blake doesn't mean that we can just leave a man out here to die. Do you have any better ideas?"

"Nope. But I have a right mind to go straight home and tell Mother what you are up to. What are you doing sneaking around Wilson Creek anyway? Up to no good with your darkie friend, most likely."

"Hey, leave Sushmita out of this. And it's really none of your business!" Carrie did not like where this conversation was headed and was getting frustrated with her dull-witted older brother.

"OK, Seth, I'll tell you what. You do what I ask, and I won't tell Mother about you and Jenny."

"Damn! How did you know? Sneaking around the barn again, are you?"

"Never mind how I know, Seth. Are you going to help me and do the right thing, or are you going to live in the barn and eat nothing but oats for the next month once Mother finds out?"

Verbally defeated, Seth stopped the horse and got down from the waggon. "Take me to this man you found—and quick—before we get home late and then there will be Hell to pay."

SETH GENTLY LIFTED THE stranger, draped him over his shoulder and walked back towards the waggon. The two girls followed behind. Once on the flat bed of the waggon, each girl sat on one side of the stranger—Carrie to the right and Sushmita to the left—and Seth drove the waggon down the dirt trail that led to the woods. At the crest of a hill they were surrounded by the towering colossuses of forty wind turbines—all silent and still. Most had their triple-blades burned and broken. Two of them had toppled to the ground.

Looking up at these relics of a bygone era, Sushmita said, "Father tells me that these were once windmills used to power Peterborough and Trenton and other cities, but they all burned because the engineers could not maintain them."

"Your father sure likes to tell tall tales, Sush", interjected Seth. "how do you think people could make things this big? Look at those blades, they are at least fifteen metres long. And the towers are forty metres tall. And how many tonnes these things weigh! Anybody who has sense knows that the Giants built them. Even Reverend McPhee says so! Do you think you are smarter than a minister?"

157

"Well, what about the topless towers of Toronto? My dad says the buildings there are 600 metres tall and on days that the clouds are low, you can only see half-way up them!"

"More tall tales!" replied Seth, now laughing.

"I'll have you know my father went there when he was a boy and saw them with his own eyes."

"Have you seen them, Sush? Have you? I didn't think so. All tall tales and damned lies."

"Fine for you to say, country boy! You've never even been as far as Peterborough!" retorted Sushmita, now in a fury for Seth calling her well-respected father a liar.

"Stop it you two, please!" hollered Carrie now fed up with their bickering. "Sushmita, you know my brother likes to pull your strings. Don't let him do it. If you had an elder brother you'd know better."

The heated discussion between Sushmita and Seth roused the stranger who, until now, was silent and apparently sleeping. "Don't take me back... please!" he said faintly in a cracking, raspy voice and with tears in the outside corners of his eyes, "they'll kill me!"

The three youths looked at each other with shocked looks on their faces. They fell silent.

"Nobody's killing anybody today, and I'll see to that!" swore Seth in the voice of a young man supremely confident in his physical strength and willpower. The girls were in awe, having never heard him speak like that before.

A FEW MOMENTS LATER, the waggon reached the end of the dirt road about 100 metres into the wood. Seth stopped the waggon and knelt down by the stranger. "Don't worry, we are taking you to a healer. We won't tell a soul. You'll be safe here," Seth assured him.

About 200 yards further into the woods stood Blake's

shack. As usual, he was sitting on his favourite boulder, but this time he was looking South, straight at them. Then he said something that unsettled all three youths: "So, the danger has come. I've been waiting for him all day. Kindly take him into the shack and I shall attend to him. I know it is getting late, so if you must leave right away, please do."

The three briefly thanked Blake and headed back to the waggon and home. They were very quiet on the road. "I told you he's a crazy old coot, sis. Did you hear what he said—dangerous? Who else would be willing to tend to a stranger especially if they are dangerous? You've got yourself into a pretty pickle, sister, mark my words!" Carrie and Sushmita kept their mouths shut thinking over and over again how Blake's prediction was coming true.

THE NEXT DAY, CARRIE stayed at home carrying out the usual burden of farm and household chores. She thought of Sushmita—how lucky she is being able to live in the village and even go to school. But she also thought how lucky she is to have Sushmita as a friend because she could read and write thanks to Sushmita's coaching. But most of the time her thoughts were on the 'dangerous stranger'. What danger was he in? Who would kill him? And why? He did not have the crazed look of a starving man or the menacing look of a gangster (she saw one up close once: he tried to rape her until her brother jumped him and broke the guy's neck). But she knew that if Blake says that there is danger associated with the stranger, she should better believe it. She stayed at home for a whole week out of fear, leaving only on Saturday for the market in Havelock. Sushmita paid her a few visits during the week and told Carrie in hushed tones that twice during that week, people in the area had seen uniformed military police officers patrolling the area but had not spoken to any locals.

159

Carrie got chills when she heard this news.

On the seventh night, Carrie had a dream. But it was more vivid than any dream she had ever had before. In fact, it seemed to be more vivid than anything she had experienced before in life. And she clearly remembered every single detail when she awoke.

In the dream, she was standing with the stranger from the creek. They were holding hands. She felt safe and secure and somehow 'complete' in his presence. They were looking at a big, strange lake. The other side was visible but a great distance away, perhaps 4 kilometers. But when she looked to the right and to the left, the shore receded as far as the eye could see. And the lake had tall grass growing out of it. The wind was gently playing with her chestnut-coloured hair and the air had strange but pleasant smell that was totally unfamiliar to her. She and the stranger looked into each other's eyes and smiled. Then she heard mature woman's voice say, "this is your home." And she woke up with a start.

THE NEXT DAY, CARRIE felt compelled to visit Blake. In the evening, she and Sushmita walked to Blake's cabin and saw the stranger sitting on Blake's favourite boulder, with Blake standing, apparently doing something with the stranger's eye.

"Hello, Mr. Blake," both girls said simultaneously when they were about ten metres from the boulder.

"Oh, hello girls. I've been expecting you, and so has our guest. I hope you are both well?"

"Yes," they both replied, "and you?" enquired Sushmita.

"Can't complain, my dear," replied Blake.

"How is the guest?" enquired Carrie, "does he have a name?"

"Indeed, he does. But he can speak for himself," answered Blake.

Thereupon the stranger introduced himself as Harold. He thanked Carrie and Sushmita for rescuing him from the bank of the creek.

"But how did you get to Wilson Creek? And you said something about somebody wanting to kill you. We've got so many questions. Please do tell!" said Carrie.

"I'll tell you what I can", said Harold, "But you may find it to be a strange story, especially for country folks like you."

"Try us!" said Sushmita, "we are used to all sorts of strange stories from Mr. Blake. We'll see if you can top him!"

They all laughed.

"Alright, I'll try," replied Harold, "but first you need to understand a bit about me. My full name is Harold Paudash. I am 24 years old. My ancestors belong to the Hiawatha First Nation, but I grew up in Toronto.

"For several generations my family lived in Toronto, mostly working on construction of the high-rise towers. Jobs were plenty. The work was good. We thought we had it made.

"Then came the hardships. First the Great Depression of '92. That was when I was thirteen years old. All construction stopped. Most of those buildings are still standing half-completed. My father was suddenly without work and had no chance of getting jobs. My uncles moved back to the Reservation around that time, but we decided to carry on in the hope that things would get better. Me and my two sisters and my parents—we all did whatever odd jobs we could to pay the rent and keep on living. Then came the Great Flu of '94. Lost my mom and one of my sisters. But because so many working-age adults died, once the flu ran its course, there was more work for my dad, my sister and me. We managed to get by. But when the power went out in '97, that's when things became really bad in the city."

At this point, Carrie and Sushmita looked at each other. The electrical grid went down permanently in Havelock and vicinity in 2070, so they had never known electricity except for a few farmhouses in the area that had rickety old solar panels and jerry-rigged small-scale wind turbines for domestic use.

"There were terrible riots. Without refrigeration and electric stoves, it became a big problem to preserve and cook food. People were quickly going hungry. Apartment buildings and condos became uninhabitable. Thousands of people were living on the streets. And then most of the street people died in the snow and the cold in the Snowstorm of January '98.

"We were lucky. We had a house. And the city kept the water and sewage systems running. We were kept really busy retrofitting houses with ice-boxes and rocket-stoves. The pay wasn't good, but it was enough to survive on and besides we were helping our fellow-citizens to survive by keeping their houses habitable.

"There was no more police force and crime became a problem, but residents found ways to pay for protection to their local gang. Armed gangs ruled the streets by night and eventually by day too. Gun-running from the US was a huge business. Everybody—and I mean everybody—in the city owned a gun and learned how to use it.

"Things were getting worse year by year and political protests became more common. If you wanted your neighbourhood to continue to survive, you had to organize politically and lobby the municipal government mercilessly—as well as pay bribes. I ended getting involved in local politics. We were doing a lot of good, especially for those who were barely surviving.

"But when 100,000 American refugees stormed the border at Niagara Falls in 2100 and came to Toronto, everything fell apart. The Mayor was assassinated and was replaced by a gangster. My group protested at the Provincial Legislature demanding that the Province declare martial law to restore order in Toronto—and then bombs went off in Queens Park, killing all Ministers of Provincial Parliament. The military police, who were stationed nearby, arrested me and thousands of others who were there at the time. We are now serving life sentences without trial."

Harold paused for a moment, obviously fatigued by telling his story. Carrie took advantage of the break to ask him a question.

"But if you are a prisoner how did you get here? The nearest penitentiary is hundreds of kilometres from here!"

"That's where modern politics comes in. In 2101, when Canada died and the Republic of Ontario was born, the newly elected President of Ontario decided to be 'creative' in solving the incarceration crisis by dealing with a new environmental crisis. Our old nuclear plants in Pickering and Bowmanville were becoming ever more expensive and difficult to maintain, even though they had not produced power in over sixty years. You see, these sites stored the spent nuclear fuel rods which, if left alone, would incinerate the nuclear facilities and then send radioactive ash and dust all over the Great Lakes area. Coal burning generators were constructed on site to generate the power necessary to prevent this nuclear nightmare from happening. And so, the President ordered that all political prisoners be involved in the transportation of nuclear wastes to a deep depository in the Kawartha Highlands."

At this point Carrie and Sushmita hardly understood a word of what Harold was saying, but they didn't want to interrupt him. And he continued with his story.

"So, for the past two years, I have been working as a slave on the underground facility to store the radioactive rods 200 metres underground near Bancroft. But that was the safe and easy work. Now that the facility has been completed, now we have started to transport this toxic cargo."

Harold saw incredulity creep into the faces of his audience, and so he paused. "But that's impossible", said Sushmita. "The only tracks between Pickering and Bancroft go right by our community. Nobody has seen any trains."

"You may be right," replied Harold, "but I'll let you in on a little secret. We have only been making these runs for the past month and always in the cover of night. Plus, when we go through a community, we turn all lights off and let the engine idle to minimize noise. And I suspect that the President's Office has been paying 'hush money' to anyone who lives within a kilometre of the tracks, as well as to local Mayors and Councils keep a lid on things.

"Anyway, I swear that what I am telling you is the truth. But you haven't heard the worst yet. What the President calls a 'life sentence' is really a 'death sentence'. The slaves who touch and transport this cargo are doomed to a horrible, horrible death. I have seen some of the first casualties with my own eyes. The 'handlers' of the cargo are the first to go. Within a few hours they get severe headaches, diarrhea and vomiting. Next comes the hair loss, weakness and fatigue. Skin irritations. And then finally, massive internal bleeding. Within three days they are dead. We all know this. And we figure that about 500 people will die this way every single month until all the fuel is transported ten years from now. That's 60,000 deaths. That will finish off all the political prisoners plus a whole lot more.

"Yesterday was just my second run, and I was already losing my hair in clumps and my skin was bubbling up into sores and peeling off in places. I figured that in another week or ten days, I would be toast. And so, out of desperation, I found a way to jump off the train. I expected to die, but a sudden death by fall seemed a lot better than dying in a huge pool of my own bloody vomit and shit.

"I managed to break free from my bonds undetected and

threw two guards off the train when they spotted me. I then took a leap in the pitch dark of night, not knowing where I would land. Somehow, I ended up in a pond and made my way up the creek as far as I could, to hide my scent from bloodhounds, until I ran out of strength. It was hard going, as I think I broke some ribs and my left arm when I fell. I must have passed out where you found me. I had probably been lying there for twelve hours, because I cannot remember travelling by daylight.

"And so, here I am. Blake has been an amazing doctor for the past week. He seems to know what can cure me of this wretched poisoning. I don't know how much longer it will take before I feel well again, but at any rate, I am immensely grateful for his services and to you two for saving my life by bringing me to him."

Blake spoke for the first time since introducing Harold to the girls. "The world is a small and strangely connected place," he said. "When I was young, it just so happened that I worked at the Pickering Plant during its final decade of operation. I learned all about radiation poisoning and found out about all possible treatments—especially herbs—because I myself experienced low-level radiation sickness and reacted badly to conventional treatments. Soon after the plant closed, I turned my back on the world. There was no use for my professional training, now that all the nuclear plants were closing. And here I have been for sixty years keeping this knowledge on how to treat radiation sickness hoping to never have to use it again."

IT WAS GETTING LATE. Carrie and Sushmita had to rush to get back home before dark. They thanked Blake and Harold for their stories and promised to return soon.

All the way back home, the two girls talked about Harold

165

and his strange tale. It seemed unbelievable, but he seemed earnest in his telling of it. And there seemed to be no good explanation of how else a person like him got to the place they found him. His story would also explained the mysterious presence of military police in the area during the past week. Besides, they had never seen bright yellow coveralls before the day the saw Harold and had never even heard that people wear such strange, ugly clothes.

THAT NIGHT CARRIE HAD the same vivid dream again. It was exactly the same as the first time down to the smallest detail. She vowed to visit Harold every day.

To keep her mother from noticing her absences, Carrie tried to keep her visits to Blake and Harold short—usually about half an hour. Sometimes Sushmita was able to join her, but not always. Carrie was able to make herself useful even during the shortest of visits: applying salves to Harold's skin, massaging his scalp with various oils, and chatting with him throughout the visits. In a way, she was glad that her mother had forced her to do endless chores since she was a little girl, because she was so used to it that she felt uncomfortable sitting still—and there seemed to be so much to do in order to nurse Harold back to health.

Each time she visited, she learned more about Harold and the life that he had lived in Toronto and the privations he had suffered as a political prisoner-turned-slave. His life had been so much more interesting than hers, but much more fraught with danger. One time she approached him from behind and touched him on the shoulder to get his attention. And before she knew it, she was down on the ground, pinned down by one arm and both legs, with Harold on top, his right hand clenched in fist beside his head ready to strike her. He immediately apologized to her and said that this was a reflex action; he made her promise to never approach him that way again. She more felt pity for him than anger at being roughly handled: it deeply impressed her about how life had become a matter of survival of the fittest—or perhaps the quickest-re-flexed—in early 22nd century Toronto.

By mid-October, all the rice in the vicinity of Havelock was harvested and farmers were preparing to plant a crop of win-ter wheat and/or fava beans. The military police had come by a few more times and spoken with locals, but nobody had seen them in two weeks. Harold had nearly fully recovered from his physical injuries as well as radiation poisoning and was planning for his departure. Carrie visited every day even though her services as a medical assistant was no longer needed; she could not bear the thought of spending a whole day without the company of Harold. During the brief occa-sions when they were alone together, Harold would kiss her. She had never felt such passionate kisses before and she felt thrilled by them.

During one warm mid-October day, while Carrie was present, Blake said to Harold, "So, where will you go to, young man, before winter sets in?"

"I have been giving it a lot of thought, old man," he fond-ly replied, "after all, I've had lots of time to think. I am fin-ished with Toronto: life there will only get worse and worse, from what I see. I think that it is time for me to return to my ancestral lands and somehow make a life for myself there. I am not sure what skills will prove useful, but I am willing to try and learn anything. But first, I feel the need to go to one of the old places that my grandparents used to tell me about: it is known as Petroglyphs. Medicine Men used to go there to receive visions and carved them into a big marble dome. They told me that it is by Stony Lake. I think that if I visit that place, I will feel either some sort of guidance or at least clarity about my future. After that, I will go either to wherever I feel guided, or if I get no guidance, I will find the way to my Reserve."

"That sounds like a good idea. I have been to Petroglyphs a few times," stated Blake. "Do you know how to get there?"

"It will be tricky because my grandparents did not use Havelock as a reference point, but if there is a will there is a way."

"It is about 25 kilometres north of here. I can take you there. I may not be fast, but I am still sure-footed, and I know all the woodland paths and river crossings between here and there. Besides, there is nothing tying me down to this place."

"Well, I don't like the idea at all," piped up Carrie, "if I am not included." By this time she had totally forgotten that Blake had associated 'danger' with Harold.

"Don't you think your mother will object, young lady?" questioned Blake, "I hear that she is a force to be reckoned with!"

"You are right about my mother," she replied, "but I am nineteen years old and can make my own decisions about my life. My mother chose her own path when she was my age, so she can't object too strongly if I follow in her footsteps."

"Then you are free to come," answered Blake. "Once at Petroglyphs you will can come back with me, unless you choose a different path."

THAT NIGHT CARRIE INFORMED her brother about her plans. If she did not tell anyone in the family, then there would be a great deal of fear and panic.

Seth was not keen on the idea, but he knew that once Carrie got something into her mind, nothing could deter her. "Though you don't know it, I have come close to crazy man

Blake's shack a few times to spy on the stranger. Blake always sees me even though I am as quiet as an owl: he winks straight at me as soon as I come and then he ignores me as if I wasn't there at all. What an odd old man! Anyway, I have watched and listened to Harold closely, and he seems like a decent fellow even though he talks a bit funny, adding g's to the end of words that don't got it—like 'nothin'. I will handle Mother while you are away, as long as it is only for two weeks or so. You'll be coming back in two weeks, right?"

"I hope so, Seth," Carrie replied somewhat choked up, "take care of yourself, and Mother, too."

Carrie managed to meet with Sushmita in the evening to tell her the news and the plans. Sushmita was excited about Carrie's adventure, but was worried that they might not meet again. Carrie assured her that they will, hugged Sushmita and headed home.

Shortly before dawn Carrie quietly slipped out of the house and headed towards Blake's shack.

SOON AFTER DAWN THE party of three set out, heading north, each equipped with a bedroll tied to a small backpack. Blake led the way, followed by Carrie, and then Harold. After a couple of hours of walking they left the level farmland behind and entered what used to be called "cottage country"—the wild mix of rocky hills and knolls, lakes, rivers and marshes that makes up the Kawarthas. Each took turns leading, with Harold usually taking the lead downhill and Blake taking the lead uphill (so that he wouldn't end up trailing behind the others). At least half the trees in the forests they walked through were dead: a matter that seemed normal to both Carrie and Harold, but it was still a horrible site to Blake who could remember the forests of his youth when dead trees were a small proportion of the total.

In the evening, the three were looking for a soft, sheltered spot to spend the night, when a movement in the distance, between some trees, caught Blake's attention. "My eyes are not as sharp as they used to be, but living in the woods as I do, I notice things. And I saw something that does not sit right with me. Be quiet and very cautious," he told the other two. They decided not to light a cooking fire to be on the safe side. When Carrie went down to the edge of a river to fetch some water, she suddenly heard a commotion at their encampment. She could hear several men's voices—Harold's and two others that she did not recognize. The volume of their voices quickly rose and by the time she got back, she saw Harold rolling on the ground with two men in dark blue uniforms. Somehow, the authorities had tracked them and were intent on turning Harold in. This was the worst possible situation Carrie could imagine.

She screamed and tried to distract the two men. She threw stones and sticks and whatever else she could find handy at them. But the two officers ignored her and eventually they forced Harold's hands behind his back and put on handcuffs. As soon as Harold was handcuffed, one of the officers quickly approached Carrie and told her, "I'm taking you in as well for harbouring a fugitive," and before she knew it, he had deftly handcuffed her. She couldn't believe this was happening.

Carrie quickly looked around and saw Blake lying still on the ground some distance away. She wanted to go to Blake to check on him, but the officer gruffly said to her, "Oh, he'll be alright. He just got in the way of the Law. He's lucky we don't take him in, too, but we'll let the old codger go… this time."

"Blake, are you alright?" Carrie said, with a louder and more panicked tone than she expected. He didn't move. Before she could think of anything else to say or do, the officers started to lead Carrie and Harold to the East. Just before they entered some thick brush, Carrie looked back one more time. "I'm sorry, Blake", she said. He was still lying down, facing her. In a flash, he opened his eyes, and then winked one eye at her. And then she was gone into the bush, puzzled at what she just saw.

The officers were rough and pushed Carrie and Harold at a relentless pace through the forest, around marshes, and past a group of half-collapsed, ruined cottages beside a lake. The officers made a lot of noise as they tramped through the woods—obviously they were more accustomed to pursuing their prey in open country. This went on for about half an hour.

They suddenly came to a clearing with a large marsh before them and steep rocky cliffs to both the left and right. The officers stopped and looked for a way around. "I don't think we've been here before," one said to the other with a slightly concerned tone. While scouting for a possible route, there came a loud crashing sound to the left: a sound much louder than even a large man could make. The crashing sound was soon accompanied by a loud, deep growl. A huge, black form came barrelling to them on four legs: a black bear!

The officer guiding Carrie let her go and put his right hand to his hip, pulling out a pistol. He fired two shots: the first went wide, but the second hit its mark. The bullet did not slow down the bear even slightly and within seconds, the bear was upon the man. With its claws and jaws, the bear mauled the officer to death. The second officer then shot at the bear four times, but before he could shoot a fifth time, the bear was upon him. He, too, met a gory end.

Harold and Carrie stood in shock as this massive beast devoured one of the officers only a few metres from them. Before long, their peripheral vision caught movement behind them—it was Blake. He was motioning them to slowly move towards him. They did so, resisting the primal urge to run

171

away from danger as fast as possible. After what seemed like hour, but was more like one minute, they were back in the woods and quickly put distance between themselves and the bear.

"Bears didn't used to be like that when I was young," explained Blake to them, "but now there is so much less blueberries and other wild foods for them to gorge on in autumn, due to climate change, and so they turn on whatever large 'game' they can find—including humans."

Both Carrie and Harold were soon wondering how they would manage to get their handcuffs off. "Don't worry about that," said Blake cheerily, practically reading their thoughts. Plunging his hand into a pocket, he pulled out a key ring. "What the...?", said Carrie and Harold simultaneously at the sight of the ring that obviously belonged to an officer. "Picked his pocket as he pushed me aside," quipped Blake, "I figured that they would come in handy!"

Freed from their bonds, the group put as much distance between themselves and the bear as they could until it got too dark to travel any more. They spend a largely sleepless night (in fear of the bear), but the bear did not make an appearance.

By noon on the second day they reached Petroglyphs. They were greeted by Peter—an Elder of the Curve Lake Nation—who performed daily prayers at the site in honour of the ancestors. Harold told Peter of his desire and Peter advised him to spend two days in fasting and prayer at the site to seek guidance. Carrie and Blake camped some distance away and waited. At this time Blake taught Carrie some skills for surviving in the woods, and Carrie confessed to Blake her strong love for Harold. Blake told her that he had seen the spark of love in her from the day she brought Harold to his shack and he was not at all surprised at how things had turned out.

On the third day at Petroglyphs, Harold told Peter about

a vision he had and the two of them talked for a long time together. Harold was convinced that his future was with his ancestral community and Peter described to him the best route to take from Petroglyphs south to the Hiawatha First Nation community.

FINALLY, WITH THE PETROGLYPHS visit completed, Harold approached the two others and said to Blake, "I guess this is where we part ways. My route is southwest, while yours is due south. You have healed me body and soul. I can never repay you for the kindness you have shown."

"No need to do that, dear Harold," replied Blake, "just remember what I taught you and whenever the occasion arises to use that knowledge, use it. That is the best repayment possible." They hugged each other for a long time.

Turning to Carrie, Harold said, "So, what do you say? Will you return to your family and the farm and all that is safe and familiar? Or will you come with me to a place you have never seen and face a future that is totally unknown to both of us? I can promise you my love, but little else in this world. The Law may still be looking out for me. I don't even know if the radiation that I was exposed to recently will come back as some horrible cancer some day."

Without a moment's hesitation, Carrie knew which path she would choose, as she had mentally prepared herself for this moment ever since their journey began. "Many girls would envy the life that I have led so far," she began, "as we have good land and a strong, supporting community. Somehow Havelock—and my family in particular—has been spared so much suffering that has been experienced over the past few decades.

"But I know that my life back home would be an empty shell without you in it. I am not afraid of hard work. I am

173

not afraid of want. But I dread a life without a good dose of adventure... and I know that life with you will bring me much of that."

Delighted with her answer, Harold took Carrie's hands in his and silently looked deeply into her eyes.

"I will tell your brother of your decision," Blake told her with a twinkle in his eyes, "but I won't tell to where you have gone. I'll just say you've gone to find your fortune. In case the Law snoops around again looking for Harold, the fewer people know about your destination the better. I see a bright future for the two of you—far brighter than for most people of your generation."

Harold and Carrie were puzzled by Blake's words, but they simply shrugged and said their good-byes to him.

CARRIE AND HAROLD MADE their way southwest: first through the rugged Kawartha Lakes region and then through the farmland and rolling hills to the south. When they came to farm country, they kept out of sight as much as possible, walking through Indian River to hide their scent in case the Law was still hunting for Harold. It was a particular relief to safely put the railway tracks and the old highway number seven behind them. Then after some time they returned to the wild country.

To Carrie, this journey was part like a dream and part like a Honeymoon. She had Harold all to herself, uninterrupted, for three days on end. They spent many precious moments together and despite the hunger and the fatigue and exposure to the elements (fortunately for them the weather was warm and dry throughout their trip) neither of them would have traded it for the world.

At long last, in the late afternoon of the third day, Harold said to Carrie, "Hold still and keep down. I need to see what's up ahead. I think that I heard something." And he walked forward into the bush and disappeared. Minutes passed by silently. Then she heard a shout of alarm, followed by a burst of laughter and three voices talking in an animated way simultaneously.

Harold appeared again, trailed by two young men of a similar age and look as Harold. "Carrie," he announced, "let me introduce you to my cousins Bob and Joe—their father is my uncle who left Toronto many years before. We are here. We've made it to Hiawatha." The two cousins practically pushed each other to be the first to approach Carrie. Small talk ensued.

A moment later, Carrie was led into a nearby cabin, where Harold introduced her to his Aunt Maxine. Before she knew it, Carrie was being warmly embraced by a bear of a woman in her late forties.

"How much I have hoped to see my nephew again—and I knew that if he was still alive, somehow he would make it back. But you are a treasure to behold."

After a while, the strangest thing imaginable happened to Carrie. She and Harold followed his cousins and aunt about one hundred metres and suddenly stopped, facing south, with the setting sun hitting the right side of their faces. Standing beside Harold and holding his hand, Carrie saw before her an immense lake with tall grass growing out of it. "Welcome to Rice Lake, honey," said Aunt Maxine to her, "this is your home."

Come Home Ere Falls the Night: a Ruinman's Villanelle

Troy Jones III

My love, my love, d'you think you might
come back from the ruins where ivy grows?
Come home, come home, ere falls the night.

The lure of riches shining bright
cause men to dig up graves like crows.
My love, my love, d'you think it right?

At home love waits with hearth alight,
and fields are ripe in amber rows.
Come home, come home, ere falls the night.

The ancient men lie dead despite
the wonders ancient science knows.
My love, my love, d'you think you might

find aught to set the world aright?
Or truths profound your spade expose?
Come home, come home, ere falls the night.

Those shabby halls, they say once bright
are tombs for men whom no one knows.
My love, my love, d'you think you might
come home? Come home, ere falls the night.

Forest Princess

Al Sevcik

As he stepped through the town's wide open entrance Bert paused for a moment and looked back. Behind him, the city hall, a handful of administrative buildings and a dozen blocks of homes and shops were encircled by the questionably protective arms of an ancient wood post palisade. Ahead, beyond the entance, tradesmen, craft shops, produce stands, and food venders ranged in ragged disorder along the pebble-paved roadway leading out of the town. The entrance no longer had a real gate. That had gone away long before Bert was born, thirty years ago. Two carved and brightly painted posts supported a wide crossbeam over the road proclaiming the community to be New Saint Augustine. Bert wondered sometimes what the original town of Saint Augustine had been like here on the east coast of Florida. That town had disappeared into the sea a long time ago.

Bert watched riders guide their mounts cautiously around mule-drawn produce carts while avoiding steam-powered trucks and through a swirling swarm of shoppers and gawkers dressed in bright spring colors. *This is good*, Bert thought. *This is healthy activity*. The town is doing well. A couple of quick steps and he caught up with a man wearing black workmen's homespun. "Morning Reverend Truble." Then Burt turned to a younger man who was following a step behind. "Roger, I forgot my notebook. Would you step back to the office and..."

A sudden shriek. A startled horse knocked over a lettuce display as a man raced out of the crowd followed by a red-haired woman yelling, "Stop that crook!" The man had almost reached Bert when the woman grabbed his shirt from behind. Dropping a cloth bag he turned and swung his fist at the woman but she ducked then grabbed and yanked his arm. Off balance, he stumbled and fell flat onto the road. Yanking a pitch fork out of a hay display she straddled the fallen man and pressed the sharp tines against his chest. "Thou shalt not steal!"

Wide eyes looked at her and then at the pitchfork. He opened his mouth and then closed it without saying anything.

In barely controlled anger she shook her head, tossing red hair, and moved the fork tines slowly up his chest until they reached his neck. She wiggled the fork. "Do you repent?"

A whisper. "I do. I do."

She dropped the pitchfork and stepped aside. The man rolled over, scrabbled to his feet and sprinted into the crowd.

Reverend Truble cleared his throat. "Freddie, you're the last person I would ever expect to quote scripture."

"Hello, pastor." She laughed, glanced briefly at Truble, then fixed Bert with unexpected blue eyes. "I felt called to show that man the error of his ways." She folded tanned and muscled arms across her chest. "Mr. Mayor, I've only been in your town a couple of months but I'm ready to help you any way I can." Her blue eyes shifted from Bert to Roger. "Hi. They call me Freddie."

Roger stood eyes wide, mouth open.

Bert's elbow poked Roger's ribs. "Roger, the lady is talking to you."

Roger shook himself and ran a hand through bristle-cut blond hair. "Uh, hi. I'm Roger." He extended an uncertain hand which Freddie grabbed.

A voice behind Bert. "Mr. Mayor, a hunter from Kingsway just arrived. Says he has a message from Princess Janice. Says he has to see you personally."

"Thanks," Bert said. "Roger, we have to get back to the office. It was, uh, nice to meet you Freddie and I'll keep your offer in mind."

Smiling, she backed into the crowd and disappeared.

Bert nodded at Truble. "A member of your flock?"

The minister laughed. "No way. I've tried, but Freddie's universe doesn't fully overlap ours. Some people say she has gods of her own."

Bert smiled. "Well, see you later Albert."

The minister smiled. "Any chance of that happening in church?"

As HE WALKED BACK through the gate with Roger, Bert looked up. "Sky's clear."

"Yep," Roger nodded. "Too early in the year for hurricanes. Hopefully they'll pass by us again."

A woman with short blond hair and wide-set green eyes poked Bert's ribs. "Admiring the clouds, Mayor?"

"Hi Stella. How's the nursing business?"

She smiled. "It's fine. Bert, I've missed you. Haven't seen you around for days and days."

"I've been visiting ranches, Stella. Problems with missing livestock."

"How about leaving all your work in your office tonight and coming over to my place for dinner? I'll show you how I've fixed up the child care center."

"Mr. Mayor..." Roger looked at him anxiously.

181

"Sounds good Stella, see you this evening. Gotta go now. Roger says there's a visitor in my office." Crossing the street, Bert ran up three steps and onto the veranda surrounding city hall. As he opened the door to his office a lanky white-haired man pushed up from a chair, his smile half hidden in a sea of tanned wrinkles. Bert thrust out his hand. "Ed! It's been a long time. How's life in the forest kingdom? You guys managing to avoid the spooks?"

Ed laughed. "We're still there. The town is, well... Bert, the Princess has some concerns and asked me to come here to speak with you."

"I'm listening, Ed. Have a seat." Bert pulled his chair around the desk and sat facing his guest.

Brown eyes studied Bert. "Lots of decades ago when a handful of ranchers and hunters started the town of Kingsway in the great forest between Old Georgia and Old Florida they figured the world would pretty much leave them alone. Except for.... You know." Ed paused. "It worked for a long, long time. Folks cleared trees away and livestock was imported though, of course hunting was always the most important. Over the years we've developed trade with other towns and the old trails in and out of the forest to Kingsway have become horse paths and a few are now wide enough for wagons. It's not that hard to get to us these days."

Bert laughed, "If you're careful to avoid the people-eating genetic monsters left over from the Old World that everyone knows roam the forest. At least that's what you would have us outsiders believe."

Ed smiled. "In big forest many strange things can hide." He leaned forward. "But, as to why I'm here. A few communities up in the Georgia area have started shooting at each other and Princess Janice is afraid that trouble could spill south into Florida. We've already had activity, shooting, livestock missing, that sort of thing."

"Ah, that could explain some of our own problems with missing animals, even though we are, what, thirty miles south of you."

Ed leaned forward, hands on his knees. "The Princess requests a meeting to discuss mutual aid between Kingsway and Saint Auggie. She suggests that a group from each community meet half way between our towns. There's a natural clearing and some large rocks"

"I've hunted rabbits there. But, wouldn't it be better if we met up at your place. At Kingsway?"

"Ed smiled. She hoped you'd say that. Is three days from now ok? She is eager to discuss closer cooperation, you know, better communication and mutual defense."

Bert turned away to look out a window. "Janice, I mean Princess Janice, and I..."

She said you might hesitate. Something about ghosts from the past.

Bert stood. "Let's do it. Give my regards to Princess Janice. I haven't seen her since the Queen died two years ago." He smiled. "That's an interesting custom your town has with queens and princesses."

Ed moved toward the door. "Yep, it's an old tradition. The story is that it started as a joke maybe a century ago, but folks kind of liked it. Our royalty is elected, of course. For a very long time the community has voted only for women and then we keep them in office forever. The titles give a thin coat of glamor to a tough job." He waved goodby and closed the door.

Bert dragged his chair back behind the desk, sat and leaned back with feet up. He wasn't sure about the meeting. His last talk with Janice had not been friendly. He looked up as the office door was suddenly pushed open. Standing in the doorway, red hair, blue eyes, a muscular but feminine shape. "Mr. mayor..."

Bert's feet dropped to the floor. "Come in, Freddie. Close the door and take a chair."

She stood by the door and took a deep breath. "Mr. Mayor I'm going with you to that meeting. It's important." She inhaled again and took a step forward. "Please. I'll be needed."

"How do you know about the meeting?"

"That man that just left your office. I overheard him talking with Roger.." She took another step. "I'm strong and I can shoot. Take me with you."

Roger burst into the room. "Boss, I..." He stopped and stared at Freddie, then at Bert, then at Freddie.

"Freddie wants to ride with us to Kingsway. What do you think, Roger?" Roger swallowed audibly, his eyes locked on Freddie.

"Roger?"

"Well," He flushed. "She... She's great with a pitchfork."

Bert smiled. "Based on that recommendation we'll just have to invite her along." He waved his hand. "Now both of you, go. I've stuff to do."

STELLA OPENED THE DOOR just as Bert's boot touched her front step. "Wait, don't come in. Let's go next door to the nursery, I want you to have a look." She grabbed his hand and led him around the side of her house to a small free-standing building set back from the gravel road. With pretended drama she pulled open the door and stepped back, smiling. Bert stepped in with Stella just behind.

"See," She said. "I put cribs over there for the tiny ones, and a big play area over on that side for the bigger kids. The floor's covering is flat so you can stack wood blocks on it." She turned. "And over there by the window is a quiet area. Well, as quiet as we can get, with books for reading." She

184

looked up at Bert, her eyes shining.

"This is amazing, Stella. We're lucky to have you in our community."

"Well, me and my army of volunteers. When everyone has to work it's important for the kids to have a safe place." She sighed. "I wonder if I'll have one of my own in here someday." She touched finger tips to freckled cheeks and studied Bert with blue-green eyes. "Or, maybe I'm not pretty enough."

Bert put a hand on each of her shoulders. "Stella, you're a fine looking woman."

"Then why aren't you kissing me?"

He closed the gap between them and held her head in his hands. She put her hands tight over his, lifted her head, and moved against him, into his kiss.

He inched his hands free and stepped back. Stella started to move with him but checked herself. She inhaled. "Well, I guess it's dinner time."

Her dining room was typical, paneled with plain planks of Florida pine. But someone had taken care to match the boards so the wood grain made a faint but pleasing background. The walls were bare except for an oversize painting of the community docks on the Saint John's River.

"Are you the artist? I like the painting."

"Thanks. It's just amateur work." She pointed to a doorless entry to the next room. "Food is on the kitchen counter. Grab a plate and help yourself."

As Bert set his dinner on the polished oak table and sat down Stella said, "I hear that Freddie girl has weaseled her way into your group on Thursday."

"Is nothing private in this town?"

"Not for long. But you already knew that." She set her plate on the table across from Bert. "Be careful Mr. Mayor. She's not what she seems."

Bert looked up, raising an eyebrow.

"That's neat. Wish I could do one eyebrow at a time." She slid her fork under homemade sausage. "I've heard people use the 'W' word, you know, 'witch'." Stella gave a small laugh. "I don't know if there even is such a thing. It's just silly. Still…"

"Still what?"

Stella shrugged. "I don't know. Freddie makes me uneasy. I'm just saying. It won't hurt to be careful."

Bert took a forkful of seasoned cabbage. "Stella, you are one great cook. This is absolutely the best meal I've had in a while."

Freckled cheeks blushed happily. "Thank you sir. Uh, does the Princess cook?"

Bert's fork dropped to his plate.

"Didn't you used to know her?"

"That's history. Ancient history."

"You're riding to see her on Thursday."

"On business. She wants to talk about our two communities protecting each other."

"I don't think you should go." Stella looked down at her still full plate. "History sometimes repeats."

MID-MORNING THURSDAY, FREDDIE WAS waiting at the gateless town entrance astride a midnight-black horse with a ragged white streak across its forehead when Bert rode up, annoyed and impatient at being delayed. Freddie's red hair, semi-tamed by a black ribbon, cascaded down the back of her cream-white rough-spun jacket. She wore dark farmers pants with worn polished boots.

"Damn," Bert said with a rueful smile, "Getting seven hunters together at one time is harder than corralling pullets." He looked up as five horsemen straggled into view from several directions. "Ah, finally! Good morning Roger." He nodded at the others, " Jim, Jose, Charlie, Alister. Let's go, it'a long day's ride."

Charlie tipped his hat at Freddie. "No black cat or pointed hat?"

Blue eyes became blue ice. "Bad joke Charles. You can do better."

Charlie touched his hat again. "Apologies. Didn't mean to ruffle anyone's fur."

"Apology accepted."

Roger said, "Which way are we going, Boss?"

"We'll go west, upland, away from the river. The last rain flooded the St. John's and roads that way north can stay swampy for a long time." His left hand flicked the reins and his mount stepped forward. As they left the graveled main street the seven horses picked their footing carefully, avoiding the larger concrete and asphalt chunks. Remnants of old paving. In places the roadway was hidden by grass and woody plants chopped short by passing wagons. After a few miles the horses relaxed and the pace quickened. Riding the horse, idly studying the broken road, Bert wondered as he had so many times what the old paving had seen. He could tell it had been wide once, and smooth. But beyond that what? How many horses and steam trucks and super powerful wagons had the road supported? What had the wagons carried? Where had they come from? Where did did it all go? He tried to visualize an Old World caravan. What would it look like? He didn't know.

The old road twisted around low hills covered with dwarf shrubs and tall grass. As they passed an area of limestone outcroppings Bert turned to Roger. "When I was a kid I hunted rabbits here."

Roger nodded. "While keeping an eye out for snakes, no doubt."

"Yep. Big ones sometimes. Mostly constrictors, though. Not poisonous."

The land rose slowly to a high ridge like a gently sloping wall running north and south. Bert led the group north along flat land and then onto a rutted, weed overgrown pathway that led up the ridge. At the crest they paused. "Okay gang. A quick lunch and then we have to move." He looked at the sky and grimaced. "Sun's already passed its peak and we've a way's to go. We'll have to push to make it by dark."

With careful steps the horses went down the other side of the ridge. The road improved and they passed isolated sheep farms. Late afternoon came and went. The sun disappeared into clouds at the horizon. Scrub growth became taller and morphed into trees and then became forest. The undergrowth thickened. Clouds thickened. Sunlight turned into gloom. Shadows lengthened and they could see for only a limited distance on either side of the road. Wind made noises in the branches. The riders brought their horses closer together and looked anxiously into the undergrowth.

Roger said, "I've heard there's strange creatures created in the Old Time still living in the forest."

"I doubt that." Said Bert.

"Still..."

Sunset passed quickly, then darkness. Freddie said, "At least we have a moon."

"Sort of," Bert said, eyeing the scudding clouds and faint shadows dancing on the road ahead.

"Hey! What's that?" Alister jerked the reins and pointed into the shrubbery. "Beyond that bush. What's that moving?!"

They all stopped. Charlie said,, "I don't see..." He squint-ed. "Maybe, something..."

Jose shrugged. "I don't see anything. I think it's gone away."

"Well," Alister said, "Sure looked like something to me. Something big."

The horses picked their way along the crumbling moonlit road. The wind strengthened and moaned through the whipping tree tops. Bert guided his horse with caution. Fluctuating shadows made the road ahead indistinct. Suddenly Charlie screamed, waiving hands around his face and neck. "Help! It's grabbing me!"

Roger spun around. "What Charlie? I don't see anything."

Charlie lowered his hands. "I felt it… something… on my face…"

Alister said, "I though I felt something, too. Guess it's gone now."

"Probably a moth," Bert said, feeling uneasy, afraid he was losing control of the group. "Okay. Everyone calm down. We've got a ways to go yet. Can't let ourselves get spooked."

"Oh no!" Alister pointed ahead. "Look! Skeletons. Dancing!"

Five hundred feet ahead where the road turned under a rock outcrop two white skeletons moved in and out of shifting shadow.

Alister said, "That does it. I ain't going no further in this haunted forest."

Suddenly Freddie was beside Bert. "Mr. Mayor, hold the group here. I'll handle this." Dismounting, alone, step by step she led her horse up the road ahead. Her figure soon disappeared into shadow but moonlight playing on her cream-white jacket made a bright spot that eyes could follow.

"Boss," Roger said. "Let me go! Freddie's in danger."

Bert held out his hand. "Wait."

As Freddie reached the curve she stopped and stood still, legs apart and arms raised, obscuring the skeletons. She stood motionless in the dark on the roadway for several minutes, then suddenly her body was silhouetted against an indistinct glow that was faint at first then slowly brightened. Frankie mounted her horse and waited as four riders came around the curve toward her carrying flaming torches.

Freddie led them to where Bert and the others were waiting. One of the riders touched his cap. "Mr. Mayor? Princess Janice thought some light would would be helpful. We're here to escort you to Kingsway."

THE ENTRANCE GATE TO KINGSWAY was fully functional and remained closed until Bert and the others rode close and stopped. Motioning Freddie to bring her horse close, Bert leaned over and said, "Whatever you are Freddie, I'm glad to have you on my team."

Freddie's face lit up in obvious pleasure. "Thanks, Mr. Mayor, but the whole thing was a gamble. I guessed that the skeletons were just moonlight shadows. Turns out I was right." She started to move her horse away then turned back. "If they had been real, well...." She laughed.

Two men with rifles pushed open the gate and the four horsemen with torches moved forward to surround a woman with brown shoulder-length hair dressed in a light green tunic and trousers.

Bert jumped to the ground. His breath caught in this throat as old memories confused his thoughts.

"Hi Bert."

"Hello Princess." Then, "Hi Janice."

She lifted her voice to the group. "Welcome everyone to Kingsway. You're tired so these guys will take you to the visitor's rooms and food will be brought. We'll meet at breakfast tomorrow."

Leading his horse Bert walked over to Janice.

"Did you have an okay ride?"

He shrugged. "Yea, except this spooky forest of yours bugged some of my men."

She didn't smile. "Bert, we're having spook troubles of

our own, but with real live spooks. Guys from tribes around the Great Georgia Swamp north of here. It's tough country. They don't have anything and have their eyes on our stuff, our livestock, whatever we have. It's become a problem and , Bert, people have been leaving Kingsway, leaving the forest. We don't have that many hunters anymore. That's the reason I asked you here."

Bert looked around. He had been here only two years ago but was surprised at how isolated and fragile the walled-in community seemed to him now. "If Saint Auggie can help, we will." He looked at Janice, into remembered brown eyes, the same deep pools. A high-pressure area formed in the air around them. Sounds stilled. He spoke in a ragged whisper. "Uh, Janice, about last time…"

She raised her hand, fingers spread. "It's too much. I can't do that now, Bert. Tomorrow." Stepping back she motioned to the gatekeepers to slide the gates closed and accompanied by two armed hunters, walked back into the compound.

The guest house was a long building with a shingled roof and walls of rough cut pine. Doors to guest rooms lined one side of the open porch. Bert shared a room with Roger next to a community bathroom that had showers and sinks with running water. As Bert and Roger came to their door several women and men appeared carrying trays of food to a room at the far end of the building. Roger stopped, "That's where I'm going! That was a wimpy lunch."

"Go on," Bert said. Then, "Wait. Where's Freddie?"

They stood side-by-side at the porch railing peering into the dark. Moonlight helped but deep shadows made the un-familiar village confusing. In a few moments a familiar figure stepped out of shadow across the street. Freddie stepped up onto the porch. "The women's house is up a couple of blocks. No food but I heard you guys had plenty to share."

Roger said, "Are you okay?"

191

Freddie leaned back against the porch rail and studied them. "I'm okay and ready to eat." She hesitated and looked at Bert. "Uh, about tonight... When I go to bed I'm only shedding my boots."

Bert nodded.

She patted her rifle. "And I'm keeping this handy."

ROGER WAS A BLANKET-COVERED lump in his bed. Bert envied the way his assistant had fallen asleep just as his head hit the pillow. Bert watched the moon crawl across the square of sky framed by the room's window. Then he dozed, his mind juggling conflicting thoughts of strange creatures and vague dangers mingled with images of Janice. He had buried his memories of her for two years, but seeing her now...

Shouting and sounds of shooting yanked him out of sleep. As his feet hit the floor he reached out and shook Roger. "Quick. Wake up. Get your boots and gun." While Roger struggled to sit up Bert jammed on his boots and checked his rifle. Roger beat him to the door.

Flames blanketed the roof of a building across the street, orange tongues leaping high against a black, cloud-covered night sky. Then a streak of light from beyond the stockade arched across the dark and crashed with a burst of sparks and flame onto the gravel road ahead of Bert. Roger ran to look. "It's an arrow stuck into a ball of tar." He looked up. "Watch out! Here comes another!"

The incoming missile arched over Roger and splattered on the guest house porch. Flames Immediately spread across the wood deck. A woman came running with a bucket. She dumped water on the fire and then stood panting, looking at Bert. "You can get buckets and water over there." She pointed then ran off as another flaming ball arched over the stockade and splashed fire against a building up the street.

Carrying his rifle Bert ran to the water trough and grabbed a bucket. A man beside him said, "Thanks to Goodness the arrows come just one at a time. There's just a handful of attackers. Georgia swamp trash. If we had a few more hunters we could clean them out."

Suddenly stockade posts near them burst into flame. The man ran over and hurled his bucket of water, but the fire continued. "Damn. They've poured tar against the other side."

As Bert bent to fill his bucket Freddie ran from an alley straight toward the stockade wall. She slowed and lifted her rifle just as a locked gate in the stockade exploded with a flash and an instant fog of oily smoke. Nearby timbers flamed. Dropping to one knee Freddie fired into the fire-covered opening, then ran closer, dropped to her knee, and fired again ignoring return bullets cracking against gravel around her feet.

"Freddie!" Roger dropped his bucket and ran towards her just as she stood, fired and then spun around and fell to the ground, her arms encircling her chest.

Bert ran towards the flame-filled gap in the stockade but was overtaken by Princess Janice. "Bert," She yelled. "Give me cover!" She ran into the flames, leaping the burning timbers and then diving out of sight into tall grass.

Bert fired over her, into the forest beyond. Three rapid shots zinged into the grass near Janice as a shadow slid behind a tree. Bert fired twice to keep the sniper in place. He watched the grass quiver as Janice crawled to reposition herself. A rifle barrel eased out from the tree but Janice was now where she could see the sniper. She fired five rapid shots.. A man staggered into the open, then fell.

The shooting stopped. In the sudden silence Bert scanned the forest's edge, swinging his rifle toward shadow after shadow. Nothing. Behind him the flames faded as they were doused with buckets of water.

Janice stood up in the waist-high grass. She looked around uncertainly and took two steps back. Kicking coals aside Bert jumped through the smashed and smoking opening. Janice paused and wavered. She jammed her rifle stock into the ground and leaned on it to steady herself. Bert dropped his rifle, forced his way through the grass and held her in encircling arms. For moments neither spoke.

He whispered. "You okay, super-woman?"

"I... I think so. But don't let go of me. Not yet."

Then Roger's agonized cry. "Boss! Freddie's been shot!"

BERT HELPED JANICE BACK through the broken stockade to Roger, kneeling on the gravel next to the sprawled form of Freddie. The right half of Freddie's cream-white tunic was now discolored by an irregular dark blotch. Roger's hand stroked Freddie's cheek. "We have to help her, Boss. We just have to." He looked up at Bert and Janice, eyes glistening.

"Help me lift her, Roger." Bert put his arms under Freddie and then stood with her in his arms.

Janice said, "Take her back to the visitor's building. I'll get medical help."

With Roger anxiously following Bert carried Freddie back to the room they had just vacated and laid her on Roger's bed. As he eased her head to the pillow Freddie's eyes flickered. She looked at Roger. There were the beginnings of a smile but her eyes closed and her body went limp.

"Boss!"

"Easy, Roger. I think she's breathing okay." There's a lamp on the table, see if you can get it lit."

Janice pushed the door open and came into the room followed by an elderly woman in rumpled work clothes. Without saying anything the woman brushed white-streaked hair aside and bent over Freddie. "Princess, let's get this jacket off and then we'll cut away her shirt." In a moment Freddie was bare above the waist revealing a gash below her right breast oozing partially congealed blood and another in her side.

Roger's face flushed. He started to turn away but Bert grabbed his shoulder. "Steady man."

The woman stood. "She's a lucky girl. Looks like the bullet skimmed a rib, probably cracked it, and made a clean exit. "You," she pointed at Roger, "Wash the blood away and bandage her up. She's going to hurt bad for some time, but she'll heal just fine. I've got to see to others now. It's a bad night." She pulled the sheet up to cover Freddie's left breast and left the room.

Janice said, "Roger, there's another sheet in that dresser drawer you can rip in strips to make bandages." She stepped to the door and beckoned to Bert.

As Bert left the room he looked back at Freddie. Was that a smile?

THEY STEPPED OUT ONTO the unlighted veranda. Janice looked up. "Rain coming." Carrying lighted oil-soaked torches, three people walked the street doing cleanup work. Janice led Bert back to the damaged perimeter wall. A man sitting by a small fire stood as they approached. He leaned his rifle against the wall and spoke to Janice. "Evening Princess. A couple of us figured this opening needed watching, you know, to keep out any rats." He smiled. "We'll take turns until morning. That's not too many hours away."

"Thanks, Pete. Let's hope the excitement is over for tonight." She led Bert to a path along the inside of the wall. "No stars and no moon but follow me. I know the way. I grew up playing hide and seek here. This will give us a chance to talk."

They walked in silence for several minutes then she

stopped. "That warrior girl, Freddie... Is she someway special? I ask because I saw her running toward that place in the wall that blew up, waiving her rifle, before the explosion happened. Sort of like she knew what was coming."

"Truthfully," Bert said, "I don't know. Sometimes it seems as if Freddie has one foot in a different world. She denies that. She says she's not a witch. One thing though, she's a good actress." He paused. "Whether she's a witch or not, I believe she's enchanted my assistant."

Janice nodded. "I noticed. I don't think Roger can be saved." She reached out and touched Bert's hand. "Speaking of saving. About you and me... Two years ago..."

"Janice, you don't have to explain anything."

"Yes I do, Bert. I owe you that. But it's not easy." She stood silent for a minute. Her face was in shadow but he sensed her tenseness. "I left so suddenly, left you so suddenly, because I was frightened, scared, confused. The queen, my Mother, had died and all at once everyone was looking at me as if I knew anything. Everyone expected me to take instant charge of Kingsway. At least until we could set up an election." She spread her hands. "Bert, I grew up here, I know everyone and everyone's secrets. My mother kept me informed and taught me about governing. But when she died I was terrified. My mind blanked. I didn't know anything at all. I couldn't handle it. I couldn't handle you. I ran."

Bert took her hand. "Janice, you gave me a couple of rough years but in your place I would have absolutely melted. Anyway, it's over now. Behind us."

"Thanks Bert. I hope you really mean it. I've missed you." She held out an open hand and looked up. "Did I feel a drop?"

Clouds overhead flashed, then a bone-shaking crash. A drop, then another, plunked on the path, then more.

"Quick," Janice said. "We're near my place. Let's run."

They ran half a block then Janice jumped two steps onto a covered porch. She stood for a moment brushing water from her hair just as a blast of rain-filled wind hit them both. Another lightening flash. Janice lifted the latch on her door. "Come inside quick or we'll drown."

As JANICE HELPED HIM shed his dripping jacket Bert made a quick study of the room. Janice's cabin was similar to his own. Smooth pine-board walls and floor. The floor softened by two multicolored rag rugs. On the far side of one rug there was a cushion and a scowling cat, grey fur fluffed up around her neck. Plain wood chairs and a pillowed settee at one side of the room were balanced by a polished dark wood dining table and chairs at the other. On the wall beyond the dining table there was a large painting of a forest scene."

"I like the picture."

"Thanks. Mother did that, but sadly she didn't pass on her artistic genes." Janice dropped Bert's jacket on a chair and turned to face him directly.

Dripping brown hair clung to her cheeks and ears. Her clothes clung to her like wet rags. She brushed a rivulet off her forehead. Bert's eyes fixed on hers. She's beautiful.

"What happened, Bert? What happened to the world? These roads with brush and trees growing through cracked and broken concrete... Once upon a time they must have run straight and smooth for hundreds of miles between towns, and even cities. Places we've never heard of. There must have been steam wagons and steam trucks that went fast for dozens of miles at a time. And tall tall buildings with safely made rope lifts moving people from floor to floor. And soft, smooth fabrics in every pretty color. Deep in the forest I know where there are rows of concrete pads. Before the trees grew there were homes there with people living in them. What happened in

197

that long ago?" She turned away. Her voice dropped. "All I know, all I've known in my life is fighting the forest, fighting the brush and the big roots that tunnel under the log wall, and fighting raiders from the Georgia swamps and from the mountains. Everything, the forest, the people, everything pushing, pushing striving to push us out, to take what we have, what we worked for, what we need to survive. It's hard. So hard."

Bert put his hands on her shoulders and turned her to face him again.

She sighed. "Bert, I want to deny it but Kingsway can't go on. Key people are leaving, like the real doctor we used to have, and our young people. Our enemies don't know it yet, but they probably suspect. After, what, a hundred years, two hundred, I don't know, Kingsway is becoming an empty shell. It's going to die."

She stood quiet, still dripping rain, un-wiped tears on her cheeks, searching his eyes. A ghost of a smile. "I guess I'm about to lose my throne."

No," Bert said. "Once a princess always a princess. Janice, I can't explain the past, what happened, why it happened. But we have years ahead. Bring Kingsway to New Saint Augustine. Join with us. There's lots of room, high ground, a river with fish, a wimpy forest but lots of brush and all sorts of trees. Problems of course, livestock thefts, river pirates, bad folks to fight off. But together our two communities can grow, even into a city." His eyes locked on hers. "I think the two of us should merge."

She met his gaze. "I accept your proposal, especially the part about us merging."

She stood quiet, hands at her sides, watching as he unbuttoned her blouse.

He said, "If a mayor were to marry a princess would he then become king?"

She laughed. "I don't know. Why don't you try and see?"

Letters from the Ruins

C.J. Hobbs

Here young Mason, have a read of these and then tell me what you think of your family," said Teacher Finch.

The sullen boy and his teacher were standing in the foyer of New Darwin University.

Mason glared, "Why should I? They just told me that I couldn't partner with the girl I love."

"I know you want to run away with her, but you should know your history before you make an irrevocable mistake." Finch replied.

Teacher Finch picked up a mouldy old book titled 'Birds of Australia' and almost forced it into the reluctant young student's hands. Mason glared. What could a lousy book on birds tell him about his family. Were the ancestors ornithologists? He was no naturalist. His fierce black eyes narrowed in anger. But all he got in return was a paternal pat on the shoulder.

"Just read. See history in the making."

Mason flipped open the book and noticed that the back of many of the photos had spidery scrawls covering the once blank pages. He sighed. He was not an historian. He was a solar scientist. He had been one of the chosen few to attend the university at the age of fifteen. That is where he had met Harriet, another genius in the science program. Mason had always liked Teacher Finch but at the moment he looked up at his teacher with barely disguised impatience. He was met only by Finch's calm gaze.

"Okay. But it's not going to change my mind."

"You can read it in the library. It is an old book so we need to take care of it."

Mason reluctantly accompanied Teacher Finch. He sat in a cane chair and despite his initial reluctance he was soon absorbed in the book.

Teacher Finch wandered out to the verandah overlooking the billabong and wondered if he had done the right thing. The boy's parents were responsible for imparting this kind of information. However they had pleaded with him saying that Mason rarely listened to their advice on anything. They thought that Mason might listen to him.

Mason started reading.

Dear Diary

It is so long since I have kept up a diary. It has been so difficult without any paper.

We lived through so many disasters while so many others perished. Who would have thought that the situation could deteriorate everywhere so fast.

I found this book in a set of solid timber draws made by Jason; bound up in plastic to protect it. It is wrinkled and mouldy around the edges but I can write on it. This book was one of Jason's favourite bird books too. Oh Jason. I miss you. You knew the vows were 'Till death do us part'. I know I was sick with the sweating sickness, but you left without even telling me. I have felt so angry, so alone. Sometimes the rage felt incandescent. But I realise I have been unfair and I miss you so much. Where are you now? I was so sure you would have at least got a message to me somehow.

I know I shouldn't have come since I defied the council's ruling about travel, but I really just wanted to see the remains of our old neighbourhood. Our house, nestled into the landscape, hasn't been completely destroyed. Samantha's bedroom and the old kitchen are still mostly intact. Comfortable enough for a while.

I even found some of her clothes in the chest of drawers that you made years ago. Those drawers are still holding together. Perhaps you should have been a carpenter like they wanted. Why did you have to argue over every little thing?

While the clothing smells I have used it as padding to make a bed. Rough, but it is more comfortable than the tiny makeshift tent I was forced to use when you left the Hub. It is a wonder I survived the sweating sickness.

The way up to our old neighbourhood is only a few kilometres but it was very difficult. Several times I almost quit; it was so hard getting through the mounds of masonry and rusting metal strewn everywhere and all being overgrown with thorny shrubs and trees. It is a wonder anything can grow in such dry conditions. There was the occasional clear path made by stray animals. I even saw fresh droppings and heard an occasional thrashing through the bush, but otherwise few animals remain near the Hub. Everyone eats what is available be it cute or cuddly or down right ugly. Rats and insects are common place items on many menus.

Only Amy, my next door neighbour, knows that I have left the Hub. However I will need to return in a few days for whatever meagre supplies I can scrounge. The conditions in the Hub are getting so much worse. There's a new Hub leader and he is particularly vindictive. He has even installed his cronies on the Council. He had Amy's boyfriend Mason, one of the farm labourers, flogged by that thug, Rider. All he did was take a bit extra from the vegetable garden for her since she is pregnant. Rider was particularly cruel and his son seems to be taking after him.

What few houses are still habitable around the Hub have been taken over by the Council members. The rest of us have had to make do. Despite all our efforts, the crops are getting worse, and more and more are taken by the Council. There have been more runners lately since the only way to object is to run. To remain and protest is to ask for a certain flogging and near starvation in The Pit. Some have been brought back and the punishment is severe. There are strong rumours the Rider makes sure that many others whom the leader doesn't like, don't make it at all.

Hopefully, a woman of eighty, despite being married to a nominated criminal, is mostly invisible. I have also been given temporary leave from kitchen duties due to the arthritis that has plagued me following another bout of the sweating sickness, so no one will be counting me absent. Amy will be happy to pick up my allocation of food. Pregnant women are always hungry.

Amy doesn't have a baby licence; too tall. The Hub council have decided in their wisdom that only short people should procreate because they eat less food. Ha! The new leader is very short but he doesn't seem to need less food. He has also licensed himself for several children. Unfortunately for him no one is offering to be his partner; more due to his evil temper than his stature.

Enough for today.

Hannah.

ANOTHER WRINKLED PAGE, WITH a Tawny Frogmouth on the

other side. Jason, wherever you are, do you remember how we used to check out the Frogmouth family at the Swamp. Every year a pair of chicks. We loved how the four of them would cuddle up on a branch of a gum tree, while you and I and Samantha watched. When did we last hear from Samantha, Gordon and the twins. I wonder where they are.

I found a family of Frogmouths in our tiny local park. I heard their funny call last night and was overjoyed to see them preparing for their night hunt. A rare sight now around the Hub with most birds ending up in a cooking pot, I wonder how many other birds have reoccupied the surrounding suburbs. I shall spend some time bird watching tomorrow and report any discoveries.

Good news. I did find a great source of water. The Duncan's concrete tank with its reinforced guttering has mostly survived. A pity they didn't survive to use it. We used to deride it as an expensive monstrosity. To those of us who survived the great calamities, forming small farming communities in the cleared swamp to grow our own food seemed like a good idea. Just like the old 'Buy Local' mantra. It wasn't much like a swamp any more but at least we had bore water. Jason. Remember the windmill that you helped to build? It is still pumping ground water for irrigation.

Jason. I had a bucket bath today. I felt so guilty as I sluiced myself all over and wondered if I would live to regret wasting it on washing rather than on drinking. When I returned to my room I wished I could have washed the bedding as well but I would have died of shame if I had gone that far. Do you remember the feeling of clean linen. How fresh that made us feel. How I long for those days.

I found some fruit trees with fruit. I picked several loquats from our old tree, the one you always wanted to cut down, and a bucket full of oranges and lemons from the Duncan plot. None of the fruit was great, but most of it was edible, if chewy.

There were even some vegetables in the Mayberrie's garden beds. Mostly just carrots and potatoes but also some spring onions and some herbs. I wondered if the trees and vegetable plots had actually been tended to some extent. I haven't noticed any recent signs but desperate people are dangerous so I hope I am alone.

I will give some of the fruit to Amy if I can carry it when I return to the Hub tomorrow. My shoulder joints are playing up. This evening I roasted the vegetables on a tiny fire that I made on the kitchen floor. I did not want the smoke to be detected. Not that anyone gets leave these days now that so many able bodied labourers have fled recently. I did not want the smoke to be detected though I didn't worry too much. In the early days everyone was happy to work and people were allowed to roam. Now the council restricts movement to stop people running.

Before I forget I need to tell you I heard a boobook calling last night from that massive Tuart tree in the park. And early this morning I counted ten species of birds. The most amazing surprise was several Ring-neck parrots. I thought I would never hear the call of the ring-necks again after they had become extinct in the suburbs of Perth even before the storms but they were there in the loquat tree competing with me for the fruit.

I miss you, Jason.

DEAR DIARY

I returned to the Hub for a few days. Only Amy was aware of my absence thank goodness. I still felt guilty about not contributing, but I was truly unable to help. I am not allowed any medications for the pain because it is reserved for the young and able bodied. I think the council would be quite happy if I curled up and died.

In some ways us oldies (as few as we are) are in better

health than our grandparents. We only get sufficient food to avoid starvation and since we have to work hard most of us are lean and fit. Little chance of heart disease or diabetes. However I would risk a little ill health if I could have a cream cake and a cappuccino right now.

Amy was happy to receive the oranges and lemons. She is six months pregnant now, in reasonable health, but has not gained the weight she should. She doesn't get the extra rations that licensed women get. Mason has not been able to steal anything extra from the farm, but he did catch a dove and cook it surreptitiously. He did not dare to roast the bird in the communal fire pit because it would have been confiscated at once. Poor Mason is still in some considerable pain from the flogging, but Amy has been cleaning the wounds daily and so far there are no signs of infection. They still obviously love each other.

Once again I am content to be back home. Remember when we first bought this modest house. It was supposed to be a temporary thing but over the years we grew to love living here. We had good neighbours as well as access to parkland and beaches. Really we were spoiled.

It is now dusk. Earlier I heard a bellowing and hunting around I found a pregnant goat in the Mayberries garden. The poor creature was startled to see me. It was in good condition but it was in labour and having difficulties. The kid's legs were protruding but nothing else happened. The creature seemed to be in extreme pain. I walked over and stroked it while I decided what I could do to assist. At first I thought it would be kinder to kill it, but I eventually remembered how long ago my uncle helped a stubborn calf be born. I found some old sailing rope in the ruins of our back shed. Strong stuff. When I returned the goat was lying down, weaker and unable even to struggle. I tied the rope around the kids legs, braced my legs on the goat's back side and waited for a contraction before I pulled. Nothing. Next time I pulled harder. A few hard pulls later, out popped the kid. The mother stayed down, utterly exhausted. The kid however wobbled to its tiny hooves as if it had not gone through a near death experience. I got a dish of water from the Duncan's tank and gave it to the mother and was relieved to see her drink and then later rise to her feet and lick her baby. Soon the kid was suckling. They made a charming picture.

Good night Jason. I still miss you so much.

Hannah

THIS MORNING I RETURNED to the Mayberries to see how the goat and her kid had fared over night. The mother was making up for lost time in the patch of weeds while the kid was busy suckling. She didn't seem to mind me at all. She just kept chewing away while keeping a wary eye on what I was doing. I gave her more water which she ended up taking in with a few swift gulps. I remember some months ago that the goatherd, Jordan, had reported the loss of one of his flock for which he had been flogged. Maybe this is it. I hope that the creature hangs around because I have designs on having some milk for breakfast. However I will wait until it has recovered from the birth and the kid is a little stronger.

I made another discovery in the afternoon. There are chickens. Of course they have become quite feral but I watched them for some time to discover where they roosted. I had eggs for dinner. Several in an old fry-pan along with some bread. Such a treat to eat until my stomach was full. I thought I would never experience that feeling again. Jason, you too would have enjoyed this meal. So like the breakfasts we shared when we camped out in the bush. Eggs kept so well that we often feasted on them near the end of a trip along those outback tracks. We were so fortunate to have had those experiences. Young people like Amy and Mason have only lived in hardship. When I asked them how old they were they told me that they were seventeen. So young. I had thought that they were several years older. The harsh living has aged them beyond their years. Mason told me that Amy's mother had taken him in when his own parents had died in one of the floods. And later when Amy's mother died from the sweating sickness the two of them looked after each other. At least our Samantha has had some good memories of what life can be like. Perhaps one day we can plan towards a gentler existence for their children or grandchildren. Or will it be great great grandchildren.

There is little news about the world outside the Hub, although a few personal messages do get passed along. I know you did not have much choice in leaving but you did leave when I was seriously ill. Where are you Jason? Did you make it past the Rider? I could forgive your desertion if I knew what you were doing. Surely you could have sent a message. I even hoped you would return for me as you had promised. Samantha's husband would have helped. I am so lonely. Your absence devastated me.

I will spend another couple of nights at home before returning to the Hub. I will scour the area for more food tomorrow. Once I would have appreciated the bush and the gardens in an aesthetic way but that is now in the very distant past. It is just a source of food now. With luck I'll collect enough fruit, eggs and greens to give to Amy.

I need to find another pen this one has almost run out. Your desk is in ruins but there are still some pens and pencils in the drawer. If none of the pens work, there are several pencils that will.

There are rats around. I can hear their scratching. I hope the boobook gets them tonight.

Jason. Please come for me!

I THINK I HAVE been so angry because I have been fooling myself that you have survived the journey to the Far North and have chosen not to return. When in truth you may have perished even before managing to catch a boat to the fishing village where Samantha and her family hopefully still live. The storms three months ago almost destroyed the farm. Did you suffer through them as well? Most of us survived because we read the weather and managed to shelter in the bunker before the cyclone hit. Fortunately there was enough dried food to last us until we could get the farm in production again.

Hannah

I HAVE COMPANY TODAY. When I returned to the Hub, Mason waylaid me and asked me about my strange disappearances. Amy had refused to tell him, and now he is afraid for her safety. If the Leader ever discovered that she had prior knowledge of my absences he may have her flogged. She would certainly lose the baby. Mason was extremely angry that I had put Amy in such an invidious position. He didn't think the extra food was worth the potential consequences to her. I agreed with him at once.

I told him that I had been going home. Through the nearby hills to my old home. He seemed surprised that I could make the distance. I could have explained how I had no family nearby and that I was only happy in a ruin of memories. I didn't say that of course; instead I told him I couldn't stop thinking of my husband and daughter and being at home kept them close. I was rather stupid and added that I would have left the Hub and gone North to follow Jason if I was sure that he had survived. Not that such a journey would be very feasible at my age. At least Jason left with two companions in crime.

I hope I can trust Mason to keep that knowledge to himself. Amy walked over at that point after completing her kitchen duties. When she understood what Mason was saying she stopped him at once. She said she was happy to help in the circumstances, and that the two of us were friends and that I had been like a mother to her. She reminded him again about the extra food and how I had checked up on how she was managing with the pregnancy. I felt touched by her words. Mason hurrumphed but settled down.

Later he asked me privately if he could accompany me the next time I came home. I said that it would be dangerous. While they never missed me they would certainly miss his presence in the fields. He replied quickly that he would return before day break in time for his work. I reminded him again that it was a huge risk but he said he would take it. He had his reasons but refused to share them.

Two days later he followed me up through the hills in the late afternoon. Most people who knew me understood that I collected fresh greens for my meal every evening. The only difference was that I had a companion on this occasion. I made out that I was teaching Mason what wild foods were safe. When we took the path through the woods towards the hills Mason took my small pack. So much easier for me. Over the weeks I had discovered the easiest path through the rubble and bush so we made good time.

As we trekked along Mason told me that he was very afraid for Amy. Only three days ago a fellow labourer had told him that he had overheard snippets from a council meeting. It seems that the Leader wants to abort or kill unlicensed babies. I was horrified. Mason had not told Amy. Instead he wanted to prepare their escape and then tell her he had a new Hub in mind. They would need to leave soon because it would be more difficult the further along Amy was in the pregnancy. I did not tell him that it would be very hard no matter what time they left. Where would they go? What about food? All supplies were allocated and closely guarded.

We arrived home in little more than an hour, just on dusk. I gave Mason a rapid tour of the rooms that I occupied and then took him around the gardens showing him what food is available and where I got my water. To my joy madam goat was still in the Mayberries garden with her kid. Mason was amazed to see them. He said his friend had lost a goat some time ago for which he had been punished. The chickens also caused his eyes to light up. More food. That's all we think about these days even though we have more now than in the early years when many starved.

We talked for a couple of hours about his plan. Mason said he had heard rumours that fishing boats sometimes still came in to the old port of Fremantle so he wanted to go there and then sail north. I had heard the same but I wondered how true they were. However the poor boy was desperate and if I could help them, I would. He said that all three of us might get a boat to Broome or even Darwin where he had heard that the living was easier. Our house would be an ideal stopping off point before setting out for the coast.

I leaped at the chance but then the better part of me had second thoughts. I told him I would certainly slow them down. I could draw a map and write out instructions that would show them the way. I was surprised when he said he had never been any further than right here at our house. Then shocked when he said that he didn't know how to read and would not be able to use a map. He implored me to be accompany them at least as far as the port.

Jason. Of course I agreed. My heart sang. Even if I found that you didn't make it, I might have a chance to find Samantha and her family.

He left after saying he would return with Amy in a day or so with some extra supplies.

Hannah

DEAREST JASON. WHERE ARE you. I am coming.

While I waited for Amy and Mason I continued to explore our suburb. It was rather difficult but I managed to find a sweet potato bed and some mulberries. I gathered as much as I could in my back pack and stored everything on one of the old bookshelves shelves. Your woodwork, Jason, seems to have survived the best.

When they didn't arrive when I expected, I really started to worry. Had they been caught or worse. Should I return to find out. Should I go on alone. Would there be any chance of me getting to Fremantle alone. I would have nothing to trade to buy passage north. Who would want to take on a frail 80 year old woman.

I was very relieved when I saw my Hub neighbours through the gloom three days later. Then I noticed that Amy and Mason were accompanied by Jordan the goatherd. Mason explained that he told Jordan of his plans to get his assistance. He wanted Jordan to explain to the council that Mason had said he was sick and unable to work for a few days. He'd had no idea that Jordan would insist upon joining them. As a consequence they had to do without anyone to provide a cover story for the next day. However Jordan made up for his presence with a donkey and sealed the bargain with one bag of flour and three of oatmeal.

I made a quick meal for them out of the sweet potatoes and some of the eggs. There was no conversation just chewing and gulping. Later we talked of how we should proceed. Mason and I thought we should spend a few days preparing the supplies. Jordan would not agree. He wanted to leave very early tomorrow. He reminded us that the Council might have them flogged but they still needed their labour. They won't want me or possibly Amy. They would send out the Rider to get us back. Mason argued that Amy might need to rest but she was adamant that she would prefer to travel as soon as possible. She wanted to reach Fremantle and give birth in a settlement. If we waited she may have the baby in the bush with no access to food or water.

I was afraid. In the old days Fremantle would once have been an hour's drive but now it could well take us two or three days.

Hannah

Dearest Jason

I am on my way. Please be alive. I am writing this while on a short break. We are sheltering from the wind behind some dunes. Jordan shared out some oat cakes full of raisins. They were stale but oh so welcome.

Before first light this morning Jordan organized Amy's and my packs on the donkey. He added three bladders of water. Then we gathered up the goat and her kid and some of the chickens. Jordan had a woven basket for the cranky hens but needed no rope for the goat once he had given her some oats and a long drink from the tank. We were well away before the council could have discovered that we are missing.

I led the party west to the sea with the aim of travelling along the coast. It will take longer but we are less likely to get lost. It will also be easier to hide from the Rider, our worst nightmare. We hope that he will not look for us in this area. Most runners want to go south east to the pasture and forest lands where they might be able to join up with a group of cattle and sheep farmers who are always scouting for herders. Few take this route because the sail to the far north is considered so arduous and dangerous with the uncertain weather conditions. With only one Rider we hope he will tackle the south east area first.

I must stop. Jordan is anxious to continue.

Hannah

DEAREST JASON

Yes this diary has become almost a letter to you. I keep it up since it gives me some peace and I can justify taking such a heavy tome with me. The day was very hard on all of us. The coast road no longer exists. It was covered in dunes and the usual building rubble, and, remarkably, in some areas, in dense low scrub. It was a battle to make our way down to the beach. The regeneration of native scrub was amazing but I was too tired to appreciate it.

The beach was not easy. It is very exposed and we are getting worried about the Rider. Walking near the dunes to give us some cover was hard in the soft sand. The gale force wind blew right into our faces so we had to cover up with scarves to avoid sand stinging our eyes and filling our noses. At times our way was barred by limestone cliffs.

Amy had to rest often so the going was slow. I was able to keep up but now my legs are one pulsing ache and shamefully I was of no help in preparing the evening meal. Most dispiriting was the fact that we had only got as far as Scarborough. There's no water here so we were grateful for the bladders of water that Jordan had so thoughtfully supplied. I hope it's not a sign for the rest of the journey. Jordan rationed our portion except for Amy's, even though she objected and said that all should be equal. I said it was equal. She was drinking for two so that was that.

Looking forward to your arms around me—much love Hannah

DEAR DIARY

It is dusk. We only made it to Floreat beach today. A tiny stump of the old flag pole is still there. At this rate it will take us several more days to reach our destination. Amy is exhausted. She needed so much help to get along. Mason and

Jordan were wonderful with her. I wasn't any help at all, but at least I could keep up by myself with the slow pace.

I could barely recognize any part of the coast except for the long sweep south and the headland at Fremantle on the horizon. Fortunately we have managed to find a sheltered spot in the dunes to spend the night. We are worried now about the Rider. He might have realized by now we took an unexpected route. No one can see us unless they actually stand on this very dune. That is is unlikely when it is just one of so many rolling sand hills extending to the north and south.

There is barely any recognizable signs of all those mansions which overlooked the beach. The destruction was worse than inland if that is possible to imagine. Another strange sight for me was the vacant ocean. The oil rigs, container ships, yachts and motor boats that were so common all those years ago have gone. Nothing apart from two dolphins and a seal lounging on the beach. Not even a fishing boat.

I wonder where Samantha, Gordon and the twins are. Did they go as far as Broome or Darwin? Gordon was so keen and successful at fishing. Is he fishing now. Jason. Have you found them? Will I find you, any of you? Did you come this way. Did Rider find you. I wish you were here to help.

Love Hannah

WE DIDN'T MOVE TODAY. Amy had her baby last night. It is at least four or five weeks early. The council would have been pleased at the early birth. They would have found it easier to kill a sickly baby.

We had no light except for the crescent moon which made everything more difficult and we couldn't afford to have a fire. Jordan and Mason left me in charge since I was a woman and had had a family. I tried to tell them that I'd had a general anaesthetic and a caesarian. I left out the bit about the complications and almost dying.

I remained by Amy's side and tried to keep my voice calm and encouraging. She only cried out towards the end. Her howls brought Mason scurrying back. I thought he was worried about being discovered but he was only concerned about her welfare. The young father to be was trembling but he took Amy's hand and apologised over and over for his desertion. He had left because he couldn't bare to see her in pain. But then realized if she had the courage to go through this, then the least he could do would be to support her. He is a good man although still a child himself.

Not too long after, the brave girl pushed her tiny boy out onto the brush that we had gathered for her bed. I tied off the chord with a scrap of cloth and then got Mason to cut it with his fishing knife. The baby mewled weakly but I placed it on Amy's chest while I fetched some sea water to wash Amy. When I returned with the dripping cloths I found Mason mesmerised by the sight of his tiny son. He was stroking the baby's back and Amy's cheek. He had tears in his eyes but Amy had only giggles at the sight of him so in love with his 'wife' and child. I only hope that the baby survives. I used some of the old material from home to make a nappy for the baby. It hung rather hugely on that little wrinkled back side but it would have to do.

Jordan returned to assist with breakfast. He had milked the goat to give Amy some extra nourishment. The goat has not suffered from this trip since there is enough scrub and dried grasses. There are animals about but only in low numbers. We have seen kangaroos and wallabies and occasionally a few cows. It just shows that if the bush is not over stocked it can recover even in a harsh climate.

I was so tired I went to sleep straight after breakfast and did not wake until almost dusk. I was glad to see Amy was busy feeding him. He was dribbling milk so hopefully he will survive despite his early birth. His milky lips were pink not blue like that baby born a few years ago at the Hub. A few painful breaths and then he slowly died.

The Hub no longer has a doctor. Old Masters died several months ago and while he did try to pass on his knowledge and skills he had few takers. So much to learn when they still had to do a full days labouring on the farm. It was even worse, since most young people can't even read. I hadn't realised until Mason had confessed to not being able to read or write. If I am spared I will teach elementary literacy and numeracy when we are settled.

While Amy and Mason busied themselves with being parents I walked down to the sea in the near darkness and bathed. It was so refreshing. The water was calm and there was barely a breeze. Such a relief after the last two days of raging winds. When I returned to camp Mason and Jordan had decided they had to have some real hot food. Jason was keeping a lookout from a sandhill. Mason was humming as he sat stirring some herbs that he had gathered earlier, into a puddle of eggs over a small fire. The chickens had done us proud despite their travels.

Good night my love wherever you are.

DEAREST JASON

We had a close call last night. Jordan was awake and heard a snuffling in the distance. After checking the goat and donkey, he carefully wriggled up the dune on his belly and surveyed the area. Our worst fear had come true. The Rider was dimly silhouetted by moonlight a few dunes over, clearly looking for a fire or any other sign of us. Jordan watched until eventually the Rider moved further off toward the next headland. Jordan immediately returned and woke Mason and I to discuss what to do. Our whispering eventually disturbed Amy and we had to let her know what Jordan had seen. She started sobbing. Mason was surprised but quickly hugged her to comfort her. I explained to Mason that it is normal after pregnancy. But it did put a sombre mood on everyone as we faced the possibility of being found by that thug.

Then something happened that so rarely happens now, it rained. A cold misty rain. Jordan suggested the rain may be a blessing in disguise, making it more difficult to see us. Mason wrapped Amy in a piece of canvas tying it around her shoulders and waist. The baby was strapped tightly to Amy's chest. At least he didn't make a sound, though whether due to weakness or from the comfort of his mother's warmth we didn't know. On the other hand the silence was to our advantage if Rider made another appearance. If the baby did cry I hoped the sling and canvas would muffle any sounds.

We trudged on barely seeing in front of us, and drenched to the skin. At least Amy and the baby kept a bit dry. It was hard. The donkey could not carry everything. Both Mason and Justin had packs. At one point I saw a thin stream of blood trickling down Amy's legs. We should have stopped, but that was not possible. Several times I stumbled, and each time I wondered if I could take another step. The only thing that kept me going was the thought of you, Jason, and Samantha and the others. The wind picked up during the morning and the waves started crashing on the beach. I could feel blisters forming so I took off my soaked shoes, and hung them around my neck. We didn't dare stop.

Finally the baby cried. It was a relief. Mason led us into the dunes and Amy fed their son, sheltered under the canvas held by Mason. We all had a lunch of soaked dry bread mixed with a few dried grapes and hard loquats. Not very satisfying but there was no way to light a fire in this misery of wet and even the smell of smoke could alert the Rider. Jordan

217

fed the goat and the donkey some oats and allowed them to graze. The chickens were clearly miserable in their basket but there was nothing to be done for them except to offer some food. We didn't delay for long. Jordan scouted around before we returned to the beach to continue.

That afternoon we stumbled down to the old harbour. Like the rest of the city, most of the buildings were levelled and sand dunes choked most of the harbour itself. There was no sign of a settlement or any boats and Mason and Jordan wondered if they had been moved to a place further up the river in a more sheltered position. After much discussion, Mason and Jordan left us in a make shift shelter to scout around.

I lay down rolled in a blanket, aching from head to toe and shut my eyes. I woke the next day to weak sunlight and a continuing miserable drizzle. I sat up in shock with Amy and the baby huddled next to me. Amy grinned up at me and said that I had snored through the baby's cries. I noticed that she had placed another piece of canvas over the three of us as a blanket.

The boys had not returned. I started to get worried but Amy reassured me. She had not eaten anything last night and when I asked her if she had any milk, she giggled and said that he was sucking on empty. She is so brave.

I soon found the goat in the grasses by the river and milked her. I soaked some oats in the milk and we ate the cold mix as is. Amy wolfed the lot so I made another bowl for her. We should conserve our food but she needed the calories. Afterwards I held 'no name' while Amy went down to the river to bathe. When she returned she snuggled down into the canvas and fell asleep, while I wrote this diary snuggled down with the baby.

All my love Hannah

OH JASON YOU ARE alive. The boys brought back the news this evening.

After a day of waiting and worry, and another meal of uncooked porridge, both men walked in just before dusk. I had got a small fire going despite my fear of the Rider. We had to have something hot to eat. The two famished men hung over the fire as I was frying up eggs with some wild mushrooms and edible weeds along with the last of our bread.

Once we had eaten Jordan regaled us with their adventures. They had gone far up river and spent a cold miserable hungry night in some ruins. Next morning they followed smoke in the distance to a small village in a very sheltered cove. A few round houses cobbled together out of old bricks along with a few small wooden sailing boats. There were racks of smoked fish hung out to dry. Careful that Rider wasn't nearby they ventured into town and were greeted by the villagers. Cold and damp, they gave the two men food until they were completely satisfied. It made Jordan wonder why their Hub had not been able to provide more food.

After they had eaten, one old man surprised them and asked if they had run away from a Hub up north. He told them not to worry, but that big brute of a man on a horse passed by the day before. He said the rider calls himself Rider and comes past sometimes when he says he is chasing a runaway. After a previous experience they always stay in an armed group when he is around. The old man reassured them saying any person who ran was welcome there and, if necessary, helped on their way. All of them had run from Hubs that had become too ridden by rules that only profited a few.

The villagers even remembered Jason, the Historian. They said he'd lost his wife to the sweating sickness. Told them he couldn't see to her because the Leader had sentenced him to death. He escaped with two others. They had had a run in with Rider. Rider killed one of the men, but the others escaped, though the Historian was badly wounded. Jason was about dead when he got there. Stayed there awhile before getting a fishing boat going north.

The villagers even knew Gordon and that he was due to pass through in a few days.

Tomorrow Mason and Justin take us to the village.

I can't wait to see you. Hannah

DEAREST HUSBAND,

We are all in a very crowded fishing boat with Gordon, heading your way. The villagers were so nice. According to the old man in the village, our Hub, 'Utopia', is not the worst. He told us so many awful stories of his and others' escapes. He is a truly exceptional oral historian. When you met him a year ago I hope that you recorded some of his views.

We stayed in the village until Gordon called in. He was so surprised to see us. We gave the villagers the goat and the chickens when we left.

All my love Hannah

MASON SOON FINISHED THE letters. They weren't so difficult to read after all. When the letters came to an abrupt stop he turned the remaining pages hoping to find another letter. There weren't any. What had happened to the escapees and why was Teacher Finch so adamant that he read this stuff.

Teacher Finch wandered up once he noticed that Mason had finished reading.

"Well what do you think of it?"

"It's interesting but what has it got to do with me."

"Haven't your parents told you about your family history at all?"

"Not really."

"Don't you recognize any of the names?"

"Only the name I share with one of the men."

"Well I'll have to give you a run down on the Mason line," said Teacher Finch wishing he didn't have to add to this boy's sorrows.

"I don't have lots of time." Mason shuffled about in the chair impatiently.

"I'll be quick." Teacher Finch put his hand on Mason's arm to restrain him or maybe to placate. It was hard to tell.

"A very surprised Jason and Hannah were reunited some weeks later in Exmouth. Samantha and Gordon and the twins were living there as well so they more or less lived happily ever after."

"How are they related to me?"

"It's complicated. But remember Amy, Mason, No Name and Jordan. No Name was your grandfather."

Mason almost stamped his feet with impatience. "That is interesting but you know that my girl, Harriet is waiting. What has that got to do with her."

"No Name was finally named Mason after his father. Mason joined the fishing fleet but was lost in a storm. Jordan later partnered Amy and adopted baby Mason."

Young Mason declared emphatically "How could she have re-partnered? I won't ever have anyone but my girl, Harriet."

"Life goes on, young Mason. I am sure that Amy grieved but she had more children and created a big family of brothers and sisters for your grandfather. By all accounts they had a good life. There's more of your family history in the new library. One of your cousins went around collecting old diaries and letters to add to the History collection. You need to read the collated volumes of Post Storms life before making any important decisions that will affect you and your family. Really you owe it to them to discuss your plans."

"I don't have time!"

Teacher Finch frowned, his forehead a mass of craggy mole ridden wrinkles. "Did you actually read it all carefully."

Mason nodded his head vigorously. Then an awful thought occurred to him. He snapped, "Are you going to tell me that my girl and I are somehow related?"

"Not at all!" Teacher Finch seemed unhappy to continue. "You have a complicated heritage. All four escapees ended up being related in one way or another. Your grandfather Mason partnered the girl of one of Hannah's twin grand sons. They all ended up fishing and farming in Exmouth."

Mason looked unhappy. "None of this makes me any less likely to partner my girl."

"What's the family name of this love of yours Mason?"

"Ryderz."

Teacher Finch stared up at the young man.

Mason pondered the Letters before asking nervously "Do you mean she is related to the Rider. The psychopath in those letters."

"That's why your parents don't want you to partner with her. There's too much history."

"But Hannah refers to the Rider not the family Ryderz. Nothing to do with my Harriet!"

"Where do you think the name came from? After the collapse of the Hub, Rider and his son came north but changed their name to avoid retribution. Harriet is his great grand-daughter."

Just then Mason looked over to the billabong and saw that his beloved had ridden up on her big black horse, Croc. She sat easily on the enormous gelding as he pranced in place not far from the water line.

Mason waved eagerly and cried out, "Harriet I'm coming."

The girl returned his wave.

Mason turned to his teacher and exclaimed cheekily. "She's not like him!"

Running to the girl he cried back, "We'll create a new family name! We're both Solar scientists. We'll be Solars! We'll be ourselves."

Teacher Finch watched them ride off. What was he going to tell his sister about her son and the girl?

The Legend of Josette

KL Cooke

Fame after death is no better than oblivion.
Marcus Aurelius

Part I: A Note Never Found

"I waited for you as we had agreed,
And since the train arrives when it arrives,
I sat all day among the rest who need
To wait and hope, we do that all our lives:

I came in fear to meet you at the rails,
With agents seeking culprits to collect:
Returning from your cause that always fails,
Two lovers greeting would be less suspect:

We had each other here, were hidden, safe;
Surviving hungry years when no rains came:
Your wife and child began to rub and chafe,
Though giving up the fight would mean no shame:
And now I think you must have been betrayed,
By going to it when you could have stayed."

Alone that year, the winter came in hard;

225

The cabin windows thickened up with ice:
Some men brought goods, but charity was marred
By village women looking at her twice:

In times of want the open hands will close;
What little came to her was bought and paid:
She had a hungry child, and so she chose
To barter with what coin she had to trade:

It was not long before the wind brought word
That gave her reason to fear for her life:
The women's grievances were being heard
By those who knew that she had been the wife
Of one they said who stood against the state:
Why did she not deserve to share his fate?

The mule that pulled the wagon had been sold;
The cow as well, the laying hens had gone
Into the pot before the stove went cold,
When there was nothing left that she could pawn:

The men still came, but carried less and less
Of food and fuel, instead they brought dark hints
Of this or else, the meaning she could guess;
Conveyed with evil grins and winks and squints:

And so in fear that she could be denounced,
She gave for nothing what they came to get:
An opportunity on which they pounced,
While she knew that hers was a foolish bet:
And so, decided she must take her child,
With little else to travel in the wild.

The town stood at a place where two roads crossed,
And so it was she had a choice to make:
Now it was clear to her that all was lost,

But still she had to think which path to take:

Should they go north or south or east or west,
When what lay up ahead she did not know?
So she could not decide which route was best,
But only knew that they would have to go:

And secretly at that, so no one saw,
And followed after them to bring them back;
Tied up in ropes and given to the law;
A few small coins made them worthwhile to track:
The women of the town would think it right,
So they would have to get away by night.

They waited past the moon when all was dark,
And quietly walked through the sleeping town;
No lighted window to see them embark
Upon their journey, now the moon was down:

For no one stayed up long beyond the sun:
When decent folk were decently in bed
Was when they said malefactor's deeds were done,
By lighted candles, making plans instead:

There was still danger though, the Civil Guard,
The watchmen walking nightly on patrol:
Appointed toughs with sticks, whose fists were hard;
Empowered by The Law to keep control:
The townsfolk knew that they were always near,
Maintaining order by the rule of fear.

The child was named Josette, not more than nine;
But when her mother gathered up to pack
A few small things, she recognized the sign
That they were leaving, never to come back:

Because she was a girl beyond her years;

Her father gone, and knowing he was dead:
A fact she realized in mother's tears;
She saw it, though there had been nothing said:

Among the things, something not seen before;
A thing of value that could not be sold:
A pistol that was underneath the floor;
She understood it without being told:
The penalty was harsh for having one,
So no one else in town possessed a gun.

Perhaps some guards were drunk, they often were;
Carousing at a post or sleeping sound:
Unpleasant consequences would occur
When agents learned that she could not be found:

This wife of a disrupter knew much more
Than common people knew about the land:
Which way would lead them to the ocean shore;
So turning south, she took her daughter's hand:

The road was rough and rutted from the carts;
The paving had been ruined in due course;
That in the Time of Magic linked all parts
By wagons that could move without a horse:
A time, so it was said, before The Fall,
Of wonderful inventions had by all.

The night was clear, the Dipper at their backs;
They needed miles before the foot fall sound
Meant guards were coming, looking for their tracks;
She knew that they could soon be brought to ground:

The smallness of the child made walking slow;
As well the pits and rocks that caught their feet:
And when they gray of dawn began to show,

Her goal of miles was mostly incomplete:

The girl was hungry, but she did not dare
To stop for rest, the town was still too near:
Nor partake of the bread they had to share;
Not for herself, but for Josette her fear:
And not long after came the sound of hooves;
The surety anticipation proves.

By luck the sound came from around a bend;
She heard before he saw and spurred his mount,
To bring their journey quickly to an end,
And take them back to settle his account:

It was the Section Guard she had slipped by,
Who found her absent when he came to pay
A visit for what she could not deny,
When he came with his threats to have his way:

Though fuddled as he was with drink, he knew
The Proctors never would accept excuse:
For they had special interest in the two,
Concerning knowledge that could be of use:
They must be found, or else it would be known
That while he slept on watch, the pair had flown.

The pack she wore, the child she pulled behind
Made going slow, as they ran to the trees;
For any hiding place that she could find,
Before the guard could bring them to their knees:

He saw them just before they disappeared
Into the woods, and stumbling on he came,
With grunts and shouts and curses as he neared
Where she had turned and stood to end the game:

He should have seen the hand hung by her side

229

That held the gun, but carelessly did not:
And so it was the turning of the tide;
She looked into his eyes before she shot:
What might have been the end of her recourse
Was not the end, and now they had a horse.

Part II: Into the swamp

They traveled for three nights and slept by day,
But on the fourth she thought the horse gone lame:
Unknown it dropped a shoe along the way;
The saying goes, a nail was to blame:

At sundown on the fifth they met a man
On foot, so not a Proctor or a Guard:
His hair was gray, his face was lined and tan;
His large, strong-looking hands were gnarled and scarred:
    "What are you doing, missy, you and her?"

He pointed to the girl who looked away:
"With every evil varmint out and cur;
A hundred of them any given day:"
The answer to this question left unsaid,
She turned attention to the horse she led:

She showed which leg seemed lame, he lifted it
To take a look, and she saw he was one
Who handled horses champing at the bit,
And kept them calm, the way it must be done:

He felt the hock and said, "All I can see
Is she has thrown a shoe, the way they do:
But I can fix it if you come with me;
While at it I will check the others too:"

He led the horse, she followed with Josette,

Along a path, and feeling some alarm:
She knew full well the consequence of debt,
Although he seemed like one who did no harm;
That is, if she knew how to read a face:
She also had the pistol, just in case.

The path came to a cabin and a shed;
It looked like there was no one else around:
"My name is John, I live alone," he said;
My woman is now ten years in the ground:"

"How is it that The Law allows you here?
Around our parts the Proctors keep their eye
On everyone, and make us all live near,
So what we do they easily can spy."

"The proctors have their breakdowns, just like you;
They need someone out here to fix their tack:
A wheel will break, a horse will throw a shoe;
These happen and it is a long way back:"
The tenor of his voice seemed to impart
That he was not a Loyalist at heart.

The shed contained a forge and many tools:
As they looked on he went about the task,
While speaking how the lawmen all were fools;
Then pointed questions he began to ask:

"I come from Fargo at the Cross, a place
The train to Jaxonville goes through:"
"I have been there," he said, "but in that case,
To ride the train had been the thing to do:"

"We have no travel papers, nor the fare:"
"Then neither have you leave to take the road:
Continuing your journey on this mare,

I do believe bad happenings forebode:
But since you have no papers for the train,
There is no more that you need to explain.

My senses tell me trouble comes behind,
But if you can turn back, I think you should:
If you continue on, then you will find
The way ahead will not bring you to good:

This road leads to The Swamp, and there it ends,
And there it marks the border of the state:
Beyond, no order that The Law defends;
A place where many have encountered fate:

The swampers are the vilest creatures known;
Far worse than any robbers you might meet:
The bodies that they hang in trees have shown
That theirs is a depravity complete:
No one with sense goes in that evil fen;
The women there are as wicked as the men."

He brought them to his cabin that was rough,
And fed them with a hearty meal of stew:
"To help you I do not have means enough,
So I have done now all that I can do:

You can stay here tonight, but then must go,
And do not tell me what you plan to do:
I cannot tell them what I do not know;
They will stop here when coming after you:"

He went to bed, she heard him start to snore;
She motioned to Josette to make no sound,
While taking food the old man had in store;
They would be gone when morning came around:
Of all that she had sold she kept one thing

That she now left, her golden wedding ring.

The horse was stepping strong, they rode all night;
Around them now the land began to change:
What had been open fields, the rising light
Revealed as country ominous and strange:

The trees grew out of water still and black,
And yet it seemed the road continued on:
There looked to be no need for turning back,
She thought, as they went calmly in the dawn:

But then a man stepped out to block their way,
And by his look she knew he could mean harm:
More followed from behind, to her dismay,
As each one held a gun across his arm:
Kentucky rifles cobbled out of scrap;
The two of them had fallen in a trap.

She thought about the pistol at her waist;
There were five bullets left, but they were nine:
Resisting she could only give a taste
To those cocked rifles spread out in a line:

They pulled them from the horse and took the gun;
Then cut the horse's reins to tie their hands,
And taking all the leather, let it run:
They had no use for horses in such lands:

Their clothes were made of hides, their hats of fur;
They spoke a tongue she barely understood,
And so she trembled for what could occur,
If they did what the old man said they would:
The men brought them to where they beached their boats,
And put them in, with knives held to their throats.

Part III: The Wild Girl

The boys were howling louder than the dog;
This time they had the raccoon up a tree,
Unlike so many they chased through the bog;
Their leader said, "This one belongs to me:"

It was the girl Josette, now twelve years old;
Taller than the boys and just as strong,
And like the boys, she wore the briefest fold
Of deerskin tied up with a leather thong:

Too young for guns, they hunted with the bow;
The rest all knew she was the best around,
To send a shaft where it was meant to go,
And peering in the darkness, there she found
Two glowing eyes a target, aimed at that,
And so she had a pelt to make a hat.

She had a brother everyone called Duck;
His age was close enough to be her twin:
An older brother Tom, a strapping buck
Who did not like her, she was not true kin:

There was a younger brother, barely three,
And this boy was true kin they all could call:
A pretty child Josette bounced on her knee;
The only one blood brother to them all:

The wife, called Mother, had not given birth
To any of them, though she had the task
Of raising them, with two wives in the earth;
The man who married her had much to ask:
The father was a fierce and giant man,
Called Rory, who was chieftain of the clan.

The high ground where the House of Morgan stood;

The Island, where the true kin of the clan,
In rough board houses made of cypress wood,
Were sworn to keep allegiance to the man:

Across the river on both sides were found
Five dozen households, give or take a few,
That took the name to live on Morgan ground;
Clan members then, by giving what was due:

Ten clans like this controlled the Waterland,
And sometimes kept the peace and sometimes fought,
When men were called upon to take a stand
To keep the chieftain's hold with rifle shot:
Among the clans, a chieftain's house alone
Stood at the highest point, made out of stone.

At fourteen seasons no more could Josette
Go running like a boy in leather brief:
Her older brother Tom would not abet
What might make others disrespect the chief:

He knew his father's woman could not help;
The girl no longer was in her control:
The only way he knew to tame the whelp;
Convince the father to declare parole:

He also knew full well she was his pet,
And so he made his case for safety's sake:
It was a duty never to forget;
At her age now there was too much at stake:
A change in her behavior would be good;
She was too far along in womanhood.

The Morgan took a rifle from the wall;
He sighted down and gave it to Josette:
It was the oldest one among them all,

And yet the finest she would ever get:

"This was my first one back when it was new;
A gift a father should give to a son:
The stock is old, the barrel still shoots true;
A woman too, should learn to use a gun:

That you are one now certainly is so,
And so you must leave off the boyish string:
Then I will teach you what you need to know,
And trade you for this necessary thing:
The better part is not to be in haste,
For powder is too precious stuff to waste.

We have a gunsmith expert in his ways,
And lead for ball quite easily is found;
Made into boxes from the olden days,
And thrown away, we find them in the ground:

The brimstone and the nitre come from caves
The Foster holds and mightily defends:
They trade the powder craftily as knaves;
The stuff on which a clansman's life depends:"

He showed her how to load and how to hold:
"When shot is fired the target has to fall;
If it is game or enemy grown bold,
To pay the cost of powder for the ball:"
The trigger pulled, the flint struck down a spark;
The gun reported and she hit the mark.

Josette tamped down the ramrod with a patch
Of linen soaked in oil to swab the bore:
A wild turkey was the morning's catch;
Her little brother watched her from the floor:

A clansman's buckskin britches she wore now,

And never would put on a cotton cress:
The reason being she had made a vow
She would not break, no matter what duress:

"Our mother gave her life to give you yours:
I was a little child, but I recall
The blood and pain that giving birth assures;
I swore that fate would not to me befall:
I will be like a man, if people stare,
So be it then, I have no need to care."

The skiff moved quietly along the slough;
At dawn, the only ripple was the wake:
Duck pushed the pole, Josette was looking to
The bank for any game that she could take:

They saw what looked to be a snag ahead,
Until it opened up two hefty jaws:
Josette looked down the sight to give it lead,
But then it disappeared without a pause:

"That must have been Old Satan that we saw;
Ten feet at least, five hundred pounds in weight:
No other gator has that big a maw;
It grew so large from all the hogs it ate:
It was around when Rory was a boy:
To take it would indeed have brought me joy."

Among the hunting dogs in Rory's pack,
Big Otis had the stoutest heart of all,
But at her heels now he was hanging back;
It was a foul scent that did appall:

For there was something hidden in the trees,
And Josette thought at first it was a bear:
Then it came out, she trembled at the knees;

237

Eight feet in height and covered with black hair:

Its face was ugly as its smell was bad;
It stood up like a man, but it was not:
It peered at her with eyes she thought looked sad;
The gun was cocked, she did not fire the shot:
It turned around and quickly disappeared;
A creature strange, but not one to be feared.

Her brother Duck was known for innocence
And gentleness, the kind of boy who sings:
A shame to Rory for his diffidence;
Josette rolled gut to make his banjo strings:

The clan encouraged boys to raise the fist,
But Duck did not, instead it was his choice,
If someone called him out, not to resist;
He led the hymn at meetings with his voice:

A churlish boy, not one who was true kin,
Once tried fight him to amuse his friends:
About to beat him when Josette stepped in;
"You had your fun, now this is where it ends:
But if determined that a fight shall be…"
She drew her knife… "Then you can fight with me."

Part IV: The Singular Woman

At eighteen seasons she had reached the age
When mothers talked among themselves to plan
Good matches for their daughters to engage;
A mother's duty was to find a man:

The wife of Rory had no part in this,
With little hope to marry off the girl;
A thing Josette did scornfully dismiss,

Nor any man think her to be a pearl:

To comb and spin and weave and sew and cook,
And women's things like these she did not do:
Nobody would give such a girl a look,
And she was bound to keep her nature true:
A woman of the clan unorthodox;
She hunted, fought and plowed behind the ox.

There came reports about a wild bull;
A larger brute than any in the herd:
Who took it on alone would be a fool,
But hearing that, Josette was undeterred:

If singlehandedly she brought it down,
There would be meat enough to have a feast:
It certainly would bring no small renown,
And so Josette set out to take the beast:

She went to where she thought it could be found,
And dropped it with a shot between the eyes:
She slit its throat and blood poured on the ground;
A spreading pool that soon brought in the flies:
But needing help to bring it in a boat,
She slit its gut to save the meat from the bloat.

Indeed the Morgan clan did have a feast;
The bull was roasted whole and fed them all:
Dawn came before the merriment had ceased;
The lively fiddles and the square dance call:

The chieftain brought out whiskey from his store;
For true kin only, though, the rest drank beer:
And mightily they drank and called for more;
In drinking every man became a peer:

A clansman deep in cups advised the host

His daughter was the equal of a man:
He claimed, In fact, the she exceeded most,
And someday could be fighting in the van:
Her brother Tom heard this announced as well,
With narrowed eyes that trouble did foretell.

    The cry was out, a child could not be found;
They searched The Island calling out his name:
His body would be floating if he drowned;
There seemed no doubt, a gator was to blame:

    Josette hid in the moonlight with a goat
Tied to a rope and staked out near the bank:
The hours went by, she saw two eyes afloat,
And from the water came a creature rank:

    This time she had her shot and hit it square;
Reloading to put three more in its head:
And though the matter was now ended there,
Five hours passed before the thing was dead:
Inside they only found parts of a hog,
But no more would Old Satan rule the bog.

    Josette had boots made from the gator's skin;
There was no finer gift that she could give
Old Rory, who had loved her as true kin,
And loved her mother too, while she did live:

    The chieftain had a gift for her in turn:
"Your mother had this when she came to me:
I kept it for the day I could discern
Who best should have it for a time to be:

    The dryland devils have them, we do not;
A dirt poor life to us they have bestowed:
We have no way to make the magic shot;

You can fire six before you must reload:
The one who has this knowledge at command
Will lead our people out of Waterland."

She studied well this fascinating piece;
Took it apart and put it back again:
She figured out the points that needed grease,
Though naming them was not within her ken:

She wondered what was in the little stack
To fire it, as there was no flashing pan:
The numbers three five seven on the back,
And makers marks around the center ran:

She wished that she could shoot a practice round,
But charges for the gun were only five:
They must be saved for danger on the ground;
For when she needed them to stay alive:
A new thought then began to come awake;
There must be these in Jaxonville to take.

A Foster trading party had arrived
To barter their black powder for strong drink:
For long between them had such commerce thrived,
And neither from hard bargaining did shrink:

With business done the chieftains played a game
Of cards, to gamble for some bits of gold,
But tempers soon from whiskey were aflame,
And trouble stirred that could have been foretold:

The Foster said The Morgan was a cheat;
The Morgan struck The Foster on his face:
Outnumbered, Fosters only could retreat,
But vowing they would answer this disgrace:
And from this incident there came a ban;

No powder traded to the Morgan clan.

A dearth of powder would disaster bring;
More than the want of game, it would be known
Among the clans, as rumor took to wing,
And soon The Island could be overthrown:

So Rory fumed while feeling his old age,
While Tom, the eldest son, advised a truce,
With gifts he said would quell The Foster's rage;
Humility might thus good will conduce:

But while they fretted, secretly Josette
Spoke to the boys who followed her back when
She led the hunt, and facing now this threat,
They pledged to follow her now they were men:
As there was powder still, if they were brave,
They had a chance to take The Foster's cave.

The powder trade had made the Fosters weak,
Despite their reputation for a fight:
The wealth it brought caused them to pleasure seek,
And ease and games produced few men of might:

The ablest were set to guard the source,
But they grew less and less each passing year:
The were about to be attacked in force,
And little aid would come up from the rear:

A foster woman to the Morgans wed,
A rumor of the raid had overheard:
Old loyalties not easily are shed;
She went in secret, bringing them the word:
But when the Morgans came to do their plan,
The Fosters met them like a one-armed man.

Their chieftain quickly gathered up some men;

A party meant to reinforce the guards:
These louts were hardly fit to leave the den
Where they were occupied with drink and cards:

The fight was short, The Foster opened first,
Disregarding how he was exposed:
With pistol fire Josette returned a burst;
She hit him square, and thus the matter closed:

They saw their leader fallen on the spot,
And thinking all the Morgans armed in kind,
The Fosters hardly answered with a shot,
But turned and ran, their leader left behind:
And he would soon be going to his grave;
It was the Morgans now who held the cave.

Part V: The King

The Foster clan would quickly go defunct;
Their chieftain dead, his son a worthless dolt:
The better ones among were not compunct,
And to the Morgan side began to bolt:

Like cats whose loyalties are prone to shift,
The women were the first to slip away:
Without them men soon found themselves adrift,
As even good men are when women stray:

More women for the Morgans was a boon,
And welcomed to The Island as they came:
New stock for wives and workers opportune,
But men were tested past the point of shame:
Before the gauntlet they were made to scud,
And swear an oath and seal it with their blood.

The Morgan now controlled the powder trade,

And to The Island wealth began to flow;
Yet mindful of mistakes The Foster made,
He would not let complacency to grow:

But rather there would be a standing force
Of men free from the need to plow and hunt;
To guard The Island and the powder source,
And always ready for the battle front:

With surplus that before they had not known,
To dedicate such men to skills of war,
And for courageous mettle she had shown,
Josette would be the leader of the corps:
Tom, the son, objected out of hand;
No fighting men would follow her command.

Josette was soon to prove this was not true,
By cleverly dividing up the men
In groups led by the ones that well she knew;
Old hunting boys, each led a force of ten:

The Kincaids were the first to try them out;
Spurred on, they were, by envy and by greed:
The fight was quickly turned into a rout,
And many were left on the ground to bleed:

The rest were hunted down like wild boar,
With each one desperate for a hiding hole:
At length they all surrendered to the corps,
And saw their chieftain's head high on a pole:
No longer would they turn to strife and moil;
In thralldom from then on and made to toil.

The clan was grown by two in land and wealth,
But Rory was made half because of age:
Tobacco and strong drink bought with his health

Had brought him now up to the final stage:

The woman wise in potions did no good,
And soon it was he could not leave his bed:
Among the people it was understood;
They would pray to Jehovah for the dead:

He called out for the closest of true kin,
To hear the final words he had to say,
And he declared as breath was coming thin,
"So it shall be now I must go away:
Although a child that I did not beget,
The chieftain after me shall be Josette."

This was a judgement Tom could not accept,
Appealing to the Elders for relief:
Traditions of long standing must be kept;
He was the next in line to be the chief:

He had a case, the all agreed, and more;
It was unheard of, what had been decreed:
No woman ever led a clan before,
But how could Tom prevail in trial by deed?

What had he done to equal her, they said;
They feared the corpsmen that were on her side:
The chieftain's word was law, though he was dead,
And now she spoke before them all with pride:
"With three clans under me I am a queen;
From here on you shall call me Josephine."

The fire of anger, envy for its fuel,
Did burn in Tom, and by the Devil stoked:
Ashamed as one held up to ridicule,
Until revenge an evil plot provoked:

Conspiring with a friend, they planed a coup;

In voices low, but they were overheard
By brother Duck, who to the queen was true;
He quickly went to her to bring the word:

    So she was ready when they came with knives;
Her pistol close, in which two shots remained:
Their treachery was paid for with their lives,
Upon the ground that with their blood was stained:
The two shots in her pistol were enough;
Their weapons proved to all theirs was no bluff.

    The queen began to rule more than to reign;
She issued proclamations backed by force,
While keeping for herself most of the gain
From trade that came in by the powder source:

    The law was what she said from day to day;
She took the gun from anyone who balked:
Dissenting ones a beating had to pay,
From corpsmen who among them always stalked:

    One day she called a meeting of true kin,
Appearing strange, but laughter none would dare:
They saw that she had fastened to her chin
A beard that had been woven out of hair:
"Do listen well and let your praises ring,
For I am Joseph now, I am your king."

    The pistol empty now, a useless tool,
The king began to think of Jaxonville:
"All Waterland could come beneath my rule,
By corpsmen armed with these to do my will:

    The dryland devils have them we well know,
And charges we do not know how to make:
But down the Merry River we could go,

For all the guns and charges we can take:"

King Joseph called the leaders of the corps;
"This plan Jehovah gave me in a dream:
Your finest men you shall select for war;
Success for us has been assured I deem:
When we prevail, great riches you will see,
And each shall be a ruler under me."

Apart among themselves, the leaders spoke;
"This king is not the one who we once knew,
But someone mad, we can no longer cloak,
And death for us is certain if we do:"

"Our fathers' fathers taught that one must kneel;
Disloyalty they held a deep disgrace,
But armaments that we are out to steal
Will be the ones that we will have to face:"

By day no more was said, the boats were filled;
Made ready with provisions for the raid:
With talk of dryland devils to be killed;
Of death they boasted they were unafraid:
To Jaxonville a hundred miles downstream,
They set off with the king to lead the team.

It was a month before they did return
To tell a tale of vain and desperate strife:
And there were some who found it strange to learn
Josette alone among them lost her life:

No longer called the king now she was dead,
And neither was she on a pallet borne:
Her royal tomb was in the river bed,
And there were few who thought it cause to mourn:

The legend of her courage, though, lived on;

With time and telling larger it would grow,
Until the battle field she died upon
Became a story everyone would know:
And brother Duck, who saw with mindful eyes,
Would be remembered as a chieftain wise.

That Which Cannot Be

David England

Beyond-the-Waters looked over the supplies nestled at the stern of his outrigger canoe one more time before drawing the blanket over them again. That blanket, woven from the fine inner fibers of one of the several varieties of island grasses, depicted the heavens of the night sky and had been a gift from the women of the village at his Naming some six moons ago. There would be many things he would be leaving behind; this gift would not be one of them.

His gaze rose and he considered the horizon where the sun-goddess Reyeh was returning to the watery house of her father, as she did near the Middle Times. The great bowl of the sky looked to be clear, both a blessing and a curse. A clear sky meant that the stars would hold themselves forth to aid his navigation. It also meant that his boat could more easily be seen in the light of the growing moon, whose rapid cycle of birth, death, and rebirth helped the People mark time along with the greater cycle of the Long Days and Long Nights.

He shook his head sharply. Success depended greatly on their departure going unnoticed until dawn, hopefully not until well into morning, but it was a risk that must be taken. Time had run out.

Turning from the beach, he made his way to the beginning of the short trail which led to the village. Behind him, his canoe had been drawn up at one end of the row of others, the full fishing fleet of the island, that fleet augmented now by the vessels of the bridegroom and the contingent of representatives from that neighboring island. He hoped that the absence of a single boat from one end of the row would be less immediately noticeable, giving them that much more time in the confusion the morning would bring.

Dances-with-Rain was the most beautiful creature to walk among the Blessed Islands of the People and the two of them had loved one another for as long as he could remember, from the time they had played as children. Now she was to be married, in accordance with the laws and customs of the People, to a young man of another village from a nearby island. Having seen five-and-ten Long Nights himself, and having achieved manhood now with his Naming, Beyond-the-Waters was sure his own betrothal and marriage would soon become a topic of conversation among the village elders. His older brother had taken a wife from the same village as the bridegroom-to-be two years before and already had a son. His younger sister had just become betrothed to a young man from yet another island and was to be married in another year's time.

The festive atmosphere of his village contrasted harshly with his somber mood. He kept his emotions carefully veiled, however, and cheerfully greeted others he encountered as he walked toward the commons, nodding and smiling with a joviality he did not feel. His heart, by contrast, was grim, desperate.

This village was the only community on this small island which was part of the outer ring of the archipelago that was the home of the People. A cluster of islands of varying sizes surrounded the large central island which bore the Hall of the Clans and the many small temples to the various gods and goddesses. Most importantly, however, that large island was home to the Great Temple of Earth and Sea.

While the People honored many different beings, the Mother-Goddess Ge and the Father-God Kos formed the axis on which the universe of the People rotated, akin to the One Star which never moved in the great celestial bowl. It was said that there was a time, long ago, when the Old Gods rested after having fashioned the Cosmos. And while the Old Gods slept, a group of Young Gods--who were clever, but not at all wise--rose to power and took the world as their own. At first, the Young Gods had respected the work of their elders, but after a time they lost that respect and came to see the world as their plaything, believing foolishly that their cleverness was superior to the Old Gods' wisdom.

As a result, the Young Gods had nearly destroyed the world: lands were drowned beneath the waves, forests as vast as the Great Water died and became waste, rivers became poisoned, and the soil lost its vitality. When the Old Gods awoke from their slumber, they became angry when it was discovered what the Young Gods had done. In his great wrath, Kos had wished to drown the Young Gods as punishment, but Ge had convinced him otherwise. Instead, the Young Gods were made mortal and forced to live in the world they had made; they and their children would inherit the fruit of their foolishness. And so, the People came to live on the earth, on the last islands that remained above the waves of the Great Water. As the children of the Young Gods, the People took great care to respect the works of the Father-God and the Mother-Goddess.

He reached the broad commons of the village and paused, trying to hide his dismay. The two ritual huts, fashioned together of bundles of dried sea-grass, had been erected on opposite ends of that open space. It was in these huts that the betrothed would spend their final night unmarried, the entrance to each hut watched over, as ritual demanded, by a member of each family: a male relative in the case of the bride and a female relative in the case of the groom. The marriage ceremony itself would take place mid-morning.

In the center of the commons, midway between the huts, preparations had already been made for that ceremony. The shallow pit had been dug, two handbreadths deep as dictated by custom, and lined with clay. The earth from that depression had been packed into a low mound on the edge nearest the bride's hut. It would be here, after water had been poured into the pit and flower petals had been scattered upon the mound, that the couple would recite the oaths of Father Kos and Mother Ge.

His beloved would be standing on that mound of earth. He would not be standing in that pool of water.

"The blessing of Kos be upon you, my son," a deep voice behind him said, breaking into his thoughts.

"And the blessing of Ge be upon you, Uncle," Beyond-the-Waters replied as he turned to face the chief elder of the village.

"How fare you this day?" the elder asked.

"I am well, Uncle," he replied, keeping his features pleasant and unconcerned.

"Tomorrow's ceremony is most auspicious. The seer stones indicate a blessed beginning," the older man observed. "It will be a time of great celebration."

"Yes, Uncle," the younger man replied. "Most joyous."

The other considered him carefully and something flickered in the elder's eyes. "I know you have a certain affection for Dances-with-Rain. Such has been apparent to many of this village for some time." A pointed pause. "It is, you must realize, *loq'una podse*," the elder stated, invoking the language of the Temple. *That which cannot be.*

In his mind, Beyond-the-Waters understood. The customs of the People were unambiguous on this point. No member of the People was permitted to wed another from the same village. Such was the will of the gods. Even when considering marriages between villages of the same island, the keepers of the Temple of Earth and Sea must first grant permission after they had consulted their charts and omens on the matter. But in his heart, the young man rebelled.

"I understand, Uncle," he replied. "I have accepted that the laws are as they are some time ago."

"That is good," the elder responded with a nod. "It is important to accept the will of the gods in these things and to observe the traditions of the People. It is this which makes one a man or a woman of the village, and no longer a child." He placed one hand on the younger man's shoulder. "We shall be speaking of your betrothal soon enough, the gods be willing."

"Yes, Uncle," Beyond-the-Waters agreed, covering his blasphemy with a smile. "I truly believe it shall be as you say."

The elder nodded again and released his grip on the younger man's shoulder. "Until the morrow, then. This celebration is greatly anticipated; it looks to be a long night."

"Until the morrow, Uncle," he replied and turned away as the elder moved on. It was going to be a long night indeed.

His hut lay on the far side of the village, befitting his recent ascension to adulthood. It was fortunate that he was somewhat sheltered by the newness of that status and had not been asked to host any of the visitors from the bridegroom's party. He would have his solitude this evening, exactly as he required.

With some relief, he managed to pass through the village without further conversation and entered the humble dwelling which offered refuge for the coming hours. Unrolling the thickly-woven reed mat on which he slept, Beyond-the-Waters sat cross-legged and stared at nothing in particular as he contemplated his heresy.

According to the elders and the keepers of the Great Temple, the Great Water surrounded the islands of the People forever on all sides. Like flecks of soil floating in a vast bowl, the cluster of islands represented the last of the lands-above-the-water, and the edges of the earthly waters merged with the waters of the sky which stretched above like a second, inverted bowl. In ancient times, before the Young Gods had been punished for their foolishness, there had been other lands above the waters on which those gods had walked, but all had been drowned beneath the waves and the wrath of Kos.

This is what he had been taught as a child, as had countless generations of children before him. This was the truth which lay at the foundation of the rites practiced by the village elders and the more complex ceremonies performed by the keepers of the temples.

And he knew it to be a lie.

Each turning of the great cycle of time known to the People was divided into four parts. The half-cycles were defined by the Long Day, where Reyeh stayed aloft and refused to enter her father's house, and the Long Night, when the sun-goddess refused to leave and declined to ride along her sky-path. These half-cycles were themselves divided into two by the pair of Middle Times, when the period of light and the period of darkness were in balance. It was the custom of the People for the rites of manhood to take place at the Rising Middle Time, before the Long Day, so that the newly-installed men of the community would have the opportunity to act in their new role during the coming fishing season. Likewise, marriage rites were held at the Falling Middle Time, before the Long Night, as the Long Nights were sacred to Mother

Ge and considered auspicious for the conception of children. His rite had started as any other the village had witnessed. The sky had been clear and the omens encouraging when he had paddled alone in his canoe out into the open water, there to spend the night alone beneath the vastness of the sky, to behold and contemplate the work of the gods, and to return the following morning. He had prepared himself as prescribed by tradition, with ceremonial washing and prayer, and had taken with him the symbols of manhood: the fishing spear and fishing net.

Then the storm had hit.

It had not been a large storm, but it had come upon him suddenly and without warning. Most devastatingly, its path drove between him and his island, between him and the archipelago of the People, and the only means of survival open to him had been to turn his vessel away from his home waters and toward the vast unknown.

Somehow, he had not capsized, his craft riding the powerful waves, but he had travelled a great distance by the time the storm had passed and the terrain of the sky had told him how very far into the Great Water he had gone. With the morning sun, he had despaired of ever seeing his village again, resigning himself to the hands of the gods who seemed determined to take him.

It was then that he had seen the shoreline. He had seen land where no land should have been. He had seen that which cannot be.

And a great *nawlu*, one of those mighty titans of the waters who were said to pull the chariot of Father Kos himself, passed just beneath his vessel. The giant had been so close; he could clearly make out the pattern of furrows and ridges in its skin. Surely, he thought, this had been a sign. Surely, the gods meant something more for him yet in this life.

He had turned into the path behind the great creature and

when night came, he was able to make out the One Star, also named in legend for the mythic animal companion of the Young Gods, the Dog. For many days, he had travelled. Rain from the storm had given him sweet-water and his net and spear had provided him food. It had been a joyous morning indeed when the islands of the People again showed on the horizon. And upon that miraculous return, he had kept what he'd seen to himself, allowing the elders' expectations of what he'd witnessed suffice for explanation.

For even then, the seed of his plan had planted itself in the back of his mind.

He woke to the waning light. A little while longer, he told himself, to allow Reyeh to complete her descent into her father's house, and then he would make his way to the shoreline and his canoe. There he would wait.

The next hours would reveal much. He had planned, but the final decision would be hers. Either she would meet him on the beach this night or else she would accept the decision of the elders and go through with her marriage come the morning. And if she did meet him and if they did make their escape under the cover of darkness, then their fate would be in the hands of the very gods whose laws they were defying. He could only believe that he had not been shown what he had seen and been allowed to survive only to have the gods snatch away the very slender thread of hope which they themselves had provided him.

The dusk deepened into dark. He rose and stepped over to the entrance of his hut, pulling aside the cloth hanging which covered it. Reyeh had gone to her rest and the night stars shone clearly. His gaze descended and he looked about the shadowed village, now grown quiet in anticipation for the festivities of the morrow. Festivities which, if his plan succeeded, would never take place.

The two of them would never see this place after this

night. Or their families, their relatives. They would never set foot on the main island; never witness the public rites of the Great Temple. They would never be a part of the People again. A tiny voice in the back of his mind asked if the gain was worth the price.

Yes, he answered himself. By all the gods above and below, yes.

With that moment of resolution, he stepped into the night air, letting the cloth fall back across the doorway behind him. He moved quietly but swiftly, skirting the perimeter of the village and then making his way along the path toward the beach. Toward the meeting place where he would discover if the woman he loved was willing to brave the gods.

He reached the shoreline without incident. The growing moon hung low in the sky yet, but was enough to illuminate the beach to such a degree that he became conscious of every shadow, every sound. Sitting in the sand on the far side of his canoe, he settled in to wait.

The very traditions they were defying provided the opening through which they might escape. According to custom, the bride and bride-groom would each spend their final night unmarried in the separate ritual hut designated, but with a difference. By tradition, the bride-groom's right foot would be tied with a particular and intricate knot to a stake driven deep into the ground, symbolizing the bond of marriage into which he was entering and also preventing any excursions in the night to his bride's dwelling.

The bride, however, was not similarly bound and the custom-within-the-custom permitted the bride, should she be willing, to visit her bride-groom during that night. The walls of the ritual huts where thinly made, easily permitting ingress and egress through the rear of the structure, and if the guardians posted at the entrances of each of the two huts heard rustling or soft moans during the dark hours, well, those were

257

likely just the night-sounds of the forest, weren't they? His beloved would be able to leave her hut without arousing suspicion, if she so chose.

He waited. And waited. The moon-god rose slowly, climbing higher into the night sky. Then, a sound. A shuffling of sand behind him. He stood slowly.

"Hello, Bey," she said as she neared, calling him by the name he'd used when they were still children.

"Hello, Dey," he replied in kind.

She reached out and he took her hand in his briefly, allowing all that could not be said to be expressed in that quiet moment.

"We need to go," he said finally. "If you are willing."

"I am willing," she replied and climbed into his vessel. Once she was settled, he pushed the craft into the low surf, taking it beyond the breaking waves before climbing in and positioning himself at the stern. Each of them took an oar in hand and propelled the vessel out to sea, away from the home of the People, and toward the vast unknown.

They paddled through the darkness, following the guidance of the bright stars above and offering thanks to Father Kos for the placement of those markers among the waters of the heavens. It was good that he had rested earlier as the strength of his back and arms were needed now to put as much distance as possible between them and the village. Dey helped in those first hours, adding her oar to the effort in the immediate aftermath of their flight, but she had not had his advantage of rest that prior day and quickly grew tired. Now, as the rim of the sky-bowl lightened with the promise of the coming dawn, she slept soundly in the bow.

He kept paddling, his body working in a steady rhythm with the water over which he and his beloved travelled. Silently, he offered a prayer of thanks to the entire pantheon of gods and goddesses for seeing them even this far.

The dawn broke and Reyeh began her ascent into the bowl of the sky, following the trail laid out for her since the forming of the Cosmos at the beginning of all things. He began to think about resting. As the air above them brightened, his beloved stirred and sat up, rubbing the sleep from her eyes. Looking at him, she smiled in that way of hers that made his chest ache with joy.

"Good morn, my love," she said.

His heart smiled. "Good morn," he replied. "If you are hungry, there are provisions in the satchel behind you." Hard cheeses and dried meats, but food nonetheless.

"I'm starving," she admitted. "But I'll only eat what I need." She looked to the brightening sky. "How many days do you think it will take us?"

He pulled his oar in and set it across his lap, relishing the momentary rest. "I'm not sure," he responded. "The storm that drove me lasted for some time and it took me many days to find my way back. It should take us far less time to find the lands I saw beyond the Great Water if we are travelling toward them directly." He looked to the satchel in her hands. "I packed enough food for the two of us for a seven-day, just in case. Plus we can fish. It is the supply of sweet-water that concerns me."

Her eyes were soft, loving. "I have faith in you, Bey." His heart swelled once more, but then her gaze slipped past him to something beyond and the smile on her face faded, replaced by a look of terror.

He heard the low-chanting rhythm carried over the water before he had turned in his seat. Sharp eyes scanned the horizon behind them before settling on a group of dots that were even then growing steadily larger.

A fleet of canoes, from the island and in hard pursuit. They had been spotted after all.

His heart sank. Even with both of them paddling, they'd

not be able to out-pace the six-man crews boasted by their pursuers. It would only be a matter of time now before they were caught. In that moment of desperation, Bey did the only thing he could think to do.

He prayed.

He prayed with every fiber of his being. He prayed to Father Kos and Mother Ge, the heavenly parents of all. He prayed to the Three Winds. He prayed to the sun-goddess Reyeh and her brother, the moon-god Reh. He prayed to Solu, the goddess of the home and the hearth. He prayed to Dem, the god of soils and fertility. He prayed to Ish, the goddess of the creatures of the Great Water. He prayed to every god or goddess he could summon to mind. "For the sake of our love," he whispered fervently. "Please. Spare us."

"Look!" Dey shouted.

He opened his eyes. The fleet was much nearer now. He could see the individual men, hear their rhythmic chant as they stroked in unison, feel the anger and outrage rolling toward him over the water. His gaze then followed the line of Dey's arm as she pointed off the right, and he lost all sense of fear in the wave of awe that washed over him.

A plume of water spouted high into the morning air. Then another. Then a third. The sign of the mighty nawlu. The giant creatures slid beneath the water, resurfacing again.

They were moving directly toward the pursuing fleet.

The angry chanting collapsed into shouts of confusion and alarm as their pursuers spotted the giants of the Great Water coming at them. The fleet broke formation, scattering in an attempt to remove themselves from the path of the creatures. The lead nawlu disappeared again beneath the waves. Long, terrible moments passed.

Then the titan of the open sea breached in the midst of the scattering vessels, rising into the sky for much of its incredible length, falling upon those of the fleet before it, crushing those vessels, killing those men. The wake capsized other canoes. The few that remained upright struggled to maintain their balance, focused now on sheer survival.

Bey and Dey paddled hard, making their way from that place. The gods had heard his prayer and chosen to intervene. Bey's heart lifted. They were not defying the will of the gods after all, but obeying it.

He glanced back. The pursuit had been broken off. Debris from smashed vessels floated on the water. The remaining vessels were circling, looking for survivors, all thoughts of the blasphemous couple gone. The cresting forms of the nawlu could be seen in the distance, moving away now. Bey said a grateful prayer of thanksgiving and kept paddling.

They travelled for days, Bey showing Dey how to guide their vessel so that he might rest. It was on the morning of the fourth day since their escape that he spied a jagged line on the horizon, something that was not water.

He woke his beloved that she might witness their arrival. Hope rose on her face like the sun goddess herself and he redoubled his efforts as she joined in. The landscape before them approached with agonizing slowness, but steadily. Some time later, as Reyeh had begun her descent, they rode onto the shore. He climbed into the surf, timing his efforts with the waves as he dragged the canoe onto the sand. She joined him and the two of them pulled the craft onto the higher beach, beyond the reach of the water.

They looked about. The air felt different and the sun-goddess rode across the sky at an odd angle. A dense forest began only paces from the beach, the heavy limbs of dark foliage strange and unknown.

A new land.

He looked further down the length of the beach and spotted a shallow tide-pool nestled among several large, flat rocks, its contents rippling and surging as the last efforts of the periodic wave surmounted the ring of stone and spilled into the center.

He stepped into the pool, the warm water sloshing about his knees. She stepped onto one of the larger stones, her face a good cubit above his. He looked up at her and she looked down at him, her eyes beaming.

"I am Kos," he said firmly, spreading his arms wide, open upward toward her. "Father of all, ruler of waters, bringer of storms, mighty and powerful. I would take you, if you be willing, to be my wife under the heavens."

"I am Ge," she responded, spreading her arms wide, open downward towards him. "Mother of all, ruler of earth, shaper of mountains, mighty and powerful. I would take you, if you be willing, to be my husband under the heavens."

He reached out his right hand and she grasped it in hers. Their eyes held one another as they spoke in unison.

"I take you as my own, my being and my breath. May the heavens bear witness to this union. May the heavens bless us this day. May the heavens smile upon us in the days to come."

And the heavens smiled upon them indeed.

About the Authors

DANIEL COWAN is a long time resident of Winnipeg, MB, and has spent most of his career working as a cook and as a plumber. He writes about appropriate technology and related topics at ecotechnicinklings.blogspot.com.

MARCUS TREMAIN has lived and worked in five different countries. A jack of all trades, he now shuttles forth between Los Angeles and London. Drawing inspiration from the absurdity of life, Marcus occasionally scribbles Irreverent mussing between bouts of intense jetlag.

CATHERINE TROUTH is an academic living and working in the Denver, Colorado area. While she enjoys writing poetry and short stories, most of her forays into writing or publishing have been in the area of Japanese studies and community colleges. She is currently working on a novel about a data analyst who specializes in supernatural events and is hoping to publish her own knitting patterns soon.

JUSTIN PATRICK MOORE is a writer and radio hobbyist. His work has appeared in Mythic Magazine, Flurb, and Abraxas: International Journal of Esoteric Studies. His transmissions have been broadcast on WAIF, Cincinnati and on international shortwave from Channel 292 in Germany. He lives with his wife in the Queen City.

TANYA HOBBS has recently started living at the end of a 3km farm track in a remote area of NSW, Australia, with her husband, young son and parents-in-law. She is still amazed by the conjunction of bushfire ravaged forests, black silted streams, showering out of a bucket and empty shop shelves with knee high green grass in the paddocks, fat cows and sheep munching the gardens, eggs warm from the chickens and working a city job via high speed broadband. She is not quite sure what the year ahead will bring but thanks to many years of reading the works of John Michael Greer is prepared to meet it armed with 10 buckets of sauerkraut and her herb garden.

BEN JOHNSON grew up in Tulsa, Oklahoma at the intersection of the Great Plains and Green Country. He is a graduate from Booker T. Washington High School and the University of Oklahoma. After college, he moved to Delaware to serve in AmeriCorps and later worked as an EMT and volunteer firefighter providing aid to those in need. He met and married his wife in Delaware, and they relocated to rural Pennsylvania. Currently, they reside in Tulsa with two dogs, two cats and three chickens. In his spare time, he gardens, brews beer and reads both history and fiction. His literary influences include Bulgakov, Babbel, Orwell and Hemmingway among many others.

VIOLET BERTELSEN has published stories in *Into The Ruins*, *Vintage Worlds*, and has self-published a short book on magical practice titled *Spiritual Cleaning and Protection*. Growing up in New England she wandered the strange ruin strewn landscape, climbed trees and followed babbling brooks hither and thither. Later she wandered near and far, worked on farms, and studied herbalism. She is an avid gardener, herbalist, occultist, and blogger whose writing can be found at https://violetcabra.dreamwidth.org/

RON MUCKLESTONE resides in Toronto, Canada, where he works as a consultant and spends his free time engaged in organic gardening, carpentry, mystical pursuits and raising a family. He has recently resumed his childhood passion of writing various genres of fiction.

TROY JONES III grew up in the future ruins of Huntsville, Alabama, where legend has it he still lives to this day. Previous stories of his have appeared in the After Oil anthologies, Merigan Tales, and Vintage Worlds. This is his first published poem.

AL SEVCIK is a professional photographer and author living in Tampa, Florida. His recent work can be found in two anthologies, After Oil #3 and Merigan Tales and in several issues of Into the Ruins magazine.

C.J. HOBBS had a career as a nurse, before becoming a primary school teacher. She now lives in Australia but spent much of her childhood in Malaya. She has also lived in New Zealand, the U.S.A. and Canada. She is now retired and loves reading a wide variety of books on natural science, birds, biographies and historical novels. She spends considerable time outdoors, birdwatching and camping out in the remote bushland areas of Australia with her husband, Andrew.

KL Cooke is a graduate of San Francisco State University, with a degree in Literature. After working briefly as a journalist, he spent 30 years in hi-tech industries, in procurement and project management, pursuing writing and photography on the side. Now retired and living on the San Mateo, California coast, he spends his time writing, taking photos, painting, fishing and attending his grandchildren's activities in sports and music. His is the author of two novels, two memoirs, poetry, philosophy, articles and short fiction.

DAVID ENGLAND grew up the son of a career Navy submariner, experiencing the wandering childhood common to military families. A life-long fan of science fiction (courtesy of his father's dog-eared Lucky Starr paperbacks), he now lives and writes in the wonderfully intimate community of Two Rivers, Wisconsin, along with his wife Anne, her incredible artwork, and the numerous voices in his head telling him what tales to craft next. His stories have appeared in Into The Ruins and MYTHIC, the e-zine Tales To Astound, and the Old Solar System anthology Vintage Worlds.

About the Editor

Born in the gritty Navy town of Bremerton, Washington, and raised in the south Seattle suburbs, **JOHN MICHAEL GREER** began to write as soon as he could hold a pencil. A widely read author and blogger, he has penned more than forty nonfiction books and nine novels. He lives in Rhode Island with his wife Sara.

Made in the USA
Middletown, DE
29 April 2020